the curators

the curators

A NOVEL

Maggie Nye

CURBSTONE BOOKS / NORTHWESTERN UNIVERSITY PRESS
EVANSTON, ILLINOIS

Curbstone Books
Northwestern University Press
www.nupress.northwestern.edu

Printed in the United States of America

10   9   8   7   6   5   4   3   2   1

Library of Congress Cataloging-in-Publication Data

Names: Nye, Maggie, author.
Title: The curators : a novel / Maggie Nye.
Description: Evanston, Illinois : Curbstone Books/
Northwestern University Press, 2024.
Identifiers: LCCN 2023058767 | ISBN 9780810147324
(paperback) | ISBN 9780810147331 (ebook)
Subjects: LCSH: Frank, Leo, 1884–1915—Fiction. | Phagan, Mary,
–1913—Fiction. | Golem—Fiction. | Atlanta (Ga.)—History—
20th century—Fiction. | LCGFT: Novels.
Classification: LCC PS3614.Y425 C87 2024 | DDC 813/.6—dc23/
eng/20231226
LC record available at https://lccn.loc.gov/2023058767

Contents

A Note about Historicity

This book contains a blend of real and imagined people and events. Among others mentioned, Leo and Lucille Frank, Mary Phagan, Jim Conley, Newt Lee, Hugh "H. M." Dorsey, Governor John M. Slaton, and Fiddlin' John Carson (here called "Fiddler") were all real people—though the book fictionalizes or imagines aspects of their lives. Note also that the "murder notes," rendered in the novel exactly as they were reported, were indeed found beside Phagan's body and much discussed in the news of the day. Fiddler's song in "Skipping Rope" is real, as well. He wrote several songs, including the very popular "Ballad of Mary Phagan," about Frank and Phagan. All information reported to have come from "the news" or from "the paper" was taken directly from the *Atlanta Constitution* (or, in one instance, the conservative paper, *The Jeffersonian*) between the dates of Mary Phagan's murder (April 26, 1913) and Leo Frank's lynching (August 17, 1915). And finally, while some of the language has been contemporized, verbiage quoted directly from news sources has not been altered and therefore contains outdated and offensive language that reflects the racist attitudes of the white public at the time of the novel's setting—much of which remains with us today.

We used to sit for hours in our clubhouse with our ears to each other's stomachs, listening to how loud our hunger could grow, until we convinced ourselves there were monsters inside us. This was in the very beginning, before anything had really happened. Before we had Mary Phagan and her murder, before we had Leo Frank and the brutal business of his fame, before we had brutal business of our own. We had only us and our huge hunger. In the end, the worst part was how it never stopped, not really. We used to call ourselves the Felicitous Five. We don't go by that name anymore.

Clayboy

The moral of most stories boils down to "don't."
I should like to write a story that is all "do."
—DIARY OF ANA WULFF

Naturally, there was another version of the golem story. All stories that have survived to retelling have another version. As many versions as tellers—or more, since tellers are not fixed to their versions and may change their stories with each retelling. Those stories that enjoy the most variation are the ones most often repeated. A different version to suit every problem, problems being the machines of stories, which are, in their humble way, offerings toward an answer. None more right than the one that came before or the one that will follow, except that acting makes them so.

It was Ana Wulff's habit never to confess ignorance. This, in part, was how she earned her reputation for cleverness. It felt good, she knew, to have a secret, to hide small pieces of knowledge away from others. Conversely, she found that if people believed their knowledge was common, they were more inclined to speak freely. And so, by pretending already to know their secrets, she quickly learned them.

This was how Ana first learned of the golem, that is, the way the others knew him. In their version, his origin was mythical: quickened by divine words and the noble cause of protection. This gilded story was not the one Ana had learned from her mother. The story she knew was of a different nature. A coarser story, a peasant's version by comparison. Nothing

3

extraordinary, only a boy made of clay. She had hated the story as a young child, but after so many years, after so many hearings and half hearings, it had worn away to a small and unremarkable pleasure.

There was an old Jewish couple—this is how her mother told it—who lived in a small village somewhere in the Pale of Settlement during difficult times, exactly where doesn't matter. The couple had no children to raise, nothing to give them hope, exactly why is none of your business. They were not generous with each other and no, they were not very happy, but they told themselves they were no less happy than any of their neighbors. In those days, in that village, happiness was not an affordable pursuit. At least they could both work, and they had butter for their bread once a year. But the older they got, the heavier was their regret.

No children! they cried. *What will become of our name? Who will tend to us when we are too old to tend to each other?* Already, they were rheumatic and wheezed on cold mornings. So, they decided to make a child out of clay. A boy, because girls are only heartache (here her mother sometimes winked at Ana, sometimes she did not). They shaped him up with a rolling pin and left him to dry on the hearth overnight. By the next morning, he was full of life. But also, he was full of hunger. At first it gave the old woman great joy to feed him, for his appetite was insatiable as she and her husband had never allowed themselves to be. She baked rye loaves and boiled porridge for the clayboy, simmered pepper stew and chicken soup.

The more he ate, the more he grew, the more he grew, the hungrier he became, until the couple could no longer satisfy the clayboy's hunger. Their hens were exhausted from laying, their cows dry from milking. Their pantry was bare, and they had spent their small savings on the rumblings of his stomach. When, at last, they had nothing left to give him, the clayboy, now bigger than a wolf, ate the hens, the cows, the old couple whole.

This much of the story was always delivered in the same way, and most often it ended with the death of the old couple in the clayboy's stomach. But sometimes, Mrs. Wulff went on telling it until the whole village was there too, chewed up and lumped together. Once, and only once, the clayboy was defeated, though not through anyone's cunning or brave deeds. In this version, the clayboy, having eaten half the village, was caught in a downpour. As the rain soaked him, he swelled and swelled. In this swelling, he found joy, for he loved nothing more than to grow. And when he had grown to the size of a small mountain, he took a happy nap. While he slept, the rain persisted, and the boy began to soften, being made of clay. And after so many hours of napping and swelling and softening, the villagers emerged from his eroded stomach, the clay that held them having thinned into red puddles. Their houses, their farms, the hens and cows, even the old couple tumbled out, all of them drowned and red. And that was all of the story.

When Ana learned of the sacred version, the Golem of Prague story familiar to the others, she asked her mother why she told her bad version.

It's how your baba told it, said Mrs. Wulff.

But what about the other way?

There is no other way.

There is, Ana pressed. *I've heard the others tell it.*

If you've heard it already, then why do you pester me for it? Anyhow, said Mrs. Wulff, wrapping lightly on Ana's forehead with her knuckles, *the other way is no good.*

I like it, said Ana.

Hard as hickory. Mrs. Wulff nodded, as though confirming something she had long suspected.

Mother!

All right, Ana, all right.

A false concession, Ana knew. Her mother never lost a fight, though sometimes she grew tired of trying to win.

You want a story about a wise and magical rabbi? What use is a story like that?

It's better than your depressing one.

You want a story where a great man does some hocus-pocus with a lump of mud and makes a magic protector who can save the Jews from their persecution? From all the men who hate them, who blame them for their own helplessness? Who want to live in a world without them? There is no such protector, there is no such great man, but fine, fine. There's your story. Now you can tell it to yourself. I'll start you off: Once upon a time. That's how all useless stories start.

It's not useless, Ana insisted. *The golem is a hero.*

Until he grows large and out of control and murders his makers, or don't you know that part?

You made that up.

All stories are made up, Ana. But the end is true.

That doesn't make sense.

The story is a story. Prague or Kyiv or Chelm. But the ending is the ending.

I've never heard it before.

There are lots of things you've never heard. People keep quiet what they wish wasn't true.

You think the golem is wicked?

No, her mother sighed. *He doesn't mean to be. The old man and woman made a child because life had made them empty, so the boy they made could never be filled, never be satisfied. Do you understand?*

Ana gave an uncertain nod.

The golem is nothing his makers are not also.

But there must be more to it. There had to be. She tried briefly to catalog her own needs: food, water, sleep, she liked books a great deal. And the others? They needed Leo, didn't they? What else was there?

Yours is just one version, said Ana. *Suppose I like the other one?* Nothing put Ana in a quarrelsome mood like her mother's certainty. In argument, as in few other things, Mrs. Wulff's attention was reliably engaged.

I don't tell you the other one because it's a story for little girls and you're not a little girl. Or, if you are, you shouldn't be one any longer. It is a dangerous, useless thing to be.

That's not fair, said Ana, swallowing her tears. Her throat ached with salt.

No, it isn't, her mother agreed.

The Leo Museum

"I'm going to live. I must live. I must vindicate myself."
—LEO FRANK, AS REPORTED BY THE *ATLANTA CONSTITUTION*

"No man with common sense would even suspect that I did it," prisoner in Fulton Tower tells attache. "It's a Negro's crime through and through."
—LEO FRANK, AS QUOTED IN THE *ATLANTA CONSTITUTION*

Our parents never talked about Leo, not to us anyway, but we knew what had happened. We followed the story with utter devotion as it broke. We felt the five of us had been charged with the collection of all the little pieces scattered across days and columns. For more than two years, we had stolen the *Atlanta Constitution* every day from the booth outside Jacob's Pharmacy. It's what our parents read. The vendor, a dopey-eyed man with greasy fingers that left smudges on the front page, went for a secret liquor break always at ten to three, just as the bell rang the school day done.

For more than two years, we had known Leo better than anyone. Certainly better than his nobody wife, Lucille. Dumb Lucille, *loose eel* for laughs. We called him Leo instead of Mr. Frank because it was more romantic to call a man by his given name. Also, Leo was Latin for lion. It was the one vocabulary word we cared to remember, and since Latin was the mother of all romance languages, his name was doubly romantic.

Once upon a time not all that long ago, we might have passed him on the street. Leo had been the superintendent of the National Pencil Company on South Forsyth, right by the cinema. His home was on East Georgia, three blocks from our school. He went to our temple.

But that was before we knew about him. Before he was accused of murdering Mary Phagan, before his trial was a national sensation, before he was sentenced to death, before his sentence was commuted by Governor Slaton, and before *The Constitution*'s front page featured his face under the banner IN HANDS OF MOB. That was the last headline of the paper's extras before it said *dead*. But we knew what "mob" meant. We knew what happened in the oak woods of Frey's Gin; they called those woods Lynchers' Grove. Our fathers said white factory workers and tenant farmers got angry at being so poor and lynching was how they blew off steam. A decade ago, they'd all gotten very angry. We were too young to remember, but our fathers said they took to the streets and burned through Darktown and Brownsville, shattering windows and tipping carriages and killing any Black people in their path. Thank goodness our fathers didn't work in factories. It must be maddening being poor. Our fathers have good jobs, they own their own stores. They're German, not Irish, like the lintheads, or Russian, like the Jews that get handouts and can't speak more than two licks of English. Our fathers are proper citizens of Atlanta.

In the two years and four months that passed between Leo's first appearance in the news and his lynching, we had learned his schooling (a fancy New York university), his dress (a club collar, always), his whereabouts (opera matinees on Sunday), and so many private things never printed in the paper: coffee black with brown sugar, Lucky Strikes, two gold-filled molars on the top left, an allergy to dogwood, a fondness for Nabisco wafers, dreams of us.

In general, he photographed handsomely—his hair perfectly slicked and the left side of his mouth smiling, though his eyes were not. They were large and unsquinting. Our hands knew the flat thinness of his face, the soft tatters from repeated handling. We passed him often between us. We knew him with a silver pin through his forehead, sun-faded on the wall of Ana's attic, which was our clubhouse.

We cut out our favorite photographs and kept them in the strap of our chemises, facing in. The left strap is closest to the heart. His gray lips crinkled and puckered against us as we moved. Afraid of dissolving him, we kept spares in the old rosewood desk in Ana's attic and in lockets around our necks. It was the first rule of the Felicitous Five never to be without him, except in the case of bathing. And we were working on a method of waterproofing to eliminate that exception.

We had planned, someday, to start a museum. We already had an impressive collection of artifacts stored in our clubhouse, but we were unresolved as to who, if anyone, should be admitted. After all, our museum would house things about Leo that only we knew.

Over time, we developed more rules:

#2   The Felicitous Five shall meet every day outside of Jacob's Pharmacy to discuss new developments.

#3   Each of us must immediately share whatever she learns, through necessary eavesdropping, about Leo Frank, the murdered factory girl, Mary Phagan, and other important figures pertaining to the story.

#4   Withholding information is a serious offense. Suspected withholders will be tried by a jury of her peers.

#5   We shall all work together to throw off adult lies and their attempts to keep us in the dark.

#6   All news clippings and artifacts are the collective property of the future Museum of Leo, which we shall direct together.

#7   The Night Witch's involvement shall be revisited as information becomes available.

#8   Above all else, our solemn and sworn duty is to have, by whatever means necessary, the complete and uncensored truth of Leo's story so that we may exonerate his noble name.

#9   All discussion between us regarding Leo and his case shall remain between us until death do us part.

#10   We now pronounce ourselves Keepers of the True Story!

And then we all signed it, which was Ana's idea. *You can't give authority to a thing until you promise it your name,* she said. She was good at saying things like that. Things that sounded true.

Ana Wulff
Rose Cohen
Sarah Aarons
Esther Fink
Franny Edelstein

All of us went to the same temple on South Pryor Street, the only one for anyone who mattered in Atlanta. And Leo had been with us every sleepy Shabbos, his vision, like ours, softening over the tissue pages of the siddur. All those boring mornings—too many to count—how had we never noticed him? How was it that we had dismissed him as just another adult? We had certainly known his name. He was president of Atlanta's B'nai B'rith chapter and a personal friend of the Rabbi Marx. But beyond that, we couldn't say.

Had he sat on the same side of the aisle? We couldn't remember. Elbowed Lucille to keep her from snoring? It was only after his arrest that we began to remember him, to distill him from the haze of our boredom, to pick out his stiff collar—never a wrinkle—from the rest; to single out his voice in the slew of prayer: a very noble timbre to it, something like a whisper blown through a shofar.

Sarah swore he spoke to her once. She said she sat behind him—she recalled the severe part in his hair—and that when he bowed his head to pray, a perfectly sharpened pencil fell from the tuck of his ear, and she caught it before it could hit the floor. It smelled, she said, faintly of the orange water her father's shop sold. She tried to return it, she said, with a tap on his shoulder. His face in profile was exquisite.

Excuse me, sir, she said she'd said. And he'd said, *Shhh, not now.*

She told us how she kept the pencil beneath her pillow and that she woke up every day to the cedar smell of shavings and found them in her hair and under her fingernails, the shreds of pink eraser rubber capping her fingers like ten pink sliver moons.

We believed her sometimes.

What we do remember, with perfect clarity, were the first pictures of Mary Phagan's dead body, her cinder-blackened face and swollen eyes. Two years later, there would be pictures of Leo's body too, hanging from a tree. He looked like the snap-neck chickens in the butcher's window. Their feet bound like his cuffed hands, crisscross. Funny how, when they're hanging there, plucked and ready for boiling, it isn't so awful. There are living, clucking chickens, and then there are the butcher's chickens. As long as you don't see one become the other—and why should you?—it's easy enough to trick yourself into believing they were always that way.

In those photographs, Leo's face and ears were covered by a white blind-fold. White to match his nightshirt, but his bare feet were perfectly visible: the surprise of them, the spines of his toes and the shadow of his high, princely arch. We kept those photographs too, but in a separate drawer from the others, one we never opened. Not because of him—because of the others. All those men gathered under his floating body. Looking out at us, some of them smiling. Saying, with their faces, *Go ahead, look. It's really something. Haven't we made you proud?*

We even knew one of them. A man called Fiddler, because he was one. He was a tall, thin man with plumes of wispy orange hair who managed to be everywhere at once and always watching. A neighborhood man, of sorts. Not that he lived in our neighborhood. He rented a place on Dekalb near Darktown when Fulton Bag gave the union workers the boot, and he peddled his fiddling in pubs along Decatur Street. More lucrative than his music, though, was his gift for gossip. He was known as a man with a nose for the newsworthy, and it was always a bad thing to be sniffed out by him. In our photograph, he stood by the oak's trunk, his face half-hidden by Leo's shadow. The other half staring out, seeing us. He probably went there just to bring back something to sell. He had a hundred skinny children and couldn't feed them more than a handful of hillbilly songs.

He'd sell his name for a dollar, said one of us.

Who'd want it? said someone else.

And his soul for half that.

It wasn't just Leo we were experts on, though we loved him best. We knew everything the paper reported and more. We knew everything there was to know.

Here's what the paper said:

Little Mary Phagan—that's what they called her—went to the National Pencil Factory on Saturday, April the 26th, 1913, which was Confederate Memorial Day, to collect the wages she was owed from Leo, her boss, and to inquire after the status of the sheet brass shortage that had resulted in her temporary layoff. She worked in the metal room. Her job was to fix the erasers to the pencil shafts, and with no sheet brass to hold the eraser, she had no job.

Here's what we knew:

Working girls got to do all sorts of things we would never get to. They could ride the streetcar with gentleman companions, if they chose. They got to go to the pictures with money they earned themselves, and since they made money for their families—who were poor—their mothers and fathers had to respect them and never made them do chores. They didn't have to go to school. They learned how to flirt, and they got to practice it on handsome older men, and who was there to tell on them? But it could be dangerous, too, which was half the fun.

Here's what the paper said:

Little Mary Phagan's body was found by an old Black night watchman by the name of Newt Lee in the basement of the factory, near the furnace, in the early morning hours of Sunday, April the 27th. Lee told the police he had gone down to the basement to use the toilets there, for Black workers, and found Mary's body, beaten and mangled. Wrapped around her neck was a length of wire and some lace torn from her petticoat. Next to her body was a set of notes the papers named "murder notes," which gave an account of how her body came to be where it was found, and who to blame for it. Newt Lee was arrested on site. And though he was only a suspect for a couple of weeks, he was held in a cell for four months. The detectives, apparently, forgot about him.

And we knew why:

Newt Lee wasn't a real man, but an illusion created by the Night Witch, whom we learned about from reading the murder notes, which were photographed in the paper. They were written as though by Mary Phagan's own dead hand. As though, once killed, she had been moved to seek out paper and write an account of her own end before lying down again and waiting to be found. We knew the murder notes by heart. When school grew boring and lecture rote, we would race to see who could write them down fastest. We wrote so fast that our hands cramped, and we would have to drop our pencils and knead the fat part of our palms:

Mam that negro hire down here did this I went to make water and he push me down that hole a long tall negro blcak that hoo is wase long sleam tall negro it wright while play with me he said he wood love me land down play like the night witch did it but that long tall black negro did by his slef!

Points were docked for corruptions of the original. And because translation from regular to witch diction hindered the speed of our scribbling, the faster writers among us retrained our minds to know the wrong spellings, the witch spellings, of certain words until the Night Witch's *hoo* replaced the resident spelling in our hands. Our marks in English suffered that year.

We all had dreams of Leo. Mostly that he let us wear his hat, but the Night Witch dreams were of another sort. The Night Witch was a Black man transformed, not altogether a man. We imagined the Night Witch not in the coveralls of a workman's uniform, but dressed in a black cloak, long and slim, its feet and hands no more than black smoke in the dark. We sometimes tried to ignore our dreams: dresses trailing in tatters, winding endlessly around our necks like spindles of wire. Other times, though, in the beds of our separate houses, we kept the Night Witch with us when we awoke. There, over our shoulders as we brushed our teeth, stroking our ankles under the table at breakfast.

Furthermore, we understood that *Newt* Lee was something of a joke, a wink that only we saw. Witches sometimes took small animals like frogs and lizards as their familiars, and familiars exist to do the bidding of their masters. Lee's arrest, we all agreed, was a diversion deployed by the Night Witch to distract the detectives, and therefore, a silly endeavor. The paper said that when they finally remembered Lee was there and released him, he returned home to find his chickens, his belongings, and his wife all gone. Proof that he'd never been a real man in the first place.

What the paper said:

On April 29th, Leo was taken into custody under suspicion of murder.

Two days later, Jim Conley, the Pencil Factory's Black janitor, was also arrested, after he was discovered washing bloodstains from a shirt in the factory's basement.

Handwriting experts were brought in to analyze the writing on the murder notes, which did not resemble Mary Phagan's or Leo's or Newt Lee's at all. Conley first claimed he couldn't write and then revised his statement, saying he had written the murder notes, but only at Leo's request. Conley said Leo had summoned him to his office and kept him shut up in a wardrobe, waiting for everyone to go home, then paid him two dollars and fifty cents to write what Leo dictated. As if a full-grown man could fit in a wardrobe. Conley's handwriting matched exactly, but he pinned the whole thing on Leo. Leo, however, swore it was a "Negro's crime, through and through." Conley blamed Leo, and Leo blamed Conley—or any Black man.

What we didn't know:

Why should it be any one kind of man's crime rather than another's? We knew our Leo was innocent, but there were many men who saw Mary Phagan, spoke to her, winked at her, paid her special attention. So many men that we thought every man in Atlanta could have played a part. We imagined how every man, receiving some signal known only to men— and there are a great many—must have helped to put Mary Phagan in the ground: one drove the streetcar, one escorted her to South Forsyth Street, one distracted while another laid a trap, one grabbed her hands, one her feet, one lowered her into the basement, one squeezed, one tore, one bloodied, one dragged the body, one stole her wages—$1.17 in all—and one, angry at arriving late, tantrumed, scattering her shoes, her parasol, her empty purse. No man cleaned up.

Coloring Book

"If social condition in Atlanta were of the best, if conditions in factories were of the best; and lastly, if children of such tender years were not forced to work, little Mary Phagan would never have been murdered," declared Dr. A. J. McKelway.

—ATLANTA CONSTITUTION

Arthur Mullinax, *a strikingly handsome youth*, according to the paper, was a suspect of particular curiosity to us, though not because of his good looks. In fact, we thought his face was distinctly goofy. You could picture him as a dancing monkey on a street corner with a round red velvet cap and a miniature set of cymbals. We happened to know it was entirely old men who ran the newspapers, and what did they know about handsomeness and youth?

He wasn't a big suspect, they only held him for a little while. The early days had been like that. New leads, new tips, new rumors by the wagonful. The queer thing about Mullinax was how he knew Mary Phagan—which was through a hodgepodge church pageant where she played Sleeping Beauty, which seems sad now. His part was some blackface nobody in the chorus, but according to Mullinax, it pleased her. She said he looked good with his face blacked, and he said he'd keep it blacked all the time then, just for her.

What a peculiar compliment, said one of us, studying his picture: a mop of wavy hair sitting high up on his long face, flanked by two jutting ears, his thick brow, a dirty shadow along his jaw. Of all his features, his long, thick eyelashes and big, dark eyes were singularly boyish and attractive.

Do you think she really preferred him that way—with his face blacked like that?

We were sitting in a circle on the attic floor with a kerosene lamp that usually sat on the desk in the middle, throwing extra light on the day's paper. The attic wasn't wired for electricity, but we liked the moodiness of live flame: candles and lanterns. It made our task feel as important, as sacred, as secret as we knew it was. Though there was plenty of daylight, there was only one window in our attic clubhouse—on the far side, just behind the desk—and our work required scrupulous attention to detail.

One of us took a pencil to his photograph, sketching lightly, darkening the line of his collar. We handed the pencil around. One of us broadened the stroke, angling our pencil so that more of the lead had contact with the paper. The thicker line was better for covering more surface, darkening more white. We colored him in, starting at the lump of his Adam's apple. The gray grew upward to his chin, then to his ears and cheeks, the shadow of his jaw disguised by graphite until we had colored him in entirely— everything but his eyes. We blacked him out.

Then we did his eyes, too. As a graphite shade in the shape of a man's face, he was not unappealing. Now that we saw it done, we preferred him that way too.

There's something romantic about it, isn't there? one of us asked. *The way her face was blacked, too, in the end? Dragged over all those cinders, so they couldn't tell what color she was. Remember? Even the detectives didn't know for certain until one of them pulled down her stocking.*

I heard they couldn't get it all off in time for the viewing and that her mother argued with the undertaker because they couldn't make her believe it was really Mary, said Sarah, our actress. *Can you imagine it?*

She tugged at the hems of our dresses like a beggar.

My little girl, she said, *my pretty little girl. Where is she? Who is that little Black child in my daughter's coffin? What's she doing in there? How could that be my Mary, my Sleeping Beauty?*

Don't do it like that, said Franny, always our sweet one, and snatched back her dress, bottom lip trembling. *It's too awful.*

Like what?

Like it's some sort of melodrama. I know they make it out that way in the papers, but it's real people. A real girl, one of us.

Well, shame on me.

Fake pouting, the whole ball of wax.

Franny-banany, don't sulk, said Ana. *Dry your eyes. I've made you a drawing.*

She's fine, said Rose. *You coddle her.*

Give it here, said Sarah, and snatched the drawing from Ana. *I'll just improve on it a bit, shall I?* she said, her pencil raised in theatrical preparation for vandalism.

We crowded around to see: the picture was of Franny, sort of. A flattering portrait, lovelier than she had ever been. A Franny she would never be. A princess, at the least, or a queen. There was something undeniably regal about the gap in her two front teeth—the only feature that identified her as our Franny—a gap that, in real life, made her look dopey and plain. Here, though, the gap made each tooth, set apart from the others, look distinguished. Two gems, set carefully in a crown, while our own teeth were common and crowded. Suddenly, our mouths were all overfull, our tongues retreating to the soft parts of our palates to seek space. We all wanted to be drawn like Franny: draped in an ermine cloak, sidesaddle on a horse with a tail down to its hooves, a rapier hanging from our hips, our teeth ennobled by gapping.

It's beautiful, said Esther, and handed the picture back to Franny, who scrutinized it under the lamplight before crumpling it up in a ball and walking it over to the open window to drop it to the ground. We all came over to the window to see where it had fallen on the lawn.

Do you think I look at all like her?

Like who?

You know who.

We did. *Little Mary Phagan,* that's what the paper always called her. We all wanted her sweet face, her golden hair, her woman's shape at not quite fourteen.

As much as any of us do, one of us finally answered.

None of us wanted to turn fourteen anymore. Before Mary Phagan, we used to call the youngest ones babies, and when it was too hot to lift a finger, we'd say, *Babies, go run and fetch us some lemonade. Babies, be sweet and bring us a damp flannel for our forehead.* After Mary Phagan, we all wished we could be babies. The older ones among us resigned themselves to the coming of fourteen; they couldn't stop it. The younger ones tried. They stayed up late, with their fingers forcing their eyelids open, as the days changed over until, one by one, we were—all but Ana—the age Mary Phagan would never turn.

Birthdays had become a solemn affair. No laughter, no singing. We crowded around the lemon party cakes our maids prepared for us. Our fathers said, *close your eyes, make a wish,* and we sighed the candles out over our mothers' squat cake stands. We were never hungry on these days, but how could we explain? How could we say to them, *I have no appetite for cake, can't you see I'm in mourning?* It couldn't be done, so we dutifully skimmed the too-sweet glaze, scalping our cakes bald with fork tines, and wiped our sticky lips clean.

I have the keenest eye of the Five, so it fell to me to
form the golem.

—DIARY OF ANA WULFF

Ana's birthday would be different because it just *had* to be! She was the
youngest, the last baby. She had clung to thirteen, Mary Phagan's dying
age, as long as she possibly could, including the addition of the three extra
days which she demanded be returned to her, one for each of the three
leap years since her birth. Every day, she insisted, must be accounted for.
Ana kept meticulously annotated calendars and was frequently compelled
to record proceedings and findings. She was the baby, but also the scribe
and scientist. Ana Wulff would not abide these omissions because she was
clever and thorough, and because once she was fourteen, all of them would
be fourteen, and then what hope was there for Leo? And because on her
real birthday, minus the make-up days she added back, they found out the
worst thing had finally happened. Even if she knew, like they all had, that
it would—that it was only a matter of time—it was still on *her* birthday,
and a not-so-small part of her feared it was some unspoken wish, lodged
deep in her bad heart, that made it happen. So, the burden was hers to find
that hope, or rather, to make it entirely from scratch, which is what she
tried to do.

The Smutch

> If anyone were to tell you that the state would expend 10,000
> perfectly good dollars in this expensive cost of living era just
> to hang a man you'd either think the state was very vindictive
> or that your friend was a liar. . . . The courthouse will soon be
> empty and the jury home. The public will take a rest, and the
> morbidly curious will turn to other fields. The Frank trial will
> go to its inevitable havens, memory and history. And nobody
> will weep thereover, especially the state of Georgia.
>
> **—*ATLANTA CONSTITUTION***

Everything was fun at the start of it, every paper flush with Leo, as though he were the only news in the whole world. To us, he was, but it didn't stay that way. Holes began appearing in the coverage of Leo's story. Pinholes, at first; he was pushed off the front page or mentioned only in brief allusions to the safety of young girls. Safety. Was there any word so dull?

But slowly the holes grew and stretched on for days, even weeks sometimes, with us inside the holes, rereading our favorite clippings to the point of blind recitation. After his sentencing, the papers lost interest in him, and we vowed not to. After all, the papers seemed to say with their silence, what more is there to report about a man condemned to die than *just wait*?

We still scanned the paper cover to cover, less out of hope than habit. And we found ways to bridge the holes. Rule #3! We made our own connections, like spiders spinning webs. When the paper reported on the blue-ribbon hog of the Fulton County Fair, for example, we said: the hog belonged to Farmer Franklin, from whom the butcher bought his beef. The butcher's wife, Mrs. Soder, was often seen in the company of Benjamin Low, an average-looking jeweler who was said to have given her the ostentatious pendant she wore daily: a squirrel carrying a bouquet of violets between his opal teeth. Mr. Soder, it was known, simply wouldn't go in for such lavish things and besides, he hated squirrels and animals of most varieties—anything that might eat his prized yellow squash. Mr. Low was kissing cousins with Mrs. Kaufmann, who was an on-again, off-again member of the Atlanta Women's Society for Charity and Advancement, to which Lucille Frank also belonged. This year, they were slated to reveal a statue depicting a peaceful handshake between a Creek Indian and a British man with the ridiculous name of Oglethorpe. This was a favorable omen. Fortune smiled on Leo in his dark cell.

Or when the Atlanta Crackers were forecast to win a match against the Barons, but Birmingham pulled out a narrow victory, we said: the pitcher, Eddie Dent, whose choleric wife often made the papers when she flew into one of her famous rages, would likely prolong his trip home and stop off at the Dixie Tavern. Waiting out his wife's mood, it was easy to predict how Dent might have a Coca-Cola or two or three, and into each glass, slip a generous nip from his flask until he was no more stable on his feet than a blade of long grass on a windy day. And further, to predict that, in an effort to get the barkeeper's attention, he would wave too wildly and knock the glass out from the hand of the man next to him, where it would shatter on the ground. And finally, to predict that this man would be Leo's prosecutor, Solicitor H. M. Dorsey, a known patron of the tavern. Such a clumsy misfortune was an unspeakably bad omen for our Leo, and we knew exactly who to blame.

In the case of this last prediction, Dent would be the Smutch. Not because he was a lousy ballplayer, though our fathers said he was, but because there had to be a Smutch; we needed one. The Smutch—a deliciously nasty-sounding word—was the name we gave to the person we decided was responsible for anything going wrong, the reason for our every problem. Once named, it was easy to blame the Smutch. We could say *Damn it, Dent!* We could say *Dent, you Smutch.* We could say *Son of a Smutch!* which was our favorite thing to say. It was fun and simple and good to know where bad things were coming from. So much better than puzzling through every bit of bad news, every ill feeling, and never knowing how to be rid of it. So much better than trying to track down the sources of such various anxieties, which, if traced back far enough, always disappeared back into ourselves like some kind of awful, unsolvable puzzle. So much better to say *Blame the Smutch* and be done with it.

The Smutch had to change often, though, because there were five of us and, all together, we had a lot of ill feelings that needed accounting for. We knew the pattern: there would come a day when one of us would pick a needless quarrel and another would burst into tears with no apparent prompting and a third would feel suddenly itchy and hot as though stung in the guts by fire ants. These were the symptoms of an overfilled Smutch and they signaled it was time, once more, to pick a new one. We lost track of how many Smutches we'd filled up. It was like tallying mosquito bites in July—impossible.

Once, we made Ana's mother the Smutch as punishment for making us shell a thousand broad beans, but then we heard her humming from the kitchen and it was so beautiful and unexpected, like hail in the summertime, that we crowded together just behind the kitchen door, in the shadow there, and listened until she burned her hand and said *chyort!* and the spell was broken.

Esther—especially taken with the assassination of Archduke Franz Ferdinand in his stately side-buttoning coat—wanted to pursue other news stories. She called us to order in the clubhouse and, passing around a picture of him cropped from the paper, put forth her proposal. Though she made a fair point about the intrigue of his pale eyes and dark temper, most of us agreed that in addition to this proposal being a blatant betrayal of our Leo, this man's gigantic mustache was not only unbecoming for the squarish shape of his face, but also in bad taste both in terms of style, and in terms of occasion—a graver faux pas. It might have been acceptable, say, if a man were something of an eccentric and a lifelong bachelor, to have a mustache the size of an eagle, but when a man had a wife to consider, such a travesty was unconscionable.

Ugh, said Rose, *imagine being his wife*. She slapped the picture down on the rosewood desk.

I do, said Esther, staring into it, her back to us.

You're telling me you want a gigantic scratchy eagle pecking at your face every day? Sarah joked and gave her a peck on the cheek.

Even Franny joined in: *I bet his children run screaming when he tries to embrace them!*

His wife's death, for she had been shot and died alongside her husband, was the final word against the archduke. Especially in the case of one's dying moments, one should be free to reflect on love and other worthy subjects. The idea that she might have been nettled by such petty thoughts as chafing was patently intolerable. So grievous, in fact, was his mustachioed offense that some of us wanted to make Franz Ferdinand our next Smutch.

It's him after all, said Ana. *Him and the stupid European War he started that's keeping Leo from the papers.*

That's not fair, said Esther. *It's not his fault he was shot.*

It doesn't have to be, said Rose. *His mustache could be the Smutch all on its own.*

Sarah said: *The mustache that launched a thousand ships!*

To which Esther replied, steadfastly: *Do what you like. He won't be my Smutch. Not ever.* She folded the archduke up and clasped him in her palm, her arms crossed against her chest.

Fine, we'll do something else while we wait for more news—of Leo, said Ana, making her eyes big at Esther.

But what had we ever done together before him? We found it was hard to recall.

Let's make a list, said Ana, who loved lists.

We fed the ducks in the Grant Park pond with stale challah. Franny wanted to get one up close to feed it from the palm of her hand.

And now we can't feed them anymore because Franny got bitten.

I still have a scar!

Only you could get a scar from a duck.

We made waxed paper boats to race on a stormy day. We folded them from newspaper with our backs to one another so that no one could cheat and copy anyone else's design, and then we raced them down the flooded alley behind Ana's house.

All but one sank like the RMS Titanic.

The SS Booger! *It won by elimination.*

It was also the ugliest.

No sail at all, no bow, just a paper box.

Fortune favored the Booger!

We picked figs from the great big trees on Washington Street.

Sarah is the best fig-picker. She always finds the ones that are so ripe they're practically bursting.

Sweeter than a Coca-Cola.

We caught fireflies in canning jars.

We had named the brightest one Mary Phagan, and when she began to die, flipping over on her back, we sliced her head off with a taut piece of thread to short her suffering. It wasn't disgusting like we had expected; her yellow blood looked like paint. Six black legs like printed Ls stopped their twitching, then we sliced her light from her body and threaded a needle to string it through. The ends we tied into a necklace for our glowing gem. From the tip of the needle to the center of the thread, the little gem painted a glowing streak of yellow—star's blood—that stayed lit for longer than we could hold our breath, so much longer that we had to catch it and hold it again.

We read each other's palms a couple of times. Esther was quite good at it.

Most of us are going to live very long lives.

We played the zoo game where you have to become the first animal you saw. Sarah saw the bear and had to act ornery—

Was that acting?

—and sleepy because hibernation season was coming, and Franny saw the monkeys first and ate nothing but bananas all day.

Remember when we went to the aviary together so that we could be birds in a flock, and we walked about all day in a V imagining what it would be like to see everything from far above?

Franny recalled composing shadow puppet plays.

They were a great laugh, she said, curving the index finger of her right hand to meet the first knuckle of her middle finger.

That won't work, Ana sighed. *It's overcast.*

But Franny ignored her, lifting and lowering her middle finger to meet her thumb, which she timed with a nasal *Quack! Quack! Quack!* But Ana was right, and her anemic shadow puppet was little more than a smudge on the wall.

I have a secret, Sarah announced. *A treasure.*

I'll believe it when I see it, said Rose, breathing onto the glass of the attic window.

Sarah went over to the mound of our bookbags where we'd shed them all in a pile near the attic door while Rose drew her own name in the fog.

From her bag, Sarah wrestled the crucifix that had hung in our homeroom. One of us gasped. Sarah laid it down in the middle of the floor and we gathered around it. Even Rose removed herself from the window to inspect it.

It wasn't really so special. In fact, it was fairly crude. The horizontal plank, to which the Jesus was affixed, was shorter on the right side than on the left so that his left arm appeared stunted or else his right arm and hand abnormally long.

What's so great about him? said one of us, turning the cross over in her hands.

He has a pleasant enough face, someone replied.

If you like that sort of thing, said another.

You shouldn't joke about sacred things, one of us frowned. *It's blasphemy and bad luck.*

It's not if you don't believe in him.

But lots of people do.

Well maybe you shouldn't have swiped him from school, someone countered. *If anything could bring bad luck, stealing a Jesus would do it.*

Yes, put him back, another agreed. *We don't need him here.*

But the homeroom wall stayed empty, except for the vague yellow outline of a lopsided cross where the figurine had kept the sun from bleaching the wall.

Easter Egg Hunt

The advance guard of the old fiddlers of Georgia began
arriving last night for the Fiddler's Convention, which opens
at the auditorium tonight. . . . The program will include such
old favorites as "Soldiers' Joy," "Billy in the Low Grounds,"
"Chickens Before Day," "Bacon and Collards," and a score
of others your granddaddies used to dance to in the country
cabins before they moved to Atlanta and got rich in real estate
and turned into grand opera lovers.

—ATLANTA CONSTITUTION

The fourth Monday in April was the very best day of the entire
school year for two reasons: one being that there was no school
and the other being that it was the first good day of spring. Not the
dreary skies and constant drizzle of early spring, but the blue-skied, warm-
morninged kind of spring where the wisteria and camellia and all the other
show-off rhyming flowers of Georgia seemed to abracadabra into full and
perfect bloom. The shame of it was that it was Confederate Memorial Day,
and everybody else was on holiday, too. As soon as they were done with
their pointless parade—the dwindling veterans were bedridden by now, so
who was it even for?—we wouldn't have a single pink petal to ourselves.

We didn't go to the parade because our parents didn't make us. *More
fantasy than history*, is what they said. Besides, it made us angry how quickly
everyone had forgotten about *our* story. The year before, there had been a

flimsy effort to commemorate Mary Phagan: her pretty face on a banner. Some of the girls carried purple parasols, like hers. Things of that nature. Not that anyone talked about it, except for us. How one year before, Mary Phagan was murdered, and the Night Witch appeared, along with our Leo. It was the anniversary of our world. Now, two years out, not so much as a tassel. We would have to make our own celebration.

Our mothers let us go to the park in the morning while everyone else was parading. *A quiet play.* The trolley didn't run on Confederate Memorial Day because everyone was too distracted with singing about cannonballs and Southern glory and blah blah blah, so we walked the empty streets under still trolley lines. Normally, they quivered all day long because somewhere down the line they were being pulled at. The air was heavy and buzzy, readying itself for summer swelter like a pot of bubbled water before the boil.

At the very top of the hill on East Georgia, one of us drew a big breath and said *Leeeee*, very low, and we all followed suit, matching her pitch as we tipped over the edge of it. Picking up speed, kicking up stones. We let our arms swing crazy and just as our legs moved into a sprint, we changed to *Ohhhh*. And we let ourselves louden as we picked up speed, whoosh! Our *Ohhhh*s changing shape as they streamed behind us, wailing sirens, and our foot slaps echoing across the morning. The trick was to let everything from your tongue to your toes be as loose as forgetting they were yours at all.

At the base of the hill where the ground leveled and stepped up to the low granite walls of the park's entrance, Franny caught her foot on a jutting tile and spilled onto the park's bronze sundial on all fours. Stones the size of freckles burrowed into her palms and the skin on her knee scrunched up like a purple-gray accordion. It held for four full seconds, until one of us said *Maybe it won't*—then, the blood welled up in spots like the darkening sidewalk when it's just begun to rain, and once it pooled up the shallow well of the scrape, it spilled over both sides of her knee in a neat red line, like a ribbon on a parcel. We walked our wounded one, an arm around both her shoulders, holding her at the waist as she limped to the spring to wash her knee, and we bandaged her wound with two soft leaves of lamb's ear, her blood matting its silver hair brown. We took turns nursing her or walking the shore of Abana Lake, though there were no paddleboats to watch.

Just beyond the spring, a Black man drew a sky-colored egg from a silver pail and nested it ever so gently in a bed of pussy willows, the round blue edge of it just visible from between the stalks. And just beyond him, skulking in the shade of the dogwood tree, was Fiddler with his hound. He watched us watch the Black man and tuned his fiddle as his dog howled at his side. We were less alone than we wanted to be.

Some kind of animal intuition guided him, wholly free of reason, to sites that would become stories of popular interest—local gossip, citywide news, Fiddler didn't seek them out, per se. Rather, he happened on them unfailingly. When the paper was dry, reporters were even known to follow him around, hoping to be first on the scene when a story broke.

And though people occasionally tried to attract his attention, mainly bored people of means who paid him a small purse to leak their involvement in this or that secret society, most folks avoided him. Besides, he was more attuned to scandal than society. Misconduct, thievery, marital affairs, brutality, and racial impropriety of all natures. These were his known attractions. People treated his presence as a sign of bad luck—they shooed him away or chased him off with a broom like a dog rooting and scattering their ripe garbage. But this was wasted effort. Fiddler didn't bring bad fortune. The bad fortune was there already, he only smelled it first.

We tried to ignore him and focus on the egg-layer.

Have you ever seen such a gentle one? one of us asked.

We couldn't remember if we had or not.

What's Fiddler doing here? said another.

Our maids are Black, someone offered.

Yes, but they're women first and Black second.

Even his sorry dog can't stand his fiddling.

I think the dog's singing along.

He gives me chills, always watching like that, like he watched Leo hang.

If you stay still for long enough, he'll go away, one of us offered.

He won't. He's waiting for the crowds to arrive so he can peddle his awful music.

Who likes that racket anyway?

Ana's maid isn't a woman. She's just got Isaac.

And he's gentler by miles than my mother, said Ana. *Plus, he knows better stories.*

What stories?

He told me about a Haitian in Darktown who's a real live voodoo woman. Isaac says her blood's as dark as India ink.

Shoo, Fiddler! Can't he tell when he's not welcome?

He's got nowhere to go. The mill's on strike. All those lintheads have nothing to do but start trouble. That's what my father says.

And she can do all kinds of magic spells. Obeya it's called.

Do you believe him?

What's that got to do with being gentle or not?

I made him swear on his wife's grave it was true.

Sure looks like trouble to me.

What do you mean?

You're so naive. There's no such thing as voodoo. Old Black folks like Isaac are just good fibbers. My father says they learned to be that way back when they were slaves because they had no other way of getting ahead.

I think it's real. He wouldn't lie to me.

I bet none of those eggs has so much as a single crack.

Scattered about the park were dozens of painted eggs in semi-hidden spots. There was one in the nook of the elm that shaded us, one in the stone crook of the spring, two in the stems of a cluster of violet irises.

We couldn't remember ever seeing one so clearly. Of course, we'd all seen Black people before. It wasn't as if they were rare, it was just that they had never seemed quite distinct to us. We liked our maids all right—when they weren't tattling on us to our mothers—but we didn't think we would mind if they all swapped houses.

Except for Isaac, said Ana.

Have it your way, said Esther. *Who wants a man fixing her hair?*

And seeing her half-naked!

He doesn't see me undressed, said Ana, very red.

Of course not, said Franny. *They're teasing.*

The Black folks on the street kept their heads down; the Black factory workers consorted only with the cogs they cranked. Like familiar sidewalks on which we never had to watch our feet because we knew, by memory, how they wound.

There were other kinds of Black folks, too. Rich ones—shop owners and businessmen. They could be found along Sweet Auburn. They wore natty suits and had neatly groomed hair. They owned their own businesses and had white men's money, far more than our fathers had. We wondered why it should be so different between them.

Why don't they all just pool their money, Esther suggested. *Then they could all be happy.*

I wouldn't, Sarah countered. *If it were mine, if I worked for it, then why should I have to give it away?*

The man was close enough to us now that we could see the tendons in his forearms. He was in shirtsleeves pushed back to the elbow. No collar, no jewelry. He looked quite young, younger than our parents, but he moved with a carefulness that suggested old age, as if his bones too were made of eggshells.

Knuckle the leaves a little until they start smelling green, he said, pointing to Franny's lamb's-ear bandage. *The juice is good for healing.*

We weren't allowed to talk to strangers, but really, who could be more familiar than a Black person?

We did as he instructed, and Franny said, *that does feel better*, like when our mothers used to blow on our burned fingers before we learned to keep our hands away from oiled pans.

Better get that washed up good, said the man. *My daughter has a scar on her elbow from a fall like that, looks like an owl.*

Sure she has, said Rose sarcastically.

Don't be rude, Ana scolded.

Scars never look like anything, except ugly, said Rose.

You ever see a cloud that looked like an owl, the man asked.

I have, said Ana.

All right then, said the man. *It looks like a cloud that looks like an owl.*

What are you doing here? Rose demanded.

Laying eggs, said the man. *Been laying them all morning.*

Easter was two weeks ago, said Sarah, reaching for a melon-colored egg tucked just behind the edge of the granite wall.

Guess the little white children liked them so much the first time, they asked the Black bunny to lay a second round for the Memorial Day.

She cracked its orange shell on the arm of the sundial.

Don't do that! said Franny. *It isn't yours.*

Sarah shrugged.

It's all right, said the man, lifting a lilac one from his bucket and rolling it to us along the grass. *Plenty more, nobody's gonna notice if a couple go missing.*

Bright slivers of shell fell across the face of the sundial, obscuring the names of far-off capitals: *Berlin, 4,767 miles; Buenos Aires, 5,011 miles; Constantinople, 5,756 miles; Jerusalem, 6,439 miles.* We never went anywhere but up and down the street. We would live our whole lives here. We would be buried here. There was a portion of the cemetery that was only for us. We would only ever know us, even once we were dead.

Ana traced her finger around the dial.

Wherever you stop is where you'll be shipped off to boarding school, Esther teased.

I'd go to Berlin, it's the closest, said Franny. *Just over ten trips to Nashville and back.* She knew the figure by heart from when she used to be our Captain of Maps, which is a game we used to play. We used to trace the train and trolley lines and mark the docks of ports along the coast. The whole point was just to go somewhere else, but we got tired of tallying miles without ever leaving. In the end, Franny was the only one with the patience for it.

I'd go to Jerusalem, said the man, brushing aside the pastel slivers.

Fiddler plucked a string on his fiddle, which made us all jump. The hound bared his teeth at the man.

Want to know where I'd go? he said.

No, said Rose.

How had he snuck so close?

Well, you ought to.

Spider's Nest

Louisa Marksfelt, a girl of 19, who has been under arrest here since
May 26, has admitted to the police that she is a German spy. . . .
The girl, who claims acquaintance with five or six European languages . . . is said to have paid visits to various military camps and
to have made extensive tour of the Canadian West.

—ATLANTA CONSTITUTION

The day's paper, though it contained nothing of our Leo, did have
an excellent story about a girl-spy who had crossed Niagara Falls!
Her name was Louisa, which we had previously thought a dowdy,
unfortunate name but now thought was genius.

Who would suspect a girl named Louisa of being a spy?

Who would suspect a girl of being a spy?

Who would suspect a girl of being a spy-der! said one of us and tickled
another under her arms.

If an old witch were to catch us stealing a cabbage from her garden and
turn us into an animal as punishment, she would make us into a spider.
Not because we would choose to be—who would choose to be a spider?—
simply because that's what we were. Hair, hair, hair, and so many legs. No
creature so horrible and wonderful as us when we tangled up, which we did
sometimes when we played spider's nest. The perfect game for playing on
rainy days when it was too gray to be alone.

We took down our ribbons and unpinned any order our maids had

41

fastened to our heads. We finger-combed through each other's hair to set every curl free and because it felt nice. Then, one at a time, we climbed into each other. Just two at first, we braided them together. A right strand from one head, a left from the other, and the middle strand, especially thick, taken from both heads and twisted together. Their braids were fastened by a strand from another scalp, coiled around the bottom and tied in a knot. We each climbed in and tied ourselves up. We each took pieces of our hair and wrapped them around the braid, coiling up the stalk until the weave of it had vanished, the design of its binding covered over by loops and calico tangles of brown that bulged at irregular joints, suggesting nothing so much as the tufted leg of a spider.

Then, we dissolved the rest of ourselves together.

Like sugar into coffee.

Like sugar into more sugar.

We tucked our legs under each other's knees and hooked our elbows. Wrapping at the wrist, we dug our fingers through the slots of each other's hands. We filled ourselves in with each other until we were one thing, and then we tested our spider. We tried to guess which pieces belonged to each of us.

One of us said, *Those toes there, in the middle, pointed at the ceiling.*

And someone else claimed them: *Mine!*

Whichever hand was closest tickled those toes and if it was a different one of us that laughed, then we knew we had done it well—lost ourselves into the spider—and none of us could know for sure what grew from us and what was only touching for now.

We could get lost like this whenever we wanted to, in any room with a locking door. Trading out our fingers, our bruises, our heads, for anyone else's. We were made up of each other and our thoughts passed freely through our hairy hearts.

We would say and say and say and say and say, and no one knew or wanted to know who said what and to whom and no one said *why?* because spiders don't care to know, and no one said *here is the solution* because spiders were simple. They simply worked. Nothing but a hundred says that rose from us then sunk back into the snarl of our body. The says never settled, we didn't let them. All says weighed the same. They moved out of us and over us in arcs and then they were gone and forgotten, all mixed up and embraced and confused for a hangnail.

The says:

If I lived on the moon, I would always be naked.   Naked as a dog and the moon's face, a man's face would stare up at me   I always wanted a different sister. I would trade her in for any of   you kissed me once on the mouth to show me what it would be like and your teeth felt slimy and cold and there was a little bit of apple between the two front ones and I'd kiss them again. I'd kiss anything.   Including your own reflection?   Are you kidding? Especially my own reflection in Abana Lake,   it's never how I'm sure I looked just the day before, in the mirror. I always look   at that knee. Whose hairy knee is that?   And I want to throw rocks at it to bust it up, into pieces, but it always re-forms, of course, and it's always the same not-me over and over and it seems like maybe if I turned off my mind, if I stayed asleep for a whole year, my body would just go on doing   the same things that get me in such trouble never get my brother more than a wagging finger. How I'd like to chop it off   Ooh! A bloody bouquet of adult fingers, mine to wag.   I've begun to bleed.   Me too.   And it isn't normal blood. It's brown blood, dead blood and I think there's something wrong with me. Something wicked inside me or else why would it be that color?   My mother doesn't know.   My mother doesn't know, she will never find out.   Can I see it?   You just wait for your own time. It's coming.   It isn't!   No, I hate it. I

never want anyone to see.   Do you feel different? Is it a lot? Like a run-
ning tap?   No, just a horrible brown leak and everything is sticky.
Does it hurt you?   Yes, it's so heavy.   Is all your blood like that when
it's happening?   No, only—   Yes. It replaces your normal red blood
and you swell up with it so much that if you prick your finger on a sewing
needle like Sleeping Beauty, you gush brown blood until you're no bigger than a
raisin shrivel.   That's disgusting.   I threw a penny in Grant Fountain
and wished my zayde would hurry and die and now I'm sad because he hasn't
and he smells of something   musty and gray.   I like that smell, it's
why I don't mind doing the wash.   Sometimes I take dirty things of my
father's. Sometimes I roll kerchiefs to stuff inside my chemise and I catch my
father looking   like what? Like he missed something or maybe he misses
something.   I'll have huge breasts one day, I know it. And they'll float
in water like two white ducks.   And eat bread scraps and bite Franny's
hand!   No names!   We'll all look like our mothers, that's what
they say.   Shame.   Why should we? Do we look like them now?   No,
don't look!   Well if we do then Sarah's out of luck because her mother looks
like—No names!   No names! No, of course. We don't have any.   We
have only one and it's Louisa.   It's Mary.   It's Spider!   Whose voice is this,
anyhow?   Whose voice is this?   Whose voice is this?   And this?

Eventually, we weren't just a spider but also a cave echoing each other's
sounds.

Whose hand is this?

One hand squeezed another, one mouth screamed its delight.

Whose big toe?

Another foot's toe curled around it.

Whose arm is tickling mine?

One set of fingers spidered down another arm's soft side, pausing part
of the way down to pluck a hair. Another yelped.

And whose thigh?

We scrambled to collect our pieces. We were pure greed, which was the best kind. When we scratched, when we pulled, when we clawed and bit, it was not for meanness and it was not in defense of what was ours. Our ferocity was simple unearthing and needed no apology, though it sometimes needed iodine.

We treasure hunted us. Whether each other's bodies or our own, it didn't matter, nor could we have made the distinction if pressed. Our only task was gathering. Whatever we could reach, we handled, we grasped with our hands and our mouths working to free it all of its belonging.

Grabbing fistfuls of cotton and hair and fingers and breasts and hip fat and pulling the blisters off thumbs and the calluses off heels and all the white-cracked skin between toes to the point of pink split and licking the grease from eyelids and tracing the shapes of small moles and pushing cloth aside to suck free, spit out belly button scum and the gray-brown threads of fingernail dirt we scraped from each other.

All of us were new.

We gleamed clean with new sweat and saliva and when we laughed, no one kept her laughter in her own mouth but let it fall freely on the tongue of whoever wanted to gulp it down. Nothing was *no*, for no such word existed to a spider in its nest, to a cave full of echoes.

We were wet and delirious and too exhausted for shame to settle in as we worked ourselves apart. These disappointing reunions with our own limbs always so cold as the sweat chilled and dried on our underwear, making them stiff. We unwound our hair with great patience and the stored gentleness we withheld in our daily lives. But always, there were pieces so bound up and fused together they had to be cut free with a knife.

Coin Toss

Predicting the close of the European war will be the signal for a tremendous Jewish immigration to American shores, Dr. Joseph Krauskopf . . . declared that unless immediate action was taken the American nation would be confronted with the problem of establishing relief associations, building dozens of tuberculosis sanatoria and increasing the number of reformatories. . . . Regardless of the outcome of the struggles the Jews must lose and, knowing the attitude of other nations, as we do, we know they will come to America.

—ATLANTA CONSTITUTION

Our make-believe games were growing tiresome. So, too, the games we knew to be popular with others our age. The domestic portraits cobbled from magazine cutouts on card stock. And the hope chest collages, which were never fun, but which other girls made, so we made too. We stacked them on top of one another. The wet paste that held the cutouts in place stuck the front of one to the back of the next. The thick, warped stack of stuck paper futures we designed for ourselves all dried together in one unruly pile, indistinct and terribly dull. Even their revival, a rascally version where we pasted things where they oughtn't go—women's stockings on men's legs, union suits on the dinner table, cigarettes in the mouths of dogs—had lost its appeal. And the last-ditch games, the ones that came equipped with a set of premade rules, that asked for no invention—games that our parents and neighbors played together, checkers and bridge and sixty-six and Hollywood gin, even with the dirty deck we found behind the bin in the school cafeteria—a real bore. No matter how many times you played, there were only two outcomes: you could win or you could lose. And then what? If that's all there was to it, what's to say winning was any better? As far as we were concerned, they were equal disappointments.

Well, what else is there? asked one of us.

We didn't know. But whatever was out there wasn't waiting in the school building under the lids of our desks.

On a May school day that was already too hot outside for cramming our heads full of useless facts—learning is really best left to the colder months when you don't sweat out every lesson as soon as you've heard it—we told our teacher *Shavuot*. Rule #5, or close enough. We had better, more useful things to learn.

Shavuot, we said. *We must be released. Our parents will expect us home after recess.*

It's the Sixth of the Sivan, said one of us, knowing that whatever we said would be Greek to Miss Albright. *No work allowed. Scripture says arithmetic is strictly prohibited.*

Punishable, even, said one of us, with honest eyes.

Quite severely, someone else added, looking believably mournful. *I ought to know. I tried to do a long division problem last year and I still bear the scars.*

Another of us said: *We must go home to let the blood from a calf for our feast.*

Miss Albright drew a sharp breath and brought her hand to cover her mouth and our joker laughed. Someone else stomped on her toes, and she yelped like a kicked poodle. We were cross with her for her stupid joke. She might have given us away.

Very well, said Miss Albright, nodding in the direction of the door. Poor woman, her color entirely drained. But of course, *very well*, what else could she say?

We left before noon. Our classmates wouldn't miss us. They only talked to us to ask for a pencil, ask for an answer, ask us to *move, kike*. Our mothers always told us, *Stick together, don't wander about alone*, and we agreed: *Like chewing gum to a chair*. What fun was there in alone, anyway? We held hands, walking west on Crumley Street, away from the schoolyard, kicking the shredded red heads off bee balms as good riddance. We were never coming back. We went to the most boring school in all of Atlanta. A person couldn't actually be bored to death because if you could, we would have died ages ago. Most Black folks and factory workers' children didn't even have to go to school. Once they were out of their diapers, they went straight on into the real world, which was the opposite of school.

In the real world, there was danger and adventure and who knows what else. In our school, there were only lines to fill in and there was only one answer for each line, which didn't make any sense at all. If there was only one answer, and no other answers could be considered, then even if you replaced the answer with a black line or a blank space or an empty box, it was still there, wasn't it? Even if it couldn't be seen, it couldn't possibly be anywhere but there, and nothing could go there but the one answer. What was the point in asking the question?

But now we were out and so was the sun, and buttercups spread butterloving shadows on the underside of our chins. We joined our hands and swung them in time with our steps, which were *all together now girls!* We sang a song we made up just for the occasion: *Crummy Crummy Crumley Street, we hate the sight of you!* The "you" a high note we raised our joined hands to boost up. *Crummy Crumbling Crumley School, we five girls are through!* We swung our arms down and stumbled, laughing. We tickled each other's palms as the school building grew doghouse small. We were fastened like a daisy chain. The first one of us to break the chain had to do a dare of our choosing. That was the rule.

The familiar sharp sweetness of linseed oil in midday heat drifted down from the Fulton Bag Mill, mixed with all the other street smells on the way. One of us in the front pulled quicker, tugging tight the arm behind her, dragging her into a run, and then we were all running away from that cotton mill smell, daisy-chaining around a pram. From inside, a baby wailed. The last of us turned around and waggled her tongue at the baby, who screamed with laughter. Around a frowning man in a well-cut suit, who clutched his hat tight to his head as we whooshed past. Into the middle of the street we whipped. A man in a buggy shouted *Watch it!* and Ana ducked around his roan horse, who bucked as she tumbled out of line. Hooves clattering on gravel. The hot hand holding hers didn't squeeze in time to keep her from unlinking herself and we all collapsed across the tracks of the streetcar and laughed, scuffed up and silly. The shadows of the telephone wires sliced our daisy chain into pieces. It wasn't losing exactly, if you pulled so hard that you basically chose to let go, but it wasn't not losing either.

We got lemon ices on Fraser and kept on west to Washington toward the Hebrew Orphan's Home, where the poor Jews went to be out of sight. Three blocks away, a pair of shoe shiners—our age? older? ancient? their hollowed-out faces made it impossible to tell—kneeled on the stoop of a drugstore closed for lunch. Their clothing was well kept but shabby from wear. Our mothers told us to keep away from boys like them. *Poor little urchins,* they said, as if the boys were chimney sweeps in a Dickens novel. *Best not to look them in the face. They don't know how to conduct themselves before young ladies.* That's what our mothers said, but we didn't want to be ladies. Not every day, at least.

Contrary to our mothers' warnings, however, it was they who would not meet our eyes, though we stared at the tops of their heads, willing our gaze to travel through their yarmulkes—silly coasters, our fathers only wore them to temple—and into their heads, willing our eyes to be magnets and pull their gaze up to meet ours. We presented our best sides, smiled over our shoulders. We threw our heads back in riotous laughter as if to say, *how deliciously wicked!* But the boys were not stirred by any of this.

Talk to them, we commanded Ana. That was the dare she earned. *Make them talk to us. They're probably your people, after all, Cossacks. All the urchins are.*

I'm not, said Ana, a weak protest. But she couldn't refuse her dare.

Hello boys, she sighed and we echoed, *Hello boys,* a chorus of silky black-birds. She said *Yoohoo!* and we said *Yoohoo!* and gave a wave of our fingers like playing down the keys of a piano. It was a gesture we imagined would have a come-hither effect but made us feel embarrassed instead because they never looked up to see it. We were not the right kind of girls. We couldn't attract gnats. Flirtation and coyness would be forever denied us: scabby, frizz-haired nobodies. If it had been us instead of pretty little Mary Phagan, no one would have given a damn.

If you couldn't make good on your dare, you had to take a new one, a tougher one. No one got away for free.

Excuse me, Ana said, trying again. *Do you boys have the time?*

But the playfulness of her first effort was gone from her voice and it sounded like an earnest question, as though she feared she might be late for supper. Without looking up from the ground, one of them jerked his head over his right shoulder as the belfry rang in the noon hour.

We licked our mouths, tongued the crusting corners, and smile-frown-smile-frown-smile-frowned to break up the tightness of the lemon syrup still on our lips, pinching and drying tight in the heat of the sun. We wanted our lips to crack and break open. We wanted to be alarming.

Poor little gutter boys, who loves you? One of us pulled a small purse from her pocket and jingled the coins within. Two or three pieces, just enough to make an audible clinking. The other boy glanced up and quickly back down. We had them. We all withdrew our purses, five of them making a tinny choir of coins. We beat them against our palms and thighs. We danced around in a circle to the drumming of our nickels and cents. Both boys were fixed on us now. Their eyes wide with longing for us, for our petty change and the ease with which we could part with it.

This was the new dare: *Give them what they want, Ana.*

She emptied her coins into her palm. Three nickels, seven pennies.

Maybe we shouldn't, she said.

You broke the chain, didn't you?

She took a step toward them as we back-and-forth chanted:

> *Russian lad in your Pushkin hat,*
> *how'd you like a dime?*
> *Give us a spin and stand on your chin*
> *before I finish my rhyme.*
>
> *One one-hundred, two one-hundred,*
> *Go Go Go!*
> *Three one-hundred, four one-hundred—*

Ana, with her fist clenched tightly around the coins, swung her shoulder, but her fist stayed coiled, little miser, as though throwing a trick pitch.

> *Three one-hundred, four one-hundred—*

She wound up again and drew a tall breath.

You're! too! slow! one of us screamed, unable to endure the torture of patience, and threw her own fistful, marvelous, into the air. The pennies

hovered above them for a moment, a copper cloud overhead, before raining down over the boys, who crawled along the ground, lurching for the
cracks in the cement, and dragged their fingers through the gutter scum to
feel them out. We had planned to throw our coins in too—add our pennies
to the merry scramble—but we no longer wanted to.

I was going to, said Ana.

But you didn't, one of us replied.

Oh, don't worry, someone said gently. *No one really expected you to
anyhow. You're too soft for all that.*

All the same, said another of us, *you're in the debt of your dare until you
make good.*

Dumpling Factory

A public meeting to protest against the appeal for commutation of Leo M. Frank was held upon the steps of the capitol Saturday afternoon at 3 o'clock. More than 400 persons, perhaps, were in attendance, some of them girls and women. Speeches deploring the interference of outside influence and the delegations from other states were made . . . The meeting was brought to a clamorous end when the crowd cheered for an encore from "Fiddlin' John" Carson, the native musician, who fiddled and sang an original song dedicated to Mary Phagan.

—ATLANTA CONSTITUTION

We were having Shabbos dinner at the Wulffs' house, and all of our parents were there, but in the sitting room, talking between themselves and our older siblings, who might as well have been our parents. We were in the kitchen making dumplings. Our mothers liked us to play at cooking and kitchen chores, though we were no longer sure if it was play or practice. They were celebrating, though they were trying to pretend as though everything was normal. We knew because they let us pick the food, and they never let us pick the food. We chose matzoh ball soup, which is usually only for Seder, but they allowed it, beaming like our mothers never did. And we knew why, too. Leo's sentence had been commuted. His life had been spared at the eleventh hour by Governor Slaton.

Never thought he'd find the courage, said our fathers, dealing congratulatory blows to one another's backs. *God looks out for his people.*

But it wasn't good news. And now the woods around the governor's house were filled with two hundred angry men and their weapons. They burned scarecrows made up to look like Slaton with signs around their necks that said *King of the Jews,* but they wanted the real thing. A body for each of their angers. For each of them, something to hurt. And everyone knows that after the eleventh hour, the twelfth comes, and the twelfth hour is the end. Our parents wouldn't know good news if we rolled it up and hit them on the nose with it.

They're a bunch of Lucilles, one of us said under our breath. She was our Smutch du jour.

Loose eels, Loose eels, we sneered. A hot, oily name slipping off our tongues. We could barely say it without gagging. The papers showed her full-body picture when Leo was first sentenced, and she fainted in the courtroom. She was a big spread on the front page. We had to see her there, taking up Leo's space, expanding in her gaudy white dress. Not at all flattering, pity no one told Loose Eel. Next to her, our Leo appeared not quite a feature of the photo, but a frame for it, for her, and she pushed him into the crease, folded him under her. Pushed him out to Milledgeville, the state prison farm (what could they possibly even grow there?) a hundred miles away, which might as well be a thousand, just like anywhere the trolley didn't go. And he was there for keeps. Stupid Lucille, her hips a thousand miles across. Lucille, fat and happy in their eel slime sheets, all hers now to spread herself over. We blamed Lucille, that oily dumpling, even though really she wasn't that bad. We all knew it. She was pretty, in her way, and probably perfectly nice. She had a kind smile, and what we wouldn't give to be her, but that didn't matter. We needed her to be terrible—to be our Smutch.

In the kitchen, we moved along the counter like an assembly line. We were working girls, factory girls, Mary Phagans, free to wield dangerous things, free to do what we pleased, and with whom. The first job—the cracker smasher—was the most coveted position because it involved the rolling pin, which most closely resembled a factory tool. We all liked the rolling pin, heavy and blunt. We took turns in this position, watching the squares of matzoh, like brittle sheet brass, turn to powder under the weight of the machinery we wielded.

Then the meal was swept into a mixing bowl and passed down the line where it was improved by pinches of salt, pepper, powdered onion, and dill. The dill station was also coveted. Whoever chopped the dill got to use the blade, the arced one, like a child's scythe. We lined up the stems and rocked the blade back and forth over the feathered leaves. The hollow, headless stems were discarded, and the cut herb made our fingers smell sweet like grass and licorice. We shoved our hands under one another's noses, or else we kept our sweet fingers to ourselves. We found reasons to pardon ourselves, go off and privately inhale them. It was not such a good job as the cracker smasher, but it was a close second.

From the other end of the assembly line, one of us added eggs to a second bowl one at a time, pouring the yolk back and forth between halves of the broken shell to sieve it from its white. A gift for the rest of us: the yolk as bright as a canary's heart. A little shell falling in with the egg, and so what? Another one of us spooned in the schmaltz. She stuck her fingers into the jar so she could dimple its white surface with her finger holes and lick the fat. Two greasy heaping mounds of schmaltz that melted into the eggs as they were whisked. Everything was gleaming yellow ribbons.

The two bowls met in the middle. One of us poured the meal into the wet bowl, a measured little bit at a time, and another stirred until the mix was thick and sticky: our cue to abandon our stations to roll the dumplings.

We wetted our hands and plunged them into the bowl, pulling at the dough, which stretched in good-natured protest until it tore. We rolled it in small circles between our palms. The smaller ones were easier to make perfectly round. Baby dumplings like pale, sticky marbles. One of us experimented, flicking a larger dumpling, a shooter, at a marble-sized one. Her aim, unusually true, landed the larger one just to the left of the smaller and they stuck together. A lopsided pair of mottled lumps, flecked with dill green, they looked a little rotten. Rose scooped them into her cupped hands and held them up to her chest, which she thrust out, her shoulders back, as she tucked her chin so that the smooshed skin underneath made more rings of skin below. She paraded in front of us, swinging her hips this way and that, like a flag on a windy day.

Guess who I am, she said, with some difficulty because her jaw was pushed into her chest.

That isn't nearly enough dough, said Esther. She took a large pinch of dough from the bowl and fixed it to the larger dough-breast so that the disproportion was downright ridiculous. Sarah added several more pinches—two to the larger breast and one to the smaller. The exaggerated lumpiness of their surfaces gave them the look of two aging heads of cauliflower.

We added and added, fixing pinches to the rest of Rose's body—her wrists, chin, her cheeks, and jaw—until the bowl was empty.

Why, Mrs. Loose Eel, Sarah played along, *are you feeling altogether well?*

How very kind of you to inquire, said Rose, in a husky dough-swollen voice, *I do believe I'm feeling ever so*—she swooned about theatrically, stumbling into each of us like a drunk.

Faint? Sarah prompted, giggling madly.

On cue, Rose, padded out in dumpling dough, tipped back and fell—*catch me!*—into Franny's unsure arms.

You're getting it dirty, said Ana. *You'd better stop it now or we'll all be picking strands of hair and loose threads from our teeth.*

But Rose, who wouldn't be told when to stop, said, *Well, look at who grew a spine. Don't think we've forgotten about your debt.*

I didn't, said Ana, though it was clear from her face that she had.

You still have to make good on your dare, said Rose. *You owe us, and I have just the thing.* She ran her dough-covered cheek along the tip of Ana's nose. *You have to make Isaac fall in love with you.*

Ana laughed.

Why would she want to do that? said Franny.

It doesn't matter if she wants to do it or not, said Rose, *it's her dare.*

It doesn't matter if it's my dare, Ana corrected. *It's impossible. He's too old, and besides he never loved any woman but his wife, and he never will.*

Then you've got to change his mind, said Sarah.

How? said Ana.

Might I suggest an accidental peek of bare leg and a fallen stocking? said Esther, dragging her skirt up her shin with the heel of her shoe as she sat cross-legged in a chair next to us. *Or you could back yourself up against him when he's cleaning in a corner. Oops!* she said, rising suddenly, and pinning Ana to the wall behind her.

We wondered what Mary Phagan had done to make so many men want to love her.

Why don't you ask the voodoo woman for a love potion? said Sarah. *Since you swear she's real.*

An excellent idea, said Rose. *Would you listen to us? We're practically doing your dare for you.*

How will she know if she's done it? asked Franny.

It was a good question.

You just know, Esther said wisely.

And what if I don't? said Ana. *What if I refuse?*

This was a bad question.

Then the Night Witch will come for your soul, said Rose and she blew a big puff of air into Ana's nostrils, which surprised them both by coming right back out of Ana's mouth and knocking Rose in the face with her own breath just like a cartoon, and we all laughed.

At supper, after we washed and said the kiddush, we grinned at each other over our soup bowls with their floating chunks of Lucille softening in broth. One of us took a bite of a dumpling and gagged. We held our laughter very well, pretending concern. *Oh dear, are you quite well?* Then another of us went *Blugh!* and one of us patted her on the back. Minutes later, two more of us gagged and one of us dropped her spoon into her still-full bowl, sending chicken broth splattering across her white linen placemat and her face. It decorated her eyelashes in yellow beads. One of the adults asked where the chicken had been purchased and another of them said, *Not at supper, please.* They carried on, ignoring us:

Soder's, if you must know. We trust Rabbi Geffen. We think he's a good man, a good rabbi.

That may be, but he's so old-fashioned, wearing his beard so long like that, he scares people.

What people? Who is scared?

And Rabbi Marx is a modern—

Good is a debatable judgment. Come Sofia, consider David's visibility in the city. Wulff's is a well-known establishment. Is that really the right choice for your—

As far as kashrut is concerned, his practices are questionable and furthermore, we won't have our daughter—

Do not speak to my wife as though—

As though what?

As though she were your wife.

What business of yours is it how I speak to my wife?

Not at supper, I beg you.

I don't see why not. Supper seems as good a time as any to address—

Then not at this supper, at least. We're celebrating, don't you remember?

What are we celebrating, exactly? A growing mob? My wife's brother in Marietta got a note on his shop door today, courtesy of a group calling themselves the Marietta Vigilante Committee—

He ought to have better sense than to live in a place like that.

That's beside the point! The note advised him to leave town at once or else they'd—

Don't. Not in front of the children.

We know! We know! we wanted to say. So much more than you ever will.

Come, now. You scare too easily. You know these people, there's nothing behind it.

Ask a Black man if there's nothing behind it.

For us, I mean.

And now, have you seen, Oscar Elsas is in the news, too? They call him a tyrant who won't settle his workers' strike.

Too many prominent Jews are making bad headlines.

Those unemployed millhands are a mob farm, mark my words. They're angry and ignorant and dangerous.

A tyrant? Elsas is a community leader, and a great advocate for Frank's release!

That's half the problem.

And those Brooklyn Jews are the other half. That petition did more harm than good. Nothing Georgians hate more than Northern interference. Listen to this fulmination from The Jeffersonian: *"Jew money has debased us, bought and sold us—and laughs at us."*

No one reads The Jeffersonian, *it's a hillbilly rag.*

You brought that rubbish paper into our home? Our dinner?

The Jeffersonian *was banned in our houses.*

I would hazard a guess the Vigilante Committee did.

We need to talk about it. Apologies, but you must listen. There's more: "Our grand old Empire State has been raped."

That's enough!

"Mary Phagan, pursued and tempted, and entrapped, and then killed when she would not do what so many other girls had done for this Jewish hunter of Gentile girls."

What wouldn't she do?

Stop this at once!

Some of our mothers fanned their blotched faces. The older brothers were red and sweating.

They're boycotting Wulff's. I got a letter midweek—

It can't be. Not here in Atlanta.

It's nothing, it's a prank.

—with over a hundred signatures. I'm sorry, Sofia, I should have told you.

We would all be better off if Frank were dead.

Rule #8, our solemn and sworn duty! It was all too much. What right had they, adults, to behave like this, going after each other, going after our Leo, and paying us no mind? What right to have such inappropriate faces? Angry, red faces, not like our parents' at all?

Rabbi Geffen, the Kosher Killer, blurted Rose, unable to stop herself from performing one of our private jokes. Not her best show. There was an urgent thinness to her voice that wrecked the bit. The adults stared at her. She stared into her own brothy face, reflected in her bowl. Half-hearted, she finished: *Four Ka-nickles gets you a klean klucker!*

With the whole game of the evening on the verge of collapse, one of

us launched into fits of illness with convincing abandon and we all followed suit. We clasped at our throats with both hands, tongues lolling. We
coughed chewed-up globs of dumpling back into our bowls, wheezing for
air. Such a good performance, we might have tricked a doctor.

Thinking us ill, our parents rushed us off to our separate houses. They
took us, not gently, by the arm, saying *Come now!*—a dog's command.
They did not look at one another as they left and we, fake invalids in recov-
ery, were not allowed to leave our houses for three days after. Of course,
we weren't ill, but we sat in our beds anyway, feeling, like dogs, obedient
and ashamed.

We sent messages to one another by whispering them to the petals of
dried flowers, which we crushed in our hands and tossed out of our windows, trusting the wind to deliver us to each other.

Making Good

Why do I feel I'm forever trying to prove myself? Sometimes
I think I'd be better off letting them get me wrong.

—DIARY OF ANA WULFF

Ana wasn't a coward, but neither was she exceptionally brave. She
had an average amount of fear, and this was to her credit, as the
exceptionally brave tended also to be exceptionally prideful and
foolish. Though she was not exempt from foolishness, from allowing her
curiosity to overtake her better logic.

She was fond of stories, and fonder still of convincing herself they were
true. Recognizing this trait in his charge, the Wulffs' hired man, Isaac, had
become an accomplished raconteur. Most affecting, Isaac discovered, were
stories of voodoo magic, which, he told Ana, was magic only Black folks
had. It was a subject about which Ana knew nothing at all and had no
means by which to learn, other than taking the old man's word for absolute truth. On matters of voodoo magic, Isaac was the foremost authority.
Particularly elaborate were his stories about Miss Zelie, the Haitian voodoo
woman who absolutely despised an untidy home. The very whisper of her
name was enough to persuade Ana to take up the feather duster and get to
work on her chores. And he ought to know a thing about it, he told her, on
account of the number of times he'd visited Miss Zelie's stall in Darktown.

I had to, said Isaac. *Who do you think had me running over there all
the time?*

Ana measured him against her dare: he was gray haired, but his cleaning rag was draped jauntily, she now thought, over one shoulder, the way a younger man might do it, and his forearms were pleasantly ropey. She loved to watch him chop onions, the iridescent slivers sailing like insect wings as his knife pared them down. There was a time, she could imagine, when he might not have been unhandsome. But whether he was, or wasn't, or had, or hadn't been, that wasn't the point of the dare, and she knew it.

You can't mean my mother, she said.

Course not.

Not my father.

No, no. Good white folks like them don't know about Miss Zelie, but with you such a sick baby, one foot in the grave until you lost your first milk tooth, it was the only smart thing to do. How do you think I cured you of that evil fever when you were knee-high to a grasshopper? he said, and whipped the rag from his shoulder to point it at her. The scent of lemon oil shot through the air.

The point of the dare was to test her, to put her in her place and make her fail, and maybe she deserved to: to be proven not attractive enough (Esther could have done it!); not bold enough (Rose could have done it!); not loyal enough to the others that she would do her dare without a second thought, without the first one being of Isaac. Not loyal enough that she would do it just because it was the debt she owed them.

Your mother can always hire a new housekeeper, Sarah had said when Ana protested. *He's old, anyhow. It's about time.*

It's a bad dare, said Franny, but she was squarely outnumbered.

Isaac had once had a wife, who had also worked for the Wulffs, but she had died of pneumonia the spring before Ana was born, and though it was unusual for a Black man to work inside the home, Isaac had asked to take his wife's place. He was very sad, and it would give him comfort, he said, to carry on the work she'd done. Mrs. Wulff was then five months into a very difficult pregnancy, and Isaac, over fifty and losing the strength for yardwork, was deemed gentle enough to handle the baby.

In fact, Isaac had never visited Miss Zelie, nor did he believe in voodoo, or any sort of magic. He only started believing in heaven when his wife died, and even then, it didn't go much beyond a place for the two of them where they could be unhurried together.

They put me in a bath of ice, Ana said. *To drive the fever down. Don't you remember? Father says I turned blue as a cornflower.*

Sure, I remember. I broke up the blocks myself, but don't be telling me you really think a cold bath cured that influenza. You were sick for weeks. He shook his head. *I thought you were smarter than that.*

It was a shorthand between them—standing in for the usual tedious series of requests that no adult enjoyed making and no child yielding to. Instead, if Ana wouldn't stop giving him grief, if Ana wouldn't set the table, if Ana dragged mud through the house one more time, he'd have the Haitian woman put some voodoo on her *and that Obeya sticks like glue.*

I don't believe you one bit, said Ana, which wasn't one bit true. Not only did Ana believe Isaac, but she picked these stories up where he left them off and kept them burning in her own busy mind, making no distinction between the end of Isaac's and the beginning of her own. It was all perfectly, marvelously true.

Besides, I have my own magic. Guess what it's called. Too pleased with her own cleverness to allow him time, she blurted *Dis-obeya! Get it, Isaac?* Ana had a laugh like the meat of a walnut. She had a nice laugh too, which she used in public, even with the others. With Isaac, though, she had always used the real one, ugly and delicious. Now, though, she wished she had used her better one. No one would fall in love with a walnut girl.

Just a little bit of your hair, said Isaac, *which Lord knows is everywhere. Don't you ever brush that bramble on your head?*

Ana swiped her palm roughly across her beaded forehead and back over her hair. The sweat slicked back the wisps near her face. She was growing irritated. What right did he have to make fun of her so, when she was trying to be beautiful?

Just one strand and Miss Zelie could make you wish you'd dusted under the sofa like old Isaac told you.

I bet Miss Zelie would side with me. Unlike you, I've got better things to do than clean the parlor. She smoothed her dress over her waist. It was a fine dress and a fine waist, and if Isaac didn't think so, well he could just—but there! He had looked just then . . . or had he? She had definitely caught him glancing, just a quick, guilty flick of the eye . . . or else it was incidental. No, he had noticed. Of course he had, he was attracted, perhaps not even consciously. It was just his nature, as a man, to be attracted. But could he really think of *her* that way? As a woman, or an almost-woman? Did she want him to?

Then she heard the faint ticking of a second hand and flushed hot. He was looking at the clock beside her. All she had to do was knock it off the wall and leave Isaac to clean up the shattered mess. It's what he wanted, anyhow. He was just waiting for her to leave so he could get on with his work. She was stupid, so stupid, to imagine she could make him . . . what? Make him want *something* from her. She couldn't even say it in her head— well, he was wrong. She mattered in the way women matter. She would not be a stupid girl forever. She was not a stupid girl now.

Mark my words, Little Miss Trouble, Isaac said. *She'd see it my way. And for all you know, she's got a hair of yours already, and she's just waiting for me to say the word.*

Then say it, Ana snarled.

She knew Isaac couldn't get to his hands and knees due to his bad back and it would only take her a second to clean beneath the sofa, but she didn't like to do it, so why should she? She didn't get paid for it like Isaac did, and those spidery threads of dust tangled her eyelashes and made her sneeze.

The others don't believe Miss Zelie's a real voodoo. They say you're a liar.

You think Obeya cares if you believe in it or not?

Why should I trust you?

Other than bringing you back from the brink of death, you mean?

Maybe it was just my good luck.

How do you know you've found a real butcher when you walk up to his shop?

That's easy. All his meat hangs in the window or sits behind the counter.

Well, it's like that with Miss Zelie, too. She's got an altar next to her where she keeps her magic laid out. Potions and herb pouches and crocus sack dolls she uses to tie the soul down. That sort of thing. Anybody with one good eye can tell it's the real thing.

Ana had two of them, and she could see what had to be done. She would make them all regret taking her for granted.

Easy peasy, thought Ana as she gathered her hair under a plain gray scarf, cast-off fabric from last winter's cuttings. *Prim and poor and pay-no-mind* was the song she sang as she knotted the corners under her chin. She was riding the streetcar to pay off her dare, riding to Darktown, a Black neighborhood where Isaac said Miss Zelie could be found (because it was a place he was sure Ana would never go). Riding alone was one of Ana's very favorite things. She liked riding with the others too. They made her laugh, but they were so loud. They would try to sing over the screech of the cable. And the cable, in response, seemed to raise its own voice. She could have taken the train all the way to Terminal Station, but she got off at Decatur Street instead. Another place she was not allowed, and certainly not alone. Well, if she was going to disobey, she might as well do it right.

It was the first time she was conscious of having walked anywhere by herself—that was to say, the first time she could recall having the thought, *it's only me.* It shouldn't have been such a remarkable occasion—hadn't she gone to the grocer's on her own before? Hadn't she run errands for her mother on her own? Walked on her own to Jacob's Pharmacy for nearly two years now? But always before she had set off alone in anticipation of her return to company, so that the solitude's objective was the end of itself.

Then there was the word itself: *solitude.* How very different it was to think herself a solitary adventurer instead of a girl alone. One word imparts: "sole" and "only" and "solid," and the other: "lone," "lonely," a frightened girl's word. Today, she decided, she would not be frightened.

She could hear the paperboy's voice in the distance, made ragged by yesterday's *Extra! Extra!* She jumped, two-footed, over a rotten newspaper, the pictures faded into featurelessness. She hopscotched: bottle, bottle, handkerchief / brown sack, linen scrap, baseball, cigarettes / Chiclets box, flower bundle, magazine, child's shoe, newspaper, until she was out of breath at the end of the alley.

Out from under the shade, the sun shone down again, drying the gutter juice splashed against her ankles. A scratch on her shin bled lightly. She tried, half-heartedly, to clean herself up using the toe of one foot to drag the dirt off the ankle of the other. Her mother said she spent too much time in her head and where would that get her but in trouble?

The sidewalk had grown busy with Ana lost in her head. That's what her mother called it, but Ana didn't feel lost at all. A saturnine man with a long black beard stood behind his cart yelling, *Fruit Ice! Hot Day! Cool Off! Fruit Ice!* His cry was from memory. You could hear in it how he had recited the English words apart from their meaning who-knows-how-many times so that they sounded strictly phonetic. A teacher's wooden pointer tapping syllables: *this* and *this* and *this* against a chalkboard.

Was this how the others heard her mother's voice? She had come to America so long ago Ana wasn't sure if her mother remembered Russia or if it was only that she knew the stories so well they seemed like her own memory. Either way, she had stubbornly retained, perhaps even practiced, her un-American accent. To Ana, her words sounded golden and honeycombed, but when the others thought she wasn't in earshot, they did impersonations of her mother's voice. Ana had seen them at it, how they pursed their lips, spilling heavy vowels into molds of nonsense scolding. *An-yyyyah*, they said her name meanly in her mother's voice, with a tongue depressor on the second syllable. *An-yyyah, what a mess you've made! She should be a broom instead of a daughter!* Once, Sarah had told her, beaming, how her father said Mrs. Wulff was the most well-bred Russian he ever met. She offered this brightly, like a piece of ribbon candy.

Peach pyramids framed the rings of pineapple that made yellow chains atop the silver-white sheet of ice on the man's cart. Their stringy flesh sweating sweetly in yellow blisters. Ana didn't eat pineapple because its skin looked like dragon hide, but the smell of the fruit, a little overripe, made her mouth water.

Ana put her hand on the ice and plunged her fingers into the cracks between blocks, simply because it was what she had wanted to do. The fruit man opened his mouth to scold her, his eyebrows drawing low and close, but before he could form the English words for his anger, two boys came barreling down the sidewalk. A man considerably larger, and unwieldy as a rogue wheel, huffed after them. The boys with their quick bodies darted around the cart, splitting apart and rejoining fluidly once past, but the man caught the fruit vendor's shoulder, knocking him into his cart as the large man chased on. The force of the fruit vendor's fall upset the pyramids of peaches and they toppled from the cart, over Ana's hand still sunk in the ice, landing on the sidewalk with a thud. There they were: three peaches presenting themselves at her feet, leaking golden pulp.

I'm sorry, she told the man on the ground, then she took a burst peach in each hand and she ran, too. Not because she was scared, but for no reason. Because they were hand-sized or because the peach skin tickled her mouth as she sucked up the juices or because her fingers had gone ice-numbed or because the boys had looked like starlings in flight or because it was too hot to be standing still or all of those reasons and a hundred more.

Her hair lifted off her neck and every leap she took invited a billow of wind under her dress. Her shoe buckles rubbed sores into the tops of her feet just under her dirty ankles where the brass chafed, and the sting of sweat in the fresh cut was bright and good like the sun in her eyes. The sidewalk unfurled before her like an illusion. Just as she thought she had the end in sight, another long stretch of city blocks came tumbling into view, and on it went right off the edge of the map.

She sailed over street-chatter, dove past barbers' *Shave and a haircut!*, weaved between a swingy skein of ragtime piano music. The Victrola rasp winked from windows thrown open in the vain hope of catching a rare cool late-morning breeze. There were, sometimes, such summer mornings here—ones that threatened, by the chilly dew they left on front porch rocking chairs, that the summer would not last forever. This morning was not that sort of threat.

The coins in her purse jingled brightly as she ran. She smiled, thinking of their small sound being played in the private chamber of her purse for an audience of stolen lipstick. She reached her hand in and scraped the coins together with her thumb and forefinger to hear the quiet *schhhhschhh* of the stamped metals rubbing one another smooth as beach stones.

The coins made up two weeks' allowance—fifty cents in six coins her father had given her *for being such a fine young Georgian lady*. Less than a quarter of Mary Phagan's wages. Her mother was not to know. It was a secret between Ana and her father—even a game. He would hide the coins in the toes of her shoes, which she left by the door, or under her cut-glass teacup and say, *Gaze into your cup, Madame Ana, greatest clairvoyant of Fulton County, and tell me what you read in the dregs*, and Ana would squint into the cup, laying her fingertips on either side of her temples, and say, *Why sir, a very good fortune indeed!* He would applaud and both of them would laugh, conspirators.

Her mother said she had her father's laugh. And whenever she said it, she would close her eyes and knead her brows. But this was before Ana left the allowance in her dress pocket one day. She hadn't wanted to spend the coins, finding them more precious as small shining gifts than any of the silly things she might have traded them for. Her mother had found them while doing her wash.

For what? cried Mrs. Wulff, brandishing the coin pouch and dropping it hard on the kitchen table. A great clatter. Mr. Wulff, who sat cross-legged in his usual reading spot, the cream and floral armchair, with a paper spread across his field of vision, cleared his throat.

These wages for what? For what work? For what labor? Zai nischt kein nar.

Sofia—Mr. Wulff began preparing words he knew would not mollify his wife—*darling*. Soft words only, each one like a drop of meringue offered to his wife for smashing. *It's only a little pocket change.*

You schmendrick, you spoil her. Mrs. Wulff whipped the still-damp dress at her husband, licking the paper from his hands with a crack, where it fell into his lap. *Can't you see that?* She stooped down to peer into his face. *Or do you need eyeglasses?*

When Mrs. Wulff was angry, sparks of foreign words burst from her mouth and her eyes were terribly alive.

Come now, said Mr. Wulff. Meaning calm down, but not really meaning it. He did not rise from his chair. For like Ana, he was more captivated than concerned.

That she should never know for what!

What's the trouble, Mother? said Ana. It was a thrill to raise her temper, though there was no real sport to it on account of ease. Ana knew it was bad of her, but was it really *so* bad?

I will have a nischtgutnik for a daughter, said Mrs. Wulff, shaking her head in mournful resignation. But no, that couldn't be the end. Ana wasn't ready to be done, so she pushed.

Yes, yes, when you were my age you worked dawn to dusk in Zayde's butcher shop, plucking feathers and pulling out chicken guts. But times are different now, Mother.

This had done it, reignited her mother, now nearly aglow with her delicious ire. Easy peasy.

You want to talk about chickens? she turned to Ana. *Fine*. She grabbed her daughter under the arms and lifted her into the air, which so surprised Ana that she did little to resist. She felt light, giddy, feathered.

Go ahead, Ana, sit on them, she said, dropping Ana on the kitchen table, atop the little pile of coins. *Sit and sit and sit! That will be your work.*

Mr. Wulff had risen now, his paper forgotten on the chair. But he only watched, smiling faintly. It was very good anger.

See if they will hatch into bigger money, she said to Ana, her small hands describing furious surges. Her cuticles, Ana could see, were ragged and red. *Bars of silver?* she huffed, and Ana wondered if her mother wasn't happy to have the occasion to rage, if she wasn't—even if she didn't know it, exactly—playing along.

Diamond eggs and golden geese and—

She could have kept going. She had the stamina, Ana was sure, to sustain her tirade with little nudges here and there from Ana, little stupid remarks to stoke her rage, but Ana broke down first—by making it a game. By jutting her chin forward and flapping her arms, hinged at the elbow, and clucking *buck buck buck buck* at her table perch, then throwing her head back and laughing her big, brash laugh. Which caught her father off guard and he, nearly choking on it, loosed his own big, brash laugh. And then what could Mrs. Wulff do but glare at her red-faced husband, her squawking daughter, who—cocking back her head—let out a giant *Ba-gawk!* at which Mrs. Wulff yelped.

Then, hands balled in fists, shoulders clenched, eyes wet, she laughed herself.

And that was Ana's last allowance. The one she'd brought here. Anyway, it wasn't so bad in this part of the city. Everybody made it out to seem as though the earth dropped off at the end of the trolley line. Obviously, the whole world couldn't be a copy of her front yard, that was just common sense. There were Black neighborhoods, and mill towns for crackers, and neighborhoods for rich gentiles, and ones for Hasids in their long coats, and ones for Chinamen, and neighborhoods with one-night-only hotels, and so forth and so forth. Every kind and color of person had a neighborhood. Sure, it was a little ramshackle, more cracks to break her mother's back, but it was all Atlanta, wasn't it?

At the border of Dekalb and Darktown, Ana asked a mill man where to find Miss Zelie, the voodoo woman, and he said, *Sure you ain't lookin for me?* She told him she was positive, and he said *Hmm. Better be Collins Street, then. Ought to watch yourself, though. Buddy of mine got a curse put on him there. Said some kind of sideways word to a Black witch and she gave him the drip just by blinking her eyes at him.* Ana nodded her confusion and hurried away.

Catty-corner to a blind tiger saloon a block off Collins Street, Ana spotted a woman in a loose white dress with skin like the space the crescent moon leaves empty. Next to the woman was a collection of assorted objects in a bundle: a glass bottle half-full of something dark and oily, a colorful square tin, a rust-tarnished silver locket, a small etched leather purse, a thin book with a vanishing gilded cover, a threadbare ragdoll. The altar? Yes, it must have been. Just as Isaac had told her.

Hello, ma'am, said Ana, approaching slowly. It was probably best not to startle her. Startled creatures will employ whatever defenses they possess. What was the appropriate way to greet a voodoo woman, she wondered. She ought to have brought an offering—a frog in a jar or something of that nature. But since she had no frog, only a little change—and what good would that be to a voodoo woman?—all she could do was curtsy. The woman didn't look up. On first glance, she was a little unimpressive. Her shoulders had the roundness of a rock that had been tumbled too many times in a river, and her hair was going white, but humble looks could disguise enormous power. Literature made a fuss of this—King Arthur and so forth. And nature insisted on it. Ants, for example, could heft their body weight several times over, and snails carried their homes on their backs.

I am Miss Alice Cheshire, said Ana, and smiled as though she had surprised herself with the spontaneity of this false name. *Practically without thinking* is what she told herself. Though she had thought of it, all the way along the streetcar ride, she had thought *curiouser and curiouser*. The woman continued to pay her no mind. And with no one else interested in being fooled, Ana continued to fool herself: it wasn't that she had wanted to deceive the woman; it wasn't cleverness that made her introduce herself as Alice, those were the words that naturally left her lips.

I'm not in my own world anymore, she told herself, so it's only fitting I should have a new name, maybe even be a new me. As a matter of fact, she didn't see why everyone should be restricted to only one version of themselves. There were times when being oneself was utterly inconvenient.

When I'm older, she thought, and out from under my parents' roof, I'll have a different me for every day of the week. Furthermore, she told herself, a false name was necessary prudence. Owing to the fame of her father's shop, there was no telling who might know the name Wulff and who might get it in their head to gossip.

Hmm, said the woman.

An unlit cigarette was wedged between her lips so that the papery threads of loose tobacco flopped about as she spoke. With her head bent, she scraped a matchstick over the ground, and it flicked alight but the flame died quickly in a wind too hot and soft to rightly be called wind. More like a giant mouth breathing a hot-toothed sigh over everybody in the city: *Ahhhhhhh*.

If one delays for too long, one is likely to lose one's nerve, thought Ana, and then one might never find the courage to say, *Are you Miss Zelie, the Haitian I've heard so much about?*

Do I look like that voodoo-casting bitch? the woman said without looking up.

In truth, she didn't. She even smelled faintly of boiled potatoes, but who was Ana to make that sort of evaluation?

Ma'am, she said, because she didn't know what came next. How exhilarating to be at a loss for words! Ana had made a study of conversation. She knew its various combinations—there were four conversation types possible in any exchange with an adult and six and a half (the half for the rare screaming match) with the others. Once she identified the type of conversation, she could usually anticipate her conversation partner's responses up to three exchanges in advance. But in this case, the unfamiliar setting of Darktown in conjunction with the use of a swear word, Ana didn't know what the woman might say next or how to plan out her responses in order to steer the conversation to her desired ends.

If I did have voodoo magic I'd use it on this damn cigarette. Light it on the first strike. That's where the real voodoo's at. I'd put a patent on that. Make me a rich woman.

Before Ana had time to think of a suitable reply, a policeman appeared and approached them with haste. Ana was equal parts irritated for being interrupted and relieved to have time to work out the correct response.

Everything all right here, Miss?

He was addressing Ana, but it was the old woman who responded: *Fine, sir, just fine. This young lady got herself lost, and I'm fixing to give her directions back to the streetcar.*

I can escort you there, Miss.

I don't need an escort, Ana snapped, her irritation overtaking her relief. *I have an errand here to complete.*

What sort of an errand, if I might ask? This can be a dangerous neighborhood. Every other person here is some sort of criminal, he said, eyeing the old woman.

I prefer not to say. She was losing patience with this intruder, this spy. *If you would be so kind as to leave me to it. It's really a matter of some urgency.*

Of course, Miss, the policeman replied after maddening hesitation. *I wouldn't dream of prying into a young lady's affairs. I'll check back in a while, if you need further assistance.*

Thank you kindly, sir, the woman answered.

I didn't need any assistance in the first place, Ana thought better of saying as he retreated down the block.

The woman licked her fingertip as she watched him go, and held it over her head, moving it in an arc, nodded, paused, and lit another matchstick, which caught and died before her face.

Shit. The smoke from the matchstick curled around her face. *Time for you to be on your way before you bring more of them here. Girls like you: moths to a flame.*

But Ana wasn't ready to leave. The scorn, the bait, the press, the brag. Ana cycled through the known patterns of conversation uselessly. How many matches had the woman lit? Three? Four? And was she the moth, or the flame?

I beg your pardon, said Ana, defaulting to politeness.

Well, you sure as shit can't have that, said the woman, *so what else are you begging? You got a list you're working from?*

Please, said Ana, adjusting her approach to include candor. *My father doesn't allow me to come to this part of town, but I've made a trip, unknown to him, just to see Miss Zelie. I'm risking quite a lot to be here, you understand*. It seemed to her a compelling tale. Furthermore, it was a true one and truth was the backbone of something or other. She could see, however, that the old woman did not care. *If you aren't Miss Zelie, then perhaps you know where I can find her?*

Ana could feel the old woman's eyes appraising her for the first time since her arrival, taking in her clothing, the quality of her shoes, the hair coming loose from her scarf, and she found she didn't know who to be.

Sure don't look like no beggar I ever saw. She made no indication of being moved by Ana's speech or indeed, having heard it at all. Instead, she scraped at another matchstick, which caught, flickered, then held flame.

Allow me, said Ana, and she hurried to the woman's side, offering a cupped hand to shield the match.

Tssss! The woman flicked her lit match, the orange head sailing before Ana's face and falling just short.

You stay where you are, she said. *Your Miss Zelie, my dumb little sister, got herself locked up in Fulton Tower from yesterday until God knows when.*

Tower. Funny choice. Towers were for storybook characters: knights and maidens and witches.

You mean the prison? asked Ana, reconsidering the woman. This word sparked a new curiosity in her, and she straightened herself to her full height, which, though it wasn't very tall, was taller every day. It was sometimes necessary to pretend oneself more confident than one felt. It wasn't a lie, exactly. It was a truth in progress.

When everybody you ever shook hands with is getting locked up there, it helps to have some imagination about it. The cops were always collecting around here. Easy money. Zelie wanted easy money, too.

Why was she arrested? asked Ana. She was fairly certain magic was not beholden to criminal law.

She wouldn't pay up. She started out as a conjure woman, but that fell out of fashion, so she switched up her rootwork for voodoo and folks seemed to like that better. Everybody except the police. They called her a fraud. Zelie said it was her business, and none of theirs. Turns out steel bars don't believe in voodoo neither, so you judge for yourself how good her magic works.

Ana couldn't focus on what the woman was saying. Why didn't she want Ana to shield the match for her? Did the woman want to keep her at a distance? What was she hiding?

What have you got on your altar there?

My what? You mean this rickety card table? Zelie used to keep shop here.

Ana nodded, surveying the objects.

These are her things, what she could hide. The police took whatever they found. The woman moved her hands over the objects on the table, not quite touching them, and her face, previously fixed with indifference, changed into an unreadable expression. When her hands came to rest over the doll, she closed her eyes and inhaled sharply.

My niece's, said the woman, *before God took her. She was younger than you are now.*

The woman struck another match, but it was out before she could bring the head to her lips. It was highly improbable that matches should extinguish themselves so many times consecutively on a day such as this, with the breeze too gentle, even, to rustle tree leaves. Almost as though the woman were putting on a great big bumbling show of "nothing-to-see-here." Almost as though she were somehow persuading the flame to go out.

Long, tall, slim, thought Ana. What was the difference between a voodoo woman and a witch? Though the woman's back was hunched and the billow of her dress hid her body, her hands were decidedly thin. Her veins looked hard, like twigs arranged beneath her skin. And they were large—hands much larger than Ana's mother's. A good indication of her height. Large and strong enough, thought Ana, to lift a cauldron. She had come all this way on a dare to get a love potion from Miss Zelie, but what if she'd found someone else instead? What if she didn't have to put a voodoo on Isaac? Rule #7! What if she could leave Isaac out of it—as she very much wanted to—and bring the other something much, much better?

Had they had the wrong idea all along? Black robes and all that. What if the Night Witch was a stooped old woman in a loose white dress on the corner of Collins and Peachtree? And if so, how sad that the old witch should have to peddle her wares like any common person. Such a solitary life—never able to tell anyone who you truly are.

I don't have any siblings, said Ana. *What's it like having a sister?*

Like nothing, said the old woman. *Might as well ask what it's like to be inside your own skin.*

Like nothing. Of course! Because witches didn't have sisters, so if she was the Night Witch, then Miss Zelie must have been invented as a cover, like Newt Lee, her familiar. Possibly the Night Witch had created a duplicate of herself to occupy her prison cell. A kind of shadow self that would appear to the guard as though she were still there, silent and obedient,

while she transformed into her familiar and slipped away. It seemed logical
enough.

Witches couldn't be younger siblings because who ever heard of a sec-
ond-born witch? And they couldn't be older siblings because once you gave
birth to a witch, you died. The mother of a witch always gave her life in the
process—that was the root of a witch's power. Witches had to be utterly
alone, except for the companionship of their familiars. No one had ever
told Ana these things. She had worked them out for herself.

Ana didn't blame the Night Witch any more than she blamed Leo.
Witches were doomed forever to witness. They came at the death hour to
watch over people because they lived their lives between this world and the
one after. *He said he would love me.* That's what the murder notes had said.
Witches must love the dying as no one else can because in those moments,
there with the departing, they are less alone. And suddenly Ana wanted
nothing more than to tell the old woman she knew. She wanted to hug the
woman, she wanted to say, *I know who you are and I will keep your secret
safer than I've ever kept anything,* but one can't just go about announcing
such things. She would have to make her understanding known subtly to
the witch.

I'd like to buy a gris-gris—

Are you deaf? said the woman. *My sister—*

—for my friend Leo, said Ana, withdrawing her personal picture of him
from beneath her slip strap. She didn't have any of his hair, but surely this
photograph, which she'd kept with her for more than two years, could
conduct magic just as powerful.

I think you'll recognize him, she said knowingly.

Of course I recognize him. The whole damn country recognizes him.

I need you to make a gris-gris to keep him alive.

I don't know what you're playing at and I don't care.

I know you can make it, said Ana. Then, lowering her voice confidentially, she added, *Madame Night.*

The woman looked at Ana with narrowed eyes as though sizing her up, taking the measurements of her understanding.

Here's the recipe for gris-gris, write this down, she said, *so you can go away and make it yourself. It's one fat sack of pigeon shit, a handful of mouse bones, and a sprinkle of head lice. But if you're trying to get one from me, I'm fresh out. So, unless there's something else—*

I know, Ana cut in. She couldn't suffer being treated like a fool. If only she could make the Night Witch understand!

I know there's more to you than meets the eye, she said, and gave the woman a slow, knowing nod. *I'm on your side.*

And just what side is that?

The right side? The good side? Deep breath, Alice.

So, you won't make a gris-gris, that's fine. Maybe they don't even work, but I know you can do other, stronger magic, said Ana—she might as well come out with it—*witch magic.* A crow cawed overhead, an auspicious sign, to be sure.

How the hell do I know which magic, said the woman. *You're the one making up this story.*

No, Ana whined. It wasn't supposed to be clumsy like this. *Witch magic. Brooms and cauldrons.*

I know you came for Zelie, but I'm not her. You don't seem to understand that.

I know who you are, said Ana, though she was uncertain again. The Night Witch was testing her determination. *And I won't be sent away until you give me what I came for.* She crossed her arms in front of her chest to show she would not be dissuaded. *I'll pay, of course, but I can offer you something better than money. I'll bet you don't even need money, do you?*

Diamonds and gold will do me fine too.

Listen, said Ana, drawing closer to the old woman, who struck a match between them, warding her off. But Ana wasn't frightened of fire. The light would illuminate her eyes for the Night Witch to look into because witches, she knew, had a preternatural intuition for character. They knew a noble person from a scoundrel as simply as knowing a bad egg floats.

I could be your confidante, said Ana, willing her eyes to lock on the old woman's. Why wouldn't she look? The match caught a breeze and a stream of smoke stung across her eyes, tearing them up. Ana wanted to scream. She wanted to take the woman's head in her hands, to force open her eyelids, to see and to know what Ana could be.

I'll prove myself, you'll see. She hadn't meant it to sound like a threat.

You know what, said the woman, glancing from Ana to the objects on the table.

Maybe even your apprentice, said Ana. *I'm the quickest study in my year.*

I think I've got something for you after all. Her hand worried over the objects until it came to rest, attracted like a magnet, to something Ana couldn't see.

Not such a tough witch to crack. All it took was a little perseverance, and now she would be a hero to the others, the most felicitous of their five. They'd forgive her debt instantly. And more importantly, she would be a hero to Leo!

I got this ten-cent tin of Nabisco wafers. Look, I ain't even opened them yet. Too sweet, I got bad teeth, she said. *They were Zelie's, but she's got bigger problems now than a missing tin of cookies.*

I'm not hungry, Ana snapped. What a maddening witch! She thought they'd understood each other. *Didn't you hear me? I want your magic for Leo. He's in dire need. Surely you know that.*

Oh, I heard you, said the woman. *These are special magic Nabiscos. I did a witching on them just last night, so they're fresh as can be.*

How do they work? Ana asked, craning over the old woman to glimpse any indication of their power. They didn't look magical, but neither did the Night Witch, at first. It made sense, of course, that she would mask her magic, hide it in plain sight, visible only to the truly worthy.

The Night Witch looked at Ana's photograph and shook her head. *He's not long for this world, I'll tell you that, and lifesaving's no cakewalk. You gotta get your hands dirty. And I've seen your hands. Whiter than Easter lilies and half as useful.*

Lilies are lovely flowers. They're fragrant and dignified.

You ever see a lily use a shovel?

I can do whatever the magic requires, said Ana, though she had no idea what that might be. She hoped she wouldn't have to hurt anyone, and she wondered if she could, for Leo. Some people would be easier to hurt than others. And did she have a choice? Now that she'd found the Night Witch, wasn't she bound by love and the duty of the Felicitous Five to keep Leo safe?

I'll write down your instructions, but don't even think about peeking them until you get all the way home.

Why not?

You know what happened to Lot's wife?

Ana nodded.

Well, you're liable to turn into something worse. Chicken gizzards, maybe, or a stack of bird beaks judging by the look of you. You ever cleaned the guts from a chicken? said the woman, making a fist around something invisible and yanking down the air like pulling the rope of a heavy church bell.

No. Was this still part of the test?

No, didn't expect so, said the woman, turning away from Ana to rip a page from the book on the table and scribble the secrets of her magic for

Ana to practice. She had very quick hands for an old woman. Perhaps that was a perk of being a witch, and where had she gotten the pencil? The Night Witch folded up the page and held it in her fist.

Pay me first, then I give you the instruction and you go. Understand me?

Yes, ma'am, said Ana.

Fifty cents, said the Night Witch.

That's it? said Ana, withdrawing the coins. She had expected knowledge so rare to come at a higher price.

Fine, ten dollars.

But I haven't got—

Too bad for you, now shoo, said the old woman, snatching the coins and turning away.

Please, ma'am. Ana tried to steady her voice, draw the beaks back into line. *I only have a little money now, but I can come back with more.* She could feel the beaks trembling, each beak ready to open its dead mouth and squawk for mercy.

You know what kind of trouble you are?

The woman looked at Ana as though she expected an answer, as though it were obvious, but the answer didn't matter. The tests didn't matter. All that mattered was that the Night Witch let her go. Ana shook her head, sniffing.

You're the kind that don't know it's even trouble in the first place. And that's the worst kind.

Look, said Ana, holding out her purse. *You can have the rest.*

You just get back on the streetcar you rode in on and take it straight back to where you came from. She pressed the tin of wafers into Ana's palm and drew another match from her box.

Get out of here, little girl, before you get a chance to upset your daddy. She struck the match, which flared and held strong, then lit her cigarette and exhaled the smoke in Ana's face.

Poof, you're gone, she said.

No! Ana growled, grabbing the old woman by her wrist as the police-man rounded the corner for a second sweep. She needed the magic, the instructions—she needed the Night Witch.

Let go of the child, the policeman barked from the end of the street. *Put your hands on the table.* He was closing in.

The woman's skin was cool and dry, and Ana could feel the tick of her pulse grow faster, all that frantic blood thrashing against her skin. The woman's eyes were wide and searching and not black at all, as Ana had imagined them. They were a deep brown edged with the faded blue halo of age, her pupils pinholes of fear searching out help or danger. A witch in danger was a danger herself. Ana loosened her grip and the woman's wrist flexed in her soft fist, urging up whatever latent magic she hid to punish Ana. What had she done?

The woman ripped her hands from Ana's grip and laid them flat against the altar, cigarette still in her mouth.

I'm sorry. Ana's voice was unsteady, a stack of bird beaks, she thought, ready to be toppled. The policeman was nearly upon them. *Please, please, don't hurt me. My father will be terribly upset.* Too loud now, and tearful, and brave Alice was gone, and Ana ruined everything, and how would she save Leo now? And then she saw it: the Nabisco instructions had fallen to the ground, blank side up, right there for the taking. She picked them up and thanked the woman with a kiss on the cheek just as the policeman tapped a call for backup into the sidewalk with his nightstick.

Ana grasped the instructions in her fist and ran. As fast and as far as she could, though no one gave chase, until she was back at the streetcar stop. It wasn't until she was seated in a row with no one beside her, no one across, and no one behind to steal a glimpse that she dared open the Night Witch's instructions:

I stood on the corner my feet was dripping wet

Song lyrics.

I stood on the corner my feet was dripping wet

She recognized the words, but she couldn't think of the song.

I asked every man I met

There would be no instructions, no guidance, no help. She wasn't even disappointed.

Can't give me a dollar, give me a lousy dime

Somehow she had known that easy wasn't how magic worked.

Can't give me a dollar, give me a lousy dime

She would have to figure it out on her own.

Skipping Rope

<u>List of Possible Ways to Activate the Night Witch's Nabiscos</u>

~~Leave the box exposed to moonlight overnight~~

~~Leave box in a fairy ring overnight~~

~~Light one on fire~~

~~Pray~~

~~Say a spell (ask Isaac what language Haitians speak)~~

~~Activate with blood (prick finger)~~

Eat one?

—DIARY OF ANA WULFF

The mob had come for Leo in the night, stolen him twenty miles north to Marietta, to the oaken woods of Frey's Gin—Lynchers' Grove, they call it. They'd taken him long after the last extra had been printed, so she couldn't have known, but she felt it somehow, right from the second she woke up in the hot blue of early morning. It was the same sort of sharp opening that pain ushers in: the quick and unintended invitation of breath and the sudden clarity of perfect focus on a single site—except that there wasn't one. She scanned her body for the source: no toothache, no shin bruise, no grease burn. Yet she felt an unmistakable longing for some remedy she couldn't name and threw open her window, as if it would be there, waiting. She hung her head out to catch whatever cool there was. A fast burst of rain slapped hot drops on her neck and was done in seconds. She wondered if the others were awake, too, waiting for the sky to spill itself.

Esther called these stirrings "intuitions." She said ladies were naturally born with quite a lot of them. Esther could be counted on to know about such things, but if this *was* an intuition, it wasn't fun or exhilarating the way she had made it out to be. Today was supposed to have been Ana's birthday, her finally-older-than-Mary-Phagan, out-of-time day, but she had delayed it. She had successfully petitioned her parents to push the celebration back to account for the three days lost to leap years, hoping for something good to happen in the lost time, for the arrival of an answer. Today, she felt something had arrived, something big, but she wished she could send it back.

She crept downstairs and opened the front door, expecting some ghastly change to have swept over the landscape. A bloodred sky or streets lined with dead dogs. She walked the length of the garden barefoot, feeling for changes to earth, but her lawn was her lawn, if a bit tawny. The streets were clean, the sky was gray, the milkman had not yet come. She ripped a handful of hydrangea petals from a blue bush in garish bloom, put them in her pocket, and left the morning to its secrets.

At breakfast, she sat with her parents and ate her cornflakes with decorum. She was frequently chided for eating them too fast—*like a starving pig*—but she hated the feel of the flakes on her tongue once they'd gone soggy.

This morning, however, she ate with perfectly moderated speed. She was mannered and silent, waiting for her parents to dole out their usual mindless morning chatter, knowing, somehow, they wouldn't. They held their hands over their coffee mugs, letting the steam sting their palms without seeming to feel it.

They appeared distractible and strange. They forgot to ask her how she'd slept, they flinched at the sound of a backfiring car and a jay's crow, they didn't even mention her birthday. Their unease confirmed Ana's waking intuition; something fearful had arrived. Recently, Ana had begun to notice how odd adults could be. They were not always so composed, so certain, as she had once thought. Her parents glanced at each other fleetingly over their china, but not at her, as though looking at their daughter might topple something fragile.

Ana finished her glass of orange juice and kissed her father goodbye, but Mr. Wulff did not rise to see his daughter off, as was his custom. In fact, he barely moved, managing only a slight angling of his cheek to Ana's lips and a flat smile, as though pressed on by an iron.

When she got up from the table to push in her chair, Ana could see the corners of the newspaper poking out from under her father's seat. She couldn't make out the words, but there it was, the arrival of the fearful thing. Adults were terrible secret-keepers, sloppy in their concealment. They thought they could keep all the fearful things in the entire world pinned between their bottoms and the seats of their chairs. Perhaps one day, they would each sit on a stack of fears so tall Ana would have to climb a ladder to bring them coffee, terror so tall that when they looked down, it would be on the warblers nesting in the tops of magnolia trees.

When she made to kiss her mother's cheek, Mrs. Wulff grabbed Ana's hand and asked her husband if he wouldn't like to stay at home today instead—they could take a family trip. The three of them could borrow the Lowmans' car and take a drive to her father-in-law's house in Decatur, a place and man Ana knew her mother detested.

We could go see your zayde, said Mrs. Wulff to her daughter. *Wouldn't that be nice, just for the day?*

And Mr. Wulff said, *Now . . . let's not—*

And Ana said she couldn't, she was awfully sorry but she had already signed up to volunteer at the nursery of the Hebrew Orphan's home. This was a half-truth—she had signed up with the others, to play with the little ones and read to them—and it was a half-lie because she knew, instinctively, she would not go. Mrs. Wulff nodded her resignation.

Be my careful girl today, she said. *The city is a dangerous place for us.*

Ana didn't ask what she meant. She knew without wanting to know, without articulating to herself what it was she knew, and she pushed the knowing aside. Instead, she pretended to hear her mother say another kind of thing. As though Mrs. Wulff had said, *Try to stay out of the sun.*

Recently, Ana had begun to feel that false things came more readily than true things, and she wondered if this was common for all adults—if truth-telling became more onerous as one grew. As though the truth was in the ground and the taller one grew up and away from it, the more difficult it became to draw. Worms told no lies, nor did ants, nor any creature that made its home in earth.

She tried to limit her lies only to the very necessary ones. Though these days, even the necessary number was quite large. More distressing, still, was the fact that no one seemed to be damaged by the lies she told, not in a real way. In the last week, she had told a handful of minor ones as an experiment, and no one had been touched by so much as a running nose. This, she thought, was the reason she'd begun losing the ability to distinguish between lies and truths. The difference used to be so stark! Had she been cursed with lies that had lost their consequence? No, it was impossible. Every lie must come at a cost, otherwise the world would fall apart. If her lies did no damage, then she would have to make her own, to maintain the order of things.

Each night before bed, she tried to recall every lie she had told for the day and the reason for telling it. If, by the end of the week, the number was greater than the day of the month, she used a sewing needle to prick a small hole in the sole of her foot for every lie that went over. If she was bad, she walked tenderly on Sunday.

Men, women, and children march past casket in undertaking parlor—crowd grows threatening when refused permission to see the body.

—ATLANTA CONSTITUTION

We met at Jacob's Pharmacy, under the striped awning, as usual—Rule #2—though it wasn't. We drank our Coca-Colas quickly, sucking up the sweet brown drink without tasting it, until we had nothing left but our fists gripped around the empty necks of our bottles, out of which we made a tuneless chorus, having only one hollow note.

Awful! We laughed, but we kept blowing until the shopkeeper asked us to leave if we couldn't be quiet. We promised we could, but why should we have to be? We were bad laughing, the kind that wears you out because you can't stop it, the kind that hurts down in the bottom of your stomach. There was something to be loud about today. After the infuriating quiet that had lasted far too long. And we were tired. None of us had slept more than in and out, like bees hovering at the threshold of an open window. It had been five days since the last good rain and the air was heavy and swollen. It sat on our chests, thinning our breath. We sweat-soaked through our nightgowns and our sheets down into the bones of our beds. We didn't know how there could be so much water in our bodies.

I don't want to volunteer today, said Esther. *Do we have to go?*

Me neither, said Franny, which was out of character.

We celebrated her selfishness with bellows from our bottles, and the shopkeeper glared at us. No one wanted to be patient. No one wanted to be gentle.

Ana handed Franny the blue flower petals from the pocket of her dress. *Whichever way the wind carries them*, she said.

Franny let them fall, entrusting them to an absent wind, and they landed in a clump on her foot, which she kicked off onto the sidewalk. One of us smeared a cluster of them against the cobblestone, streaking zig-zags with her boot heel, one of us drew her initials, one of us drew a blue arrow in no particular direction and we followed it away without pausing for why.

Not eight blocks into the arrow's course we came upon a growing crowd of excited people. They were rattling at something and amplified by midday heat, a crowd of cicadas. We were small enough that we could weave between their shrinking gaps, and when we could no longer weave, we shoved into the thick of their commotion and added to their rattle with our own.

We didn't yet know why they had gathered, but we had been drawn to this place. Sarah hoisted Ana up on her back to get a better look, which was a game they used to play a lot. Sarah said Ana was the piggy and Ana insisted Sarah was. You have it wrong, she would say. It's *piggy's* back.

It's the funeral parlor, Ana reported, and slid down from Sarah's hips. It was not a good place, but it was the right one.

Someone important must have died, she said, but she knew who because we all did. At least now he had come home.

And then we saw him, he was everywhere. Our Leo, his last picture, our last glimpse of his face hidden by blindfold. Flattened out in black-and-white, rolled, folded, and tucked under every sweat-slicked arm, fanning every red face in the crowd. Up, down, up, down went his small, gray body, which floated feet above the ground.

Ana reached out for him and traced her finger up the line of the oak trunk, printed parallel to his hanging body.

He's inside.

How could she touch him like that?

I want to see him.

The man holding the paper must have felt the weight of Ana's finger, for he jerked the paper out from its perch under his arm, and our Leo was gone.

One of us drew a sharp breath, and we all squeezed hands until it hurt. Gone meant real gone, not Fulton Tower gone, not Milledgeville gone, not pushed aside in our heads gone, which—shame on us—happened too often when we were thinking of nothing at all. We didn't even know what kind of gone this was. Gone like milk teeth, perhaps. If the milk teeth were small knives lodged so far into your gums that pulling them out would rip out your jaw.

There were so many gathered there—men, women, whole families, even, waiting to climb the stairs to the funeral parlor. Why were they here? What right did they have to see him? What need? Some of the very youngest had grown cranky and hot and refused to stand any longer. They sat right on the ground, yanking at the hands of their mothers and older siblings, and the hands they reached for recoiled and shook off the smaller ones before reaching under their arms and heaving them to their feet. Everyone recoiled from one another, they flexed when touched as if hit by a doctor's mallet. Yet no one resigned their post. No man put an arm around his family and led them home. Instead they crowded closer, urging their bulk up the stairs where the policemen had made a fence of their batons, which looked quite flimsy in the presence of this crowd.

From the back of the crowd somewhere, a group of men had taken to singing a hillbilly song about poor sweet dead little Mary Phagan and how Leo had gotten his comeuppance now, and we wished they would get theirs. In the center was Fiddler with his namesake, standing on a soapbox a head above the crowd. Beside him was his mangy hound, Trail, barking the men up into a wildness they wanted. *Come on all you good people,* was how Fiddler started them off, though they didn't look like good people to us. Then he went:

> *There's a dear old oak in Georgia, the one we all wish well,*
> *As the sun was just arising there, old Frank was sent to Hell—*
> *There was people there from Georgia, Alabama, and Tennessee*
> *To view the body of Leo, as it hung there on the tree.*
> *Little Mary is in heaven, where the streets are paved with gold,*
> *While Frank is in the pits of Hell, kicking with the coals.*
> *Two years we have waited and tales of innocence we have listened to,*
> *But the boys of old Georgia had to get that brutal Jew.*

Everyone bellowed the last line with their fists punching the air, their mouths in big screaming grins while Fiddler's skinny children set to work hawking broadsides of the tune for a dime apiece, and the "good people" bought them to bring into their own homes, to holler about brutal Jews around their own pianos while bouncing their young ones on their knees.

We had read about crowds like these. Crowds that got called animal things like *drove* and *horde* and *swarm.* A vexed monster in whose matted fur we were hiding. The next day, the papers would say there were ten thousand in all. Ten thousand people had walked in, witnessed, and left the room of Leo's body before he was taken to Brooklyn for burial. But it ought to have read 9,995 because we ought not to have been counted. We hadn't come for the same reason as the animal crowd. We had come by coincidence, and yes, we had stayed by choice, but how could we leave our Leo to be picked over by them? We had to see him, to be with him. It was our last chance after the last chance was over.

We knew we couldn't be alone with him, but we didn't have to be one of them, either. We could choose. The funeral parlor would be our gallery and the crowd would be like tourists moving through our museum. We hated that we had to share him, the most important display. His other artifacts, we decided then, would always belong in our private collection. These faceless gawkers would stream in and out of our museum. We would let them come and go by our grace, indistinguishable, and we would stand by him, in stillness as perfect as his, and have just as little to say, and as much to ask, as if he were still alive.

After a half hour of Fiddler's song, the wild men were too restless to tolerate another round.

We didn't come here to stand around and sing, barked one man.

Let us at him! came a cry from the group of them. They removed Fiddler from his soapbox and another, larger man stepped up.

We want proof he's dead, the man called to the police, and the animal crowd cheered him.

It's no more than we're owed, another man cried.

Officers, the larger man called to them, *you have a duty to keep the peace, so let us at him or we'll force our way in.*

Whatever response the policemen gave was lost to the jeering crowd, which lurched forward, thrusting its great body up the steps of the funeral parlor. It moved us with it.

It's our right, the large man spoke again. *Let us in or you'll meet the same fate as Frank.*

The crowd exploded in a roar of brute chaos that beat at our chests and we couldn't tell if we were screaming too, or if the sound was passing through us.

The crowd was admitted, a few at a time, up the steps and through the double doors of the parlor.

The men were instructed to form a line on one side, the women on the other. A policeman escorted us down a narrow hallway carpeted by a crimson runner that divided our gendered lines. The wood floor peeked out on either side, but we tried to keep our feet on the carpet, letting it absorb our footfalls. We would not add to the clacking of heels, the scuffing of toes.

The two lines emptied out into a wider room featuring a leaning grandfather clock with a yellowed face. The wallpaper was a drab olive printed with flowering vines and urns, and the whole place stank of talc and tonic.

Set back against the wall, lofted on a table covered in a heavy black drape, a body lay in a pine box with brass handles like a dresser drawer for a giant. The table was low enough that we could discern its contents from our distance—how, tucked into the dresser was a small man of extreme pallor, though his cheeks appeared oddly flushed. He didn't look the way we imagined a dead man to look. There was nothing morbid in his aspect. No fusty stench, no spiders, no flies buzzing about, nothing that declared decay had set in. As gruesome as such a sight would have been, these were the conditions we had braced ourselves to witness. But this Leo, this pale man in a pine box, what was he?

As our queue moved closer to the body, we recognized some of the features that had grown sacred to us. The dark, tidy arches of his brow and his decisive cleft chin moved us to minor tenderness. Just a little of our Leo, just a shade. But there was more that was strange to us than familiar. The mortician had applied a hasty layer of powder to mute the horror of his injury, which was significant. His bottom lip was split and swollen, his nose was bent, and his nostrils were rimmed in the black-red of old blood. The color in his cheeks, which we had taken for a flush, was the perfect scarlet crescent of a bootheel edged in deep purple. Twin bruises, one on each cheek, aligned as though his attacker had taken great care to land his blows symmetrically. The left side of his face was sunken, though, so his features sloped to one side, as if fixed in a smirk. As if he were fooling everyone with his pine box trick and if we pinched his nose, he would gasp for air. These marks of assault—the terrible violence carved into his face—ought to have engendered sorrow or rage or something we could grab at and tear into. He had been ours, after all, but we could make ourselves believe neither his ourness nor his deadness. How could his dead face look so wrong?

What if we just don't know what a dead person looks like? one of us whispered.

Why did they have to go at him so? said another. *Now he'll look like that forever.*

His face looks like hers looked in the paper.

There was a cast-looking appearance we had assumed was a result of the photograph's poor quality that had transformed Mary Phagan into a battered version of the porcelain dolls we used to receive on our birthdays but had since outgrown. The same glazed, immutable whiteness. A small collection of them still perched atop a certain shelf in Ana's attic, all out-fitted in cobwebbed gowns of lace or velvet, something women of the last century might have worn to the opera. The man in the pine box had the same look, as though he might have sat with them, as their chaperone. Though his costume would not do for the opera. Instead of the formal black suit we had thought was a requisite for the dead, the man wore only a loose and low-collared white silk nightgown that managed to be oddly elegant, entirely too intimate, and somehow antique looking.

We had seen dozens of photographs of Leo—standing with Lucille, posed with the stem of a tennis racket tucked under his arm, looking somber in the courtroom. We knew his face better than we knew our own, which appeared considerably changed each time we saw them—our noses were growing regrettably longer, our foreheads now shining with oil. Leo's face, though, had been a source of consistent satisfaction. Yet when we looked at the face displayed in the drawer, and the body—a body ten thousand people would confirm belonged to Leo Frank—we could think of him only as Dead Man.

The girls of our dollhood had porcelain limbs and heads and necks, but if you were to unbutton them collar to navel, you could find the hidden place where the porcelain was fixed to the leather chest plates of their stuffed bodies. Unlike those dolls, the Dead Man's seam was visible in his clothing. Cresting the low rumpled collar of his shirt was a terrible red gash left unpowdered by the mortician. Freshly vexed scar tissue, wormy and shining.

His eyeglasses and hat had been removed and his face laid bare in a way it never had been in the photographs. And yet there was a gaudy, done-up quality to it. The thin wire eyeglass frames that had bridged over his nose had been a permanent feature of the face we'd seen for two years, and without them, Leo appear stripped, almost indecent. The eyes, which were shut, were fringed with thick black lashes, and doubled in length by the shadow they cast, so that they spidered over the thin gray skin of his under-eyes. The symmetry of his battered cheeks, in stark contrast to the pallor of the rest of his face, gave him the look of an applied blush, a heavy-handed suggestion of coquettishness. Worst of all were his lips. Their plumpness had always seemed gentle, nearly tender in photographs, but now they were swollen and overfull. Dried blood had settled into the cracks. Even his cupid's bow seemed to shimmer salaciously, as though whetted by eager drool. We touched our own hot faces, pressed clammy hands to our cheeks as hot tears burned over them. We wanted to cover the lid of his casket and shut him away forever.

How many times had we gazed on his face in photographs and wished for his paper eyes to be endowed with sight? And now, close enough to lay our fingers on his lids and pry them open, we were relieved he could not look at us. This was not our Leo, but the Dead Man. They had transformed him as a cruel trick. They had taken him in his gown, they had hanged him dead and beaten his face until it looked greasepainted. They had done him up, not in porcelain, we now saw, but like a coarse ventriloquist's doll, to leer and disgust, playing to a full house, turning our museum into a vaudeville show. The way they heckled and jeered, they couldn't have him just once, swinging on his oaken stage. They were so thrilled by him they needed an encore performance.

When these onlookers thought of Leo Frank, it wasn't the same Leo pasted on the backs of our eyelids like a stamp on a letter. It was this Dead Man, with his unnatural face, in their mind's eye. These features, large and ripe with swelling, this skull fitted with this grotesque mask. Seeing the Dead Man here, we understood how the horror of this face satisfied them, with its resemblance to the villain of their imaginations.

They were all in on it. All those men from Marietta, the prison guards, the mortician, the journalists, the solicitors, the detectives, the onlookers, the big-bellied cameraman with his tripod set up in the back of the room. His camera overwriting the living Leo Frank, making the Dead Man the only version, his camera witnessing everyone's agreement and setting it down the wrong way for all of time.

They all wanted him to look this way—for people to see him this way and know in their rotten hearts they had been right all along. We hated them for it. And now we hated this Dead Man's face, too. And we hated ourselves for thinking such cruel thoughts, and we hated one another for knowing our own cruelty.

I wish we could take him away, Franny whispered. Our line of women was already moving past him, toward the exit at the back of the room. We had to walk backward to watch him growing smaller.

We should, said Sarah, half-heartedly.

Take him where? said Ana.

How? said Esther. *He's surrounded by people.* We were moving away without meaning to go, halfway past him, twelve paces to the door.

Just take him, said Rose, a little too loud. *We could lift him.* She had stopped walking and stepped out of the line, which slowed against her disturbance. *All of us together*, she said, though she wasn't really talking to us. She was working herself backward through the line now, moving in the wrong direction through the tightly packed room. And what would she do when she got there?

There was little time for us to wonder before a policeman approached. He moved quickly and took her by the elbow.

Come away now, miss, he said. *We've had two women faint already. Let's not make it three, shall we?*

We moved toward her, but only so much. We braced ourselves for what she might do, and whether it would be bad enough to get her taken to prison. In the fourth grade, Rose had punched another girl in the face just for touching the bow in her hair—new and pink and velvet. We had all wanted to touch it.

That tickles, Rose giggled.

The policeman's rough hands must have grazed the underside of her arm, a notoriously tender spot. Esther told us that stretch of skin was called "the lady's mile," and it was meant to be engaged only in serious flirtation. And then Sarah laughed, because we had been expecting something so much worse, and it wasn't a quiet laugh either, it was a great hen-ish squawk that made the rest of us laugh. And suddenly everyone had turned away from the Dead Man to look at the laughing girls. We could feel their eyes, the whole room, even the cameraman's lens, trained on us.

They were supposed to be tourists moving silently through, seeing Leo and leaving. But they stopped to stare at us, as though we were on display instead. And then one of them, a beastly young man, laughed too. A flabby burst of it. As though we had invited him to. All wrong! *We didn't*, we wanted to say, *stop laughing!* but then others started laughing too. Snickering, first, then it tumbled, hurly-burly, into a mean racket. The camera saw it all.

Dead as a duck, a scrawny man said, breaking his line to peek over the open casket, *and he still looks like a pervert*.

Frank's sitting with the devil down below, said an old wire-haired crow with baggy eyes, hobbling over toward the Dead Man. *I just know it*. She rapped the end of her cane against the wood floor and we jumped.

We hated the stupid hot holes of their mouths and their eyes, slivering with laughter. We hated that they could make us afraid. Their orderly lines and museum silence were dissolving. They were moving in on us, on him.

All the better perch to glance up a little lady's skirt, said a man we hadn't known was so close. He gave the hem of Ana's skirt a small lift with his boot. She yelped and batted it down. Then everyone was slapping each other's backs, going off with their donkey *haw-haws*. We could have whipped them just as if they had been. We were the unwilling centerpiece of their show now. Their mouths, their laughter, eating us up, scarfing us down. Some of them didn't even look strange or ugly. They looked normal, like our fathers. And once we were out of this place, how could we tell who was decent and who would have paid for tickets to his hanging?

From the corner of the room, the big-bellied cameraman guffawed, and some of the gawkers looked up and waved.

Don't mind me, pretend I'm not even here. His mustache twitched cheerfully. One child looked into the camera and pantomimed strangling another, and the cameraman winked at him. Who was on display and who was not and who saw who watch who? Not us, that was for sure. They couldn't have us anymore, we wouldn't let them. Even though we knew—because we could feel it too—what brought them together: how to feel so angry you could rip anything apart.

Rose broke free of the policeman's grip, and we all tore out of the parlor, knocking through the crowd to keep from doing worse. We spilled through the back door and ran around to the side alley of the building, resting our backs against the brick as we panted in the sunshine.

Our last chance, our last, last chance, our only chance, and we'd ruined it. We had run from our Leo, abandoned him to his box; we had made nothing better. Nothing was finished, because it couldn't finish like that. The crowd was still there, seeing him, hating him, after we had fled. No one to change their hearts, wrong and horrible. No one to stop them bringing it wrong to their families, their friends, Atlanta, the world.

As if we could have done anything about it.

One of us said, *We shouldn't have gone at all.*

We had to try.

Try what?

What did we think we could do?

No one was crying. No one was even sad.

Not even us, not then. And now our tears weren't the right kind. Not for sorrow. We anger-wept, huffing through flared, runny nostrils. It didn't even feel like crying. It felt like fighting to breathe. We rubbed our fists against our eyes and dragged our palms roughly across our foreheads, kneading the bad feeling free.

On the street facing the road, a man in a flat hat with a thin brim was working the funeral gawkers, shouting at passersby:

Get your souvenir lynch rope! Cut down on site! One hundred and ten per cent awe-thentic. Why waste a hard-earned quarter dollar on a flimsy, run-of-the-mill photograph when you could have the genuine article for twenty cents?

We weren't the only ones with a Leo Frank collection. Now everyone could have a piece of him. And here was a man selling him off, and not even him, but his death. It was his death they wanted to own.

Sir, he bellowed, pointing to a stout man with cuffs rolled to his elbows. *Why sir, come see for yourself! It's the real McCoy! Cut down from the very oak where they hanged the devil! Came down from the hills of Marietta just this morning!*

Wait just a minute, sir, the peddler hollered, jogging around the stout man to block off his path as he tried to pass, *you're a man of good Southern stock, anyone can see that.*

We wondered what kind of stock we were, how we would boil down.

I'll tell you what. I'll cut you a deal—fifteen cents, that's practically highway robbery!

The man with the rolled sleeves reached into his trouser pocket and flashed his photograph postcard at the peddler: the cocoon of Leo's bound body hanging from the tree. He pocketed his souvenir, wiped his brow on the back of his arm, the hair matted with sweat, and walked off.

We were glad the peddler had failed. Why should the rope, something our Leo had touched, be in his wicked hands?

Goddamn, said the rope seller. When he thought no one was looking—but we were, we were!—he took a flip knife from his breast pocket and shaved three segments from a coil he pulled from the left sleeve of his cheap jacket. From his right pocket, he pulled a bottle of red dye—forged blood—and gave the pipette two shakes before pocketing it again. We couldn't stop the mob, the crowd, we couldn't stop the stupid cameraman, but we had this pretender caught, this tragedy profiteer. We would stop him.

Buy a piece of history for your lady, crooned the peddler to a young man shepherding his companion down the sidewalk. She was a couple of years older than us and had taken on a kind of prudish elegance we hoped never to develop. The long stem of her neck reached out from a high lace collar. Her face, the pinched bud of a late-blooming flower.

Blood's still fresh! said the peddler, brandishing the dye-flecked rope as though it were a flaky pastry still hot from the oven, and he a pâtissier instead of a snake. To our amazement, the lady stopped and turned to look. Her flower face, shut off to sunlight, began to quiver and open for the peddler and his hoax. A weed, we thought, not a flower at all, and weeds must be plucked. The peddler saw it too. He had them, he knew it, but *we* had *him*.

Virtue is Georgia's most valuable commodity, he said to the weed's companion, *wouldn't you agree, sir?*

It was a question that didn't need asking between one man and another because, like a line on a school test, it had only one answer.

Yes, well yes, of course I would. The young man stuttered his agreement, prickling at the question, as though the peddler had suggested he hadn't studied.

The peddler's smug performance made us want to dig our backs into the alley's hard wall. We ground the knuckles of our spines over the bricks, searching out jagged edges. Why did a man like him get to give out lessons on virtue? And we could think of a hundred things more valuable.

Hairpins, said Esther, *are infinitely more valuable than virtue.*

So is a ball of earwax, said Franny.

And dog shit, said Sarah.

We tried to laugh but our chests were filled with cement.

And justice, said Ana, *only Georgia hasn't got any.*

Anger, said Rose. *And bricks.* There was a small pile of them next to her feet. Leftover materials abandoned by the bricklayers. Materials waiting for anger to turn them into weapons. She stooped to pick one up. We hoped she would do it, that it wasn't just to show off her rage. We didn't need a demonstration. We had our own.

Before I send you on your way, the peddler was saying to the young man, *I'm obliged to tell you that this rope I have in my hands is the same blessed rope that brought justice to that lecherous Frank—*

We would scream a warning to him, to make it fair, and then watch the blunt brick hurl through the air, each edge fighting to lead, to be the one that would strike him.

—a man who thought he could rob a beautiful Georgian flower of her virtue, and her life, and pay his way to salvation.

This very rope? said the weed. *Remarkable!*

Pluck her. Stomp her. Get her at the roots.

I've been following the story for ages, she said.

Our story, our story, give it back.

I asked Robert to take me inside the funeral parlor, but he wouldn't do it.

It's not proper, said the young man, *for a lady to be exposed to something like that.*

I've a right, said the weed. *Like everybody else. To see him true and dead.*

No man can deny Georgia her justice, and son, said the peddler, *this fine lady is demanding hers.*

Oh please, Robert. It's only twenty cents. Begging, glowing weed. *What a marvelous souvenir it would make.*

It's a hoax! bellowed Rose, and she ran out from behind the alley, still clutching the brick. The three of them looked at her with the usual adult glance of dismissive amusement. She turned the brick over in her hands gently, embarrassed, as though it were a homemade gift or an apology, something soft. And they waited to be presented with it.

Don't buy it, she said weakly, looking down at her soft brick. What a disappointment.

He's got a whole length of it up his jacket sleeve, said Sarah, stepping out of the shadow, also with a brick. Hers turned Rose's back into a weapon.

And a vial of red dye in his pocket, Esther joined them. Three bricks, three targets.

What do you kids want? said the peddler.

We watched him doctor up the rope just before you came along, said Rose.

Is this true? said the young man.

What a sucker. What a dupe.

On our virtue, said Ana. Four bricks.

You can't seriously believe these little girls.

If you believe him *you're a fool.* And Franny made five.

Five girls, five bricks, five weapons: felicitous.

I don't know what you're up to, pal, said the young man, seizing an opportunity at false bravery, *but you're not pulling one over on us. And shame on you for trying.* He took the flower, pinched shut again, by the elbow, and led her away.

I'm not giving any one of you a chipped nickel, the peddler spat at us as he watched them hurry away.

We laughed at him. It was easy, we discovered. We were light.

Keep your pocket change, said Rose. *We don't need it.*

Then scram, girlies. You're killing business.

And how do you plan to make us? Esther giggled. *Are you going to lynch us?*

We laughed and laughed and slapped our bricks.

What? the man stammered and stuffed his coil back into his jacket. *Now, why would you say a thing like that? Pretending's one thing . . .*

Get the rope back out, said Ana. *We want a five-yard length.*

Ha! said the peddler. *Ha!* As though he were reading it from a script. *Forget it, girlies. That's my product.*

If you don't give us what we want, said Esther, *we'll scream that you're a phony and the police will have you arrested.*

They wouldn't bother a hard-working man, said the peddler, without a trace of certainty.

Who cares about the police? Sarah drawled.

She had something good, and we wanted in.

Us girlies *have* brickies!

We cackled hard and raised them up. Five girls with bricks for faces.

Give us the rope. Give us the rope. Give it to us now (or else or else or else or else or else, that's how bricks talk).

Guess you little sleuths have changed your tune, the peddler said and tried to laugh, but no sound came out, and he looked like he was gagging instead. *Now you want a souvenir.*

Ana held out her palm to show the peddler *stop speaking* and *give me what I have asked for.* It was something we'd seen Franny do with her family's old spaniel, Charity. She called the dog hers, but it was really her sister's. Franny had tried to train the spaniel to obey hand signs, the mark of true obedience. When Franny held her hand in a fist with her fingers even with the floor, Charity wagged her tail and walked away. When Franny opened her palm, when she pointed to the ground, when she snapped her fingers, Charity wagged her tail and walked away. When Franny gave Charity a spiteful kick to the ribs, not very hard, the dog walked away, and Franny cried.

The peddler, however, yielded to Ana's palm. He knew the command, obedient peddler. He jerked his head toward the alley, and we followed him there, bricks still raised (or else or else). Once, twice, three times, he looped the coil between the hook of his thumb and the crook of his elbow, and then made a cut. He delivered us the length, just as we had asked. And now it was ours. We had our rope, we had bricks, we had seen a dead man in the flesh, and he was our Leo.

It's not a hoax, the peddler said, cutting a length for himself before returning the coil to his jacket. The act seemed to rekindle the bumptious spirit we'd wanted to snuff out, and he droned at us: *It doesn't matter one lick the rope's fresh from the spindle.* Our rope now. *These folks know they're paying for a phony. But they buy it anyhow, and once they hold it, it's as good— better even—than authentic lynch line.* We passed it between us, fingered the fraying ends. *Blood on the real thing's probably brown, if you can even find a spot of it. That's the trouble with the real thing; it doesn't feel real. It isn't good enough. My rope is realer than real.* Much heavier than we'd expected. *None of my rope was the stuff tied to the tree.* So heavy it weighed our hands down. *Each and every piece of rope I sell was wrapped around his neck. Each and every piece was the one that killed the pervert Jew.*

We didn't want to listen, but we had. It did feel real. Real and heavy. Such a real, killing weight. Having regained himself in full (adults are always galvanized by their own lecturing), he went off from us to con some more people or drown in the Chattahoochee. We didn't care which.

Franny and Esther took up the ends, wrapping them several times around their palms like boxer's gloves, and started to turn the rope. The weight of it made its rise sluggish at first, but they worked it high with their shoulders until it reached its peak and then brought it crashing down to the ground. Rose and Sarah watched it go, their bodies lurching in time with the arc and smack of the turn. We had done it a hundred times and a hundred times more. We knew every song there was, and every skipping pattern, but now we were tentative, almost nervous. The rope hit the ground with such force. What if the turners' hands slipped? What if the jumpers missed a beat? Anything could happen. If we did it wrong, we'd be hit by lightning. If we did it wrong, the road would crack open and swallow us up. If we did it wrong, our fathers would be taken away by a mob of angry men.

Then Sarah rushed in and cleared the rope, her knees pulled up to her chest. Two more turns and Rose was with her. The rope slapped and their feet double-jumped and we held our breath as the wind kicked up. And Ana called it:

Right / foot, left / foot, right / foot, left / foot, both / both / both / both

It was good to be told, good not to have to decide how to keep on going.

And the rope went turn / turn / turn / turn / turn / turn / turn / turn

Faster!

Right/foot, left/foot, right/foot, left/foot, both/both/both/both

Turn/turn/turn/turn/turn/turn/turn/turn

Le/o, lynch/rope, Le/o, lynch/rope, dead/dead/dead/dead

Over and over and over and over, just the same, always our feet crashing down and down, the jolt of it feeding up to our back teeth how the sidewalk beat our soles and we beat it with our rope. We weren't getting high enough. We needed more height, more air, straight up we lifted—spring! And our wrists turnturnturning double, triple, time and we jumped higher, higher than a measuring stick, street sign, tree-top high, because jumping was the fix for fall and down. We would spring up up spring up so high that we got stuck because what goes up goes up goes up goes up

Swapping Stories

Caesar Sheffield, a negro prisoner in town jail at Lake Park, was taken from the prison and shot to death last night by unknown parties. No trace has been found of the slayers. Sheffield was arrested yesterday, charged with stealing meat from the smokehouse of Elder A. B. Herring.

When Arthur Ross, a big burly black of 358 West North Avenue insulted Miss Bessie Jenkins of 40 Emmett Street late Sunday afternoon . . . a mob of over 200 white men quickly answered her screams, and, catching the black after a chase of several blocks, threatened to lynch him.

DEFIANT BLACK LYNCHED BY MOB NEAR GROVETOWN: NEGRO WHO THREATENED WHITES TAKEN FROM OFFICERS AND RIDDLED

—ATLANTA CONSTITUTION

B ack in Ana's attic we milled about, unsure of how to mourn. Some of us looked at old clippings from our Leo collection, shuffling through our drawer of favorites: a very scholarly robed Leo smoking a pipe at university, a startled-looking Leo in a thick sweater with a coffee mug, a distracted Leo standing before a magnolia tree in Grant Park, his eyes cast down into Lucille's chest, and somehow through her. We wondered if we had already seen the last new picture of him we'd ever see. His gaze was always brooding in photographs, but now it seemed especially tragic. We thought we detected a noble and prophetic acceptance of his doomed fate. All of our noses ran from trying to cry quietly. We sniffled the tears back so they hid behind our faces, puffy and stinging. Something had to be done.

We should sit shiva, said Franny. *It's only right.*

Little Miss By-the-Books, said Rose. *A regular worm.*

None of us had ever been mourners before. Sure, we knew old people who had died. Sarah's grandfather had died three years ago, but she hadn't known him well—he had stopped speaking English when she was still young. When you get old, Sarah's mother had explained, you want to be comfortable. Apparently, he thought German was comfortable, though we found it bulky and rough, like a wool sweater. Sarah only knew a handful of German words, and hugging him, she said, was like hugging a sack of twigs. Besides, at ten, she had been too young to mourn formally. And Franny had wanted to mourn when Charity got rabies and died, but her mother wouldn't let her because you weren't supposed to mourn for pets or for any animals. Except that humans are actually animals too, and we had liked Charity more than we liked lots of people. Our teacher, Miss Albright, for example, though she wasn't dead.

When Charity got sick, she wouldn't drink any water and her tongue grew dry and dark with dirt, blistered like charred wood. Franny's father wouldn't let Charity out of her crate even when her legs stiffened and she seized and her whole body was rigid and shaking. It was awful to watch and we wanted to set her free, but we were scared. When we came near the crate, she snapped at us with her black tongue and tore at the bars or her own thin legs. And though Franny had no civilizing command of the dog when she'd been healthy, now Charity was only peaceful when Franny was nearby. Her dying dissolved the grudge Franny had harbored at the

family spaniel's disobedience, and Franny sat with the dog for hours, singing prayers from the siddur or from her own head. She sang so quietly that
only Charity could hear, because dogs could hear things people couldn't,
and maybe Franny could too. Both of them, listening to each other's blood
as they looked up, past the ceiling, into the sky.

How do we do it? Ana asked.

We mark out a week of mourning from the day of the beloved's burial, said
Franny.

He's going north to New York today to be buried, said Sarah.

Don't say that, said Esther.

Well, he is, said Rose. *Tell what you know, Rule #3. Cover your ears if you
want to be a baby about it.*

Franny continued: *We sit on the floor and tear our clothes over the heart
and say the prayers. I've read them. I could lead them.*

And then what happens?

For all her study, all those musty volumes she was ruining her eyes
over—already she had an older woman's squint lines, bookmarks, we called
them—what did she really know?

And then we refuse to bathe, she concluded weakly.

*Our Leo gets lynched by a mob and you want to sit around stinking and
sweating in a ripped-up dress for a week?*

Pointless. We were all thinking it.

Baruch dayan ha-emet, said Franny. *Blessed is the True Judge.*

Oh yeah, said Sarah. *And who's that?*

You know who, said Franny.

Well, it wasn't the court judge, said Ana. *Clearly, he didn't have the final
word. And it wasn't Governor Slaton. Neither did he.*

So, I guess that makes the lynch mob the True Judge, said Sarah. *Did I get
that right, Franny?*

The same day they took Leo, did you see, said Rose, *they shot a Black man a hundred times in Decatur. Dead a hundred times and they lynched him anyhow, but I guess that's the nature of the True Judge, right? He can be everywhere at once.*

You know those were different men, said Esther.

The paper just said "lynch mob." And one in Macon too, said Rose. *If it had said Franny, or Night Witch, or God, even, it'd be the same Franny, same Night Witch, the same God.*

Blessed is the True Judge. Franny repeated the phrase, to forgive or to condemn. We didn't care which.

And the response you're supposed to give, said Franny, steadfastly, *is "This is also for good."*

Why sit around for a week, if firing a gun is also for good? said Rose.

We don't have a gun, said Sarah.

What I mean, said Rose, *is if it's all meant to be, if it's all the will of the True Judge after all, then why shouldn't we do exactly as we please?*

I bet we could get one, said Esther. *We could all pull the trigger together.*

Order! said one of us, rapping her fist on the desk like a gavel. *I would like to address the Felicitous Five.* The formality of the request made us feel silly and buoyant. The first huge gasp of air after holding your breath for too long.

Permission granted! said someone else.

Have your mothers told you this story?

In fact, they had, or versions of it. They did it before bed, coming to our rooms like the mothers of children in a book might, tucking in our sides like bread dough. They would kneel down beside us and say, *Whenever you're afraid, think of the Golem of Prague*, as though it were a story we had always shared. But that wasn't so. Only in the last two years, ever since Leo's picture first made the paper, did they start telling such bedtime stories.

It used to be they would tell us, *No nonsense before bed. Imagination is a foolproof recipe for nightmares.* Now, this. It was strange to hear them tell it, a story so moldy with superstition. Why had they dragged it out now from the dusty corners of their memories? What was Prague to us but a page in our history books? What was it to them? The story was ancient and a little childish, like an ugly fairy tale. Still, we agreed, it was a good one. A story with instructions, if we could piece it all together, and what did we have to lose?

We sat crisscross with our bare feet touching like praying hands. One of us said we all had a bad case of cold feet. We laughed, and our feet began to sweat. Then we went around the circle and each one of us said whatever we knew. Some of us took extra turns, some of us were shy to speak. Ana was the last one, so she wrote it all down:

Golems are like men but made from dust.

And far stronger than any ordinary man.

They're made from clay, actually.

They're made of mud, everybody knows that.

Golems protected the Jews in the Prague story when the pogrom came, like the mob, to drive them out of their villages.

To hunt them down.

To kill them.

But sometimes golems go bad, like milk.

They can't speak.

They just couldn't answer the rabbis who made them.

But only rabbis *could* make them.

So, they probably couldn't speak Hebrew or Yiddish or German or Czech or any of the old bubbe languages.

Anyone could make a golem if they could write down the correct shem on a bit of paper.

Which is the secret name of God.

Which is the truest thing in the whole world.

Which only rabbis know.

The shem is 42 letters long.

No, the shem is 72 letters long.

The shem is 216 letters long and that's that.

Then you carve it into the golem's forehead.

No, you feed it to him.

That's how he comes to life.

On Shabbos, golems need sleep.

On Shabbos, the golem must die.

None of us know why, none of us know how.

To make a golem is to bring yourself closer to God, or something like that.

Hide and Peek

"Jim, did the man of whom you speak wear a hat?"

"Yes, sir."

"Did he take it off?"

"I don't remember."

"Was his head bald?"

"I think it was—a little bit."

"Did you observe his head closely?"

"Did I do what?"

"Did you get up close so you could see his head?"

"No, sir, not exactly."

—JIM CONLEY'S TESTIMONY ON MARY PHAGAN'S ALLEGED KILLER, AS PUBLISHED IN THE *ATLANTA CONSTITUTION*

W e drafted him on a page of Ana's sketchpad paper, because obviously none of us had ever made a golem before and we wanted to be certain he looked just right, a pleasing likeness of our Leo. *A betterness*, one of us suggested. Impossible. The rest of us voted to remain faithful—*to the last freckle*, though he didn't appear to have any. We owed it to our Leo to render him as faithfully as possible to the divine original. We scoured Esther's mother's magazines for advice on the golem's formation, and discovered a great deal about the ideal lady's figure, from which we made guesses at a man's:

A straight back and good posture were important.

A low waist-to-chest ratio was preferred.

Bright skin was the nicest, though this would be difficult to achieve owing to the fact that golems don't have proper skin, only mud.

A long leg was attractive. The perfect leg-to-body ratio was 5½:4½.

Softness was supposed to be very pretty on a woman, so we imagined hardness to be a desirable quality in a man. We would pat him down, pack him tight as brown sugar.

In our first attempt at drawing him, we made the waist far too narrow and the legs overlong, but we made adjustments, widening our cautious lines until the body looked just thick enough. Sufficiently manly and stout, yet elegant, in a manner. One of us took the pencil up and drew a small circle on its stomach with four dots like the holes of a button, but no one laughed at the joke. This poorly drawn navel, sitting slightly left of center, was the first mark of his nakedness. Before it, the sketch had only been an outline—like a tin cutout for a gingerbread soldier. This crooked navel, however, called attention to his other missing features—the embarrassing matter of the more intimate parts of the anatomy.

Too silly, one of us finally said, pretending teacherly scorn and rapping the joker's knuckles with the pencil she'd dropped.

Damn you, said the other, surprising us with her sharpness and nursing her punished hand. *That hurt.*

Do you suppose we ought to make him up as though he's already dressed? Just sculpt his clothing on to him? one of us asked, erasing the button and blowing the graphite-blackened rubber across the page.

The scatter of rubber returned our sketch to a featureless outline and brought us some relief, though we weren't certain relief was what we wanted.

It was a possible solution. Having never seen one up close, none of us knew exactly what a naked man looked like down there.

Won't it all turn into flesh? one of us said. *What if he just has skin in the shape of a pant leg, then, or a necktie?*

We agreed this was a potential complication. Still, some of us favored clothing him. Sculpting a shirt for him, a collar, shoes, slacks, and even a hat, all made from dirt. We thought it might be funny to see a strip of necktie-shaped skin flapping about like a tie in a gale, though we knew magic, by its nature, was not intended to be funny. It was even possible that humor diminished the power of magic. We agreed, as well, that nakedness seemed to increase the power of magic, as long as one could take it quite seriously and manage not to laugh.

It's elemental, said one of us, sounding very wise.

Just take the witches of Salem, for example, someone else agreed.

Our history teacher called it a hoax, but we knew better. Why else would a judge condemn twenty women to hang? It was so like adults to try to make everything boring. Witches, we knew, practiced their craft completely naked, shoeless even, in the moonlit woods. Did this mean *we* had to be naked for the magic to work properly? One of us suggested that stripping to our nightgowns would be a sufficient gesture.

What we didn't say—because we all knew it—was that we wanted him absolutely and completely functional. We wanted all of him. Without censorship, without secrets. It was all part of the story we needed to understand.

We stared at the sketch to avoid looking at one another, and our eyes sloped down the column of his torso into the pit of its absent anatomy, then we looked at each other to avoid looking into the empty V where its legs met, until one of us took up the pencil once more and made a wild scribble there, frantic and sharp.

We agreed to spy on our brothers and fathers. To open their bedroom doors just a crack as they dressed for the day. To steal the towels from the washroom before they bathed so that they had to call out for one. We would take only the briefest glimpses as they rose from the tub, no prolonged observation. Not a study, exactly. Just enough looking to know the shape of it.

Invisible Ink

After having been shut out from the sunlight for more than a year, the first words yesterday of Leo M. Frank, upon emerging from the courthouse in which he had been sentenced to die . . . were, "Oh, but isn't the sunshine wonderful. I feel it tingle all over me."

—ATLANTA CONSTITUTION

Ana's fourteenth birthday would be a slumber party, which is where a group of ladies all sleep together in the same room, but not in the same bed. We read about a whole society up in Nashville utterly devoted to them. They called themselves "The Secretive Seven," ladies who took turns giving elegant suppers, probably stuffing themselves full of French foods—foie gras and iced madeleines—and then dozing off together, with their tulle hats still pinned to their heads. The newspaper didn't reveal the reason for these group slumbers or the exact details of their unfolding because, of course, it was a secret.

We thought it was a dream-sharing society. We'd never slept close enough to anyone else to know for certain, except when we were infants and our nurses slept in our rooms, but our minds were probably too small then to know the difference between our dreams and theirs. It made perfect sense, though. A person could easily catch a cold or a cough or a sour mood, so why not a dream?

Our parents slept close enough together to pass their dreams between themselves, but really, their minds weren't equipped for it. Their hum-drum heads, the insides of which looked exactly like our houses in minia-ture, were made up of rooms—the drawing room, the powder room, the kitchen, the study—and each room occupied entirely by one very dull thought, like the price of linen or how best to punish us or the particulars of kashrut or the damn European war. And if they passed dreams at all, which we doubted, they were of a very ordinary sort.

It wouldn't be that way with us. Our dream-sharing society would be flooded with wild and fantastic dreams. We would go only places we'd never been and meet only people we weren't allowed. We would carry daggers and vials of poison. We would know a hundred languages and dress only in red. That way, we'd know one another even if our faces and bodies changed, as they sometimes do in dreams. If it was frightening—and we very much hoped it would be—we red girls would know how to find each other.

There was some early debate as to the naming of our society, but since it was Ana's birthday—she was the last of us to turn fourteen—she was allowed to choose.

Our invitations, when they came by mail, were impeccably white and sealed in white scalloped envelopes. They were addressed to each of us in calligraphy so looping that if we were to read them aloud, our tongues might become tangled around the letters of our own inky names. Even before we opened them, we could smell the lemon, and we knew.

Dear [Each of Us],

You are cordially invited to attend a ceremonial meeting of the Felicitous Five. On the evening of Saturday, August 21st, 1915, after Shabbos (my mother made me include that), there shall be a small birthday celebration in honor of Miss Ana Wulff at her home on 43 South Washington Street. Following cake and refreshments, Miss Wulff will host a Slumber Party for her distinguished guests,

each of whom will be formally inducted into the society in a manner of the host's
choosing. Guests in attendance shall be strictly limited to Miss Rose Cohen, Miss
Esther Fink, Miss Sarah Aarons, Miss Franny Edelstein, and, of course, Miss Ana
Wulff. Bring a sleeping gown and read this message by candlelight.

    Felicitously Yours,

    Miss Ana Wulff

There was the signal. *Read this message by candlelight.* Our suspicions were
gleefully confirmed. Recently, we had spent many hours in the attic at
practice, perfecting a method for invisible ink—lemon juice in an emptied
fountain pen—to be used at a yet-to-be-determined time. And here it was!
We read about it in the *Fireside Boys Companion* Sarah had stolen from her
brothers. The genius of the trick, once the note was safely in the hands of
the intended recipient, was the warming of the note over flame, at which
point, and not a moment sooner, the message revealed itself. A barely visible brown, the color of a bitten apple. But only if you knew what you were
looking for, and how to find it.

    We weren't much good at patience; we thought it was a foolish virtue.
Still, we waited until we were alone. All in our rooms, in our own houses,
we unsecreted our message by fire. Holding it close, and then closer, to the
lamp as the hidden words emerged with agonizing measure. A too-patient
goldening of the white card, fragments of letters—loops and squigs like
hair trimmings in the sink—flirted to the surface of the still-indecipher-
able page. Just a little closer, just a little lick of flame and a small gold ring
appeared in the white. A sign, it seemed, until it coughed up burnt-lemon
smoke, and the fire we weren't quick enough to blow out burned a hole
through the center as big as our fathers' thumbs. The black of it snaked
down the page. The message, excusing the hole, now read with perfect
clarity:

TO IGHT!
FOR   EO!
FOR   OVE!
F   EVER!

Fever! Fever! Fever! we whispered in our beds and checked our foreheads with the backs of our hands. *Fever! Fever! Fever!* until we felt a hot, dizzy flush.

And so we waited the whole impatient day, threads of challah melting on our tongues. We waited at the windows of our kitchens for the stars to come and end the Shabbos so we would be released. We squinted up at the sky. Our eyes were good at finding stars before the sky had sunk into its night colors, and we pointed them out for our mothers—*one, two, three, free*—who brought their reading glasses to their noses. *All right*, said our mothers, *you may go.*

We never imagined—who would?—all the trouble bound to him. Half real, half invented, half planned, half chaos, half mine, half mine, half mine, half mine, half mine. Too many halves made it more than the whole we thought we could keep for ourselves. As if we could say *just like that* and snap our fingers and make it so. As if we could snap again and undo it all.

Mudman

NEW ENTERPRISES STARTED WITH GREAT BUILDING ACTIVITY

—ATLANTA CONSTITUTION

We made him in the early dark hours of Sunday morning, hours stolen from the night before. They were the first hours we were, all of us, fourteen. Our time spooling away from us like thread from a bobbin.

We lay on our bellies with our ears to the floor of Ana's attic and kept them there until we were sure the adult whispers below had died away completely and nothing but the scuttering of mice came from between the floorboards, then we tiptoed down the stairs, through the kitchen and the foyer, holding our breath for sixty seconds, maybe more, until all ten of our feet were out the front door and we could breathe again: we breathed in honeysuckle for beauty, roses for love, sweet wisteria, our favorite flower, for youth. In the dark, they were steeped together with the night-bloomers—moonflowers and four o'clocks—and their fragrance had a bitter snag.

We had one pillow slip between us, a lamp from the attic, and a spade we found propped against the hedge. We passed the spade around, each of us digging a shovelful of dirt, cool and moist, from the underbelly of the hydrangea bush, where no one would notice the hole we'd made. When it was not our turn with the spade, we held the pillow slip open or the lamp high, or else we dug with our hands. Our fingers tore open

127

the wall of the hole, widening its mouth as we scooped up fistfuls of loose dirt. Fraying bits of mulch and root wedged themselves between our fingernails and the infant skin below. Night creatures watched from their perches on the oak tree, but we stayed brave. Our ten hands, not even as large yet as our mothers', seemed to grow in the dark to the size of men's hands. We dug and scraped with men's strength, and our pillow slip was quickly filled.

We hosed down hands and feet, and wrung our hems so as to leave no evidence of ourselves behind. It was the part of the night when the air shrugs off the last heat from the day before to prepare for the next morning's warming. We goose-pimpled and scratched at fresh bites on our ankles and elbows as we waited for our hems to dry enough to cease their dripping, then one of us said *it's time* because too late can come quite suddenly and then what have you got?

Back into the house we went, soft-stepping once more. But damp now, dirty now, carrying with us now an unmade body. Back in the attic, we shut the door and stripped down to the chemises our mothers made us wear under nightgowns. We balled up our filthy nightgowns and tossed them all in together as if to say *so there*. We knew we would be punished for ruining them, but the heap of soiled white things, steaming on the floor, made us feel bold and agitated. We kicked at the heap with our bare feet until flecks of dirt leapt from them, spraying our faces.

We picked dirt from our eyelashes and emptied the contents of the pillow slip onto the floor. We dialed up the wicks of the brightest lamp so that it gave off broad light. It was a pretty kerosene marriage lamp with a glass base, twin fonts, and twin chimneys with faintly ruffled edges. The glass of the chimneys was an icy blue, and it cast double-cold blue light.

Each of us laid a hand on the mound, a silent gesture whose meaning no one bothered to articulate. Then we dug in. Working quickly, we pushed the dirt into a column, very thick at first. Then two of us took to making a division midway down, pushing the dirt into two tapered lines with a foot-length of space between them where the wood panels of the streaked attic floor shone through.

Two of us began to cleave two thinner lines from the column, one flanking each side and ending roughly where the first, thicker set of lines began to diverge. We pushed the thinner lines away from the column several inches, so that the whole thing looked like the fletching of an Indian's arrow. When the dirt became too dry to handle without crumbling, we wetted it with the tea we'd been served before bed, sugared lavender, a slumber party treat from Mrs. Wulff.

One of us scraped upwards from the column, rounding at the top edges as we collected dirt for the piece that would become his head. The rest of us hovered, redistributing the soil when it became too bald in any place. Some of us raked through the soil with our fingers, picking out earthworms, pill bugs, and other noncompliant matter, which we collected in the now empty pillow slip. Later, we would shake the sack of bugs out the attic window and watch them plummet.

After some time at it, we managed to divide our sculpture into the six identifiable sections of a body: two arms, two legs, one unshaped torso strip connecting arms to legs, and atop it all, a circle of uncommon symmetry for the head. But here we paused our work, each of us unwilling to take charge of the finer bodily details of our creation.

Though there was little yet to see, we stood back to evaluate our work. We squinted and nodded as though we could see it taking form, the promise of our man in the mud. In truth, we all knew we were stalling. Our sculpture was black by the moonlight and very small for a man—half the size of the smallest one of us. We had only enough dirt to make a man of this size.

We don't have to do that *part yet*, said one of us.

Yes, we could do the hands, someone else offered. *Fingers that small will take a while.*

I'll do it, said Sarah, stepping forward, her toes between the spread of his legs. Though we had planned to spy and see and know how it should look, we only ever glimpsed it so briefly that none of us could recall, with any replicable certainty, what it had looked like. Just a little extra something, a jumble of pink and hair. Sarah had two older brothers, and we were happy to entrust her with the rendering of a man's down-thereness. She got to her knees and used her forearms to sweep the angle of his legs wider until she could wedge her shins into the space between them.

She knelt over the empty space and set to work scooping the dirt from the thickest part of his legs and the lower portion of his torso column into a loose mound, which she piled between the V of empty space, dividing it. Then she rolled the appendage with great care, patting and moistening it periodically to keep it from going dry and breaking off. We all watched her fingers work, worrying our own fingertips over the dark new hairs on our thighs in imitation. She urged the thing to bind with gentle pressure and some pinching where it met the legs, fusing the soil of the appendage with the soil of the body to which it now belonged. At the end of the thing that now filled the empty space, she made another, very small shape, which came to a soft point so that the whole thing looked like a candle held upside down with its flame pointed perfectly to the figure's feet.

When she was done, we helped her up and she brushed the soil from her arms.

Not really so different from a necktie, one of us said. We giggled and one of us poked it with her big toe. But it was very certainly different from a necktie. It was an intrusion on the form we were familiar with. We had always thought of people as looking more or less the same underneath their clothing—smooth and predictable, loose duplicates of one another, like the paper dolls we played with when we were babies. Or rather, we were just beginning to think how people might look once out of their clothing. People wear clothing nearly all of the time, which doesn't leave much room for thinking about them undressed, but we were making room. We looked at one another, imagining what deviations from the paper doll body might be hidden by our own clothing. And for the rest of the night, when touching each other, we let our hands glance skin-prickling parts, lingering a second too long.

They truly believed I could do it, that I could make it all real.

So I did, I had to.

—DIARY OF ANA WULFF

The face, Ana knew, was what would make him real, what would make him Leo.

It has to be just right, Esther said. *I couldn't stand for it to be coarse.*

Ana. Rose volunteered her name. *She could do it. There's no one more precise in the whole world.*

Yes, Ana the artist, Franny agreed. *In school last year, remember how she made a portrait that looked just like herself?*

Maybe even more so, said Sarah. The attic had begun to take on a buzzy heat that fogged the window. They were five honeybees, their ten wings beating with frantic excitement.

Even Mrs. Wulff, so thrifty with her approval, had smiled and issued a good-natured tsk at her *vain art project, but skillfully done.*

I recall Esther spent a full quarter-hour chatting to the portrait about a boy she was keen on before she realized it wasn't talking back, Rose added to the joke.

It's true, said Esther, *"How patient she's being," I thought. Imagine my surprise.*

Everyone wanted to play along. Everyone wanted to be teased, to laugh.

So Ana said *OK* and everyone cheered *OK!* and they tried to stay still, stay quiet, let Ana concentrate on her task, but they were eager to see, to watch his face take shape. They craned into the corners of her sight, and she tried to blink them gone. If she could only vanish them for a minute or two, if she could only be alone with him, she could rewrite the Dead Man's face. Remake it to her satisfaction.

Esther offered up her locket photo of Leo for reference, but Ana had her own (Rule #1), and they were both too small to be helpful. Franny offered up her personal picture—the one she kept touching her skin, face-side down. In the photograph she brandished, a pale stripe ran down his face. His mouth and chin nearly erased by the constant rubbing of Franny's chemise strap dissolving Leo into the tender purse of skin between her collarbone and shoulder. Ana shook her head and tried to shudder off her sudden jealousy. It was kind of them to offer, said Ana, but *no* and *thank you.*

After all, she had seen him in person, in color, and even if the color was somewhat more purple than she had imagined, the flesh was his own. She had been close enough to touch him. Why hadn't she touched him? For a moment, she thought of changing him. She could shorten his forehead, rob the dimple from his chin. She could make him just a little bit wrong. And eventually, his wrong face would overtake the memories of his face in the others' photographs, and only she would remember his real face.

But she wouldn't. Of course, of course, of course she wouldn't. She had wicked thoughts sometimes, about the others. She didn't mean to, they just happened. And she could always shake them off, but sometimes they felt good, like a numb foot just before it turns to pins and needles.

First, she attended to the general shape of the head, which was like a gem in its construction—having many angles. The cheekbones and chin that always caught the light, and the dark shadowed spaces they carved. She gave these bones particular attention, raising them from the flat bed of his face by wedging small stones beneath the surface of the dirt. *Clever!* someone gasped, and the others said *Shhhhhh*. With only the glow of the lamplight, the shadows were doubled, a dramatic effect that was not undesirable. A severe face suited him best. She built his nose straight and Roman, though in some photographs it appeared beak-like, bent.

Everyone's got a bad side, Esther had said when they came across the first one. *Tragic but true.* Her mother subscribed to several ladies' magazines, and Esther sometimes managed to lift an issue of *Mirabella* or *Holland's*. She had found this information in an article titled "How to Put Your Best Face Forward," which recommended a thorough evaluation in full light and then a course of selective presentation, including diversionary hats and hairstyles.

For weeks, they had all scrutinized their faces in the mirror to determine which of their sides was the bad one. They stopped engaging one another squarely and conducted all of their conversations with their chins angled up or down, toward one collarbone or the other. They became very geometric.

Eventually, they agreed to discard the bad-side pictures when they came across one. They had upwards of seventy-five pictures in their growing collection and they could afford to be choosy. Now and then, Ana snuck an unsanctioned photograph for her private stash, which was in violation of Rule #6, but the others called them unfit for the museum's collection, which wasn't fair. Shouldn't they seek to preserve him in his entirety? In these "unfit" photos there was an uneasiness about Leo's eyes, the gaze too direct, a little coy, or else the nose pitched, as though following a rotten smell. Ana liked these bad Leos best because she had them all to herself.

For his hair, she used a real comb, and someone said *nice touch*. She cleaved a part deep on the left side and dragged the teeth through the dirt edge of his head, grooming a crown of thinly spaced lines like slicked hair. For his mouth, a simple hole into which the shem would be fed.

His eyes gave her the most trouble. It was easy enough to make his eyeglasses, to carve the shape of their small round lenses, but she didn't even know if Leo was brown-eyed or blue-eyed, and she didn't want to ask the others for their input. His face would be her effort alone. In the pine box, his eyes had been closed. She flinched remembering the long, feminine lashes that had cast spider-leg shadows across his beaten face.

In the cast-off things they had rejected from his body, there were brown and black shapes—twigs, pebbles, ants, beetles, rotten leaves—but there were also hydrangea petals, shaken loose from their branches by digging. Small blue flowers peeking out from the dark monochrome. Ana plucked two and blew them clean of dirt dust before nesting them into twin sockets she'd made with her thumbs.

Before the others could contest the decision, she said *wait* and sorted through the heap of soiled nightgowns until she found her own and fetched a single Nabisco wafer, which she had wrapped in a scrap of gauze for drama, from the square front pocket.

It was her last chance to draw out the Night Witch's magic. Yes, she had failed on her own, with only some stupid song lyrics to guide her, but now the others could help. Maybe they already were just by being there together. They were making their own magic now, and maybe the golem magic would wake up the Night Witch magic, which was the kind of magic that hid in plain sight—camouflaged in a tin of Nabiscos. It made sense. Such magic must be cautious in order to survive. But the others, she knew, would need convincing, a little something to push them in the direction of belief. So, in service of their belief, Ana had resorted to a small lie: she had drawn a couple of spirals and Xs on the tan wafer with a pen, and the ink had bled and enhanced her lie, turning her simple marks into an elaborate web of black that looked like a sinister language. She felt a pang of guilt for fibbing up the Night Witch's magic, but she was fourteen now and too old to be in the debt of anyone's dare any longer. And furthermore, she told herself, the Night Witch's magic was necessary. Sure, the golem magic was ancient and Jewish and noble, but Night Witch magic was Atlanta magic, here and now and Leo Frank magic.

To settle my debt, said Ana, unwrapping the wafer. *I got this proof from the woman in Darktown, whom you know as the voodoo woman, Miss Zelie.*

Of course that's how we know her, said Sarah. *That's what you told us her name was.*

Well, she's not Miss Zelie, Ana stumbled. *She's much more than that.*

What do you have there? asked Esther.

You've never been to Darktown, said Rose.

Have so.

Who is she, then? said Franny.

Is that a cookie? said Sarah.

She's the Night Witch, Ana said, with all the conviction she could muster. *The real thing.*

The Night Witch isn't real.

Why not?

I think she is.

What's that you're holding?

It's Haitian Obeya magic, said Ana. *Extra potent.*

The Night Witch isn't from Haiti, said Sarah. *She isn't from anywhere.*

Everyone's from somewhere, said Esther. *Even witches.*

Haven't we already got Jewish magic? said Franny. *Don't you think that ought to be enough? It's enough in the story.*

Ana could feel the sacredness of their ritual dissolving into a squabbling heap. They had come too far to fail, and she swore a silent oath to Leo: I won't let you be gone.

Considering that a minyan is a basic requirement for a Jewish ceremony of any importance, Ana said to the others, *even run-of-the-mill prayer at temple, it's got to be required for making a mudman, which is a great deal more complicated than prayer. And a minyan is ten. We're only five, which means our magic can be only half-strength. It seems to me we can't afford to be picky. We need all the magic we can find, wouldn't you agree?*

Do you even know how it works? said Franny, always the worrier. *What if it's dangerous?*

I know it's Haitian Night Witch magic.

Then maybe it should stay Haitian Night Witch magic, said Franny.

I vote we use it, said Esther.

Rose pretended skepticism; Sarah, disinterest. Their brows pushed high, making ridges on their foreheads, but Ana could tell they were curious by the way their eyes tracked the wafer as she swished figure eights in the air. She had said the right things.

Besides, Jewish magic only works fully if you're a man. A rabbi, actually, Ana persisted, *a really old one. Night Witch magic is women's magic, though. Magic only we can do. Men probably can't do it at all. If a rabbi so much as tried,* she continued, filling with confidence in her own lesson, *his tongue would swell up, and he wouldn't be able say the spells or speak at all for three full days. Which isn't to say, Franny*—she could see her friend's mouth pinching in protest—*that we're abandoning the Jewish magic, we're just improving our odds.* It all tumbled so easily from her mouth, like flowers or truths, that maybe it was.

And we ought to do it now, while we've still got the moon, she continued. *It so happens the moon is the source of power for all Night Witch magic.* The others—having no insight into the matter of Night Witch magic, as Ana knew—said nothing. But their silence said *do it, make it alive.*

Ana traced the golem with a corner of the wafer, starting and returning to the top of his head. She crawled around him on all fours whispering the only witchy word she knew: *Obeya Obeya Obeya,* she chanted, feeling a little silly. She was not a natural performer, but she kept it up: *Obeya Obeya Obeya,* she whispered, until she almost believed it, until she almost felt the moon beating in her chest, until the word almost had meaning, almost meant *life.* She let the *Obeyas* rise from a quiet rattle to full voice, and her throat went icy, as if she'd swallowed the moon like a snowball. The attic too went cold with their nerves, their greedy hope. Ana wasn't thinking—because thinking is the opposite of believing—when her fist pounded the golem's chest, when she smashed the wafer over him, crushed it into the part of him that on her was her heart.

The young woman of today has so many interests that very often, she seems to neglect that all-important object called man.
—ATLANTA CONSTITUTION

For a full minute, none of us spoke. There was only the faint hiss of our held breaths letting go. Then someone said, *Did you really need to do it like that?* Too soft to be asking an answer, it was an apology.

I guess not, Ana answered anyway, her teeth clenching her bottom lip. It's what she always did when she was trying not to cry. Poor Ana, she had really believed she could do it. Always overbelieving in her own talent. We had wanted to believe it too, of course, but we weren't surprised it didn't work.

Without looking at us, she swept the crumbs gently from his body into her open palm.

Maybe Night Witch magic only works if you're Black, Esther offered.

You tried at least, said Sarah. *You really went to Darktown, so I think your debt's off, even if it didn't work.*

Sure, sure, said Rose. *You made good, but if that little show hadn't been free, I'd ask for my nickel back.*

Sarah laughed like she always laughed for Rose. Then we all laughed, glad, in a way, that it hadn't worked. Glad to return to something less exotic—a fussier, more prudish magic. Something we suspected we owned a little of just by being born.

It's a good thing, said Franny, prudish and fussy herself. *Who knows how a Black mudman would have behaved?*

Who knows how any *mudman would behave?* said Sarah.

Will behave, Esther corrected her. *The night's not over.*

They're protectors, said Franny, *guardians of the Jewish people. Rabbi Judah Loew made the first one in Prague during the sixteenth century because the townspeople were attacking Jews and burning their houses.*

But that was hundreds of years ago, said Sarah.

There are still pogroms in Eastern Europe, said Ana. *My mother told me so.*

Then I guess the golem's not doing a very good job, said Sarah.

That's all the way across the Atlantic. We aren't in any kind of danger here, are we? said Esther. *What'll he do if there's nothing to protect us against?*

What does a hammer do without a nail? said Sarah.

Be bored, I imagine, said Rose, poking at his thick trunk with her big toe. *Join the club, Mr. Mud.*

We didn't know when she started thinking bored was a good game, but she played it all the time.

If we haven't got anything for him to do, he might do anything, said Esther.

He'll be our honored guest, said Rose, *so as I see it, we'll be obliged to make some trouble for him.*

Oh no we won't! Franny protested.

All I mean is, if he can't do his job, he could be unpredictable, said Esther, *hard to manage.*

He'll be whatever we need him to be, Franny assured her. *That's how the story goes.*

But what do *we need?* Esther asked.

What if he's hungry? said Ana.

For being so smart, that's a pretty stupid thing to say, said Rose. *You wouldn't feed a doll, would you?*

We need the shem, said Franny.

We didn't know the shem, no one knew the shem. It was guarded by holy silence.

I'll bet my father knows it, Sarah bragged. *I could ask him.*

He doesn't and that's a fact, Rose answered. *And if he did, he couldn't tell you anyhow. If he said it out loud, he'd go up in flames and you would too for asking.*

Besides, said Ana, *it has to be tonight.*

I could try, said Franny.

Most of us didn't know any Hebrew beyond the letters of our own names, but Franny was mousy in that way, interested in all that tedious religious stuff. She did all the singsongs like she really meant them. At Shabbos, with our one puny candle lit, we had peeked long ago, but Franny, our good girl, always kept her eyes shut tight, like the ritual asked. She didn't know that when she wheeled her arms, three scoops of the candle flame, nothing happened. Nothing more than a yellow flicker. For all she knew, the face of God appeared at the top of the candlewick and winked at her.

Sometimes she scooped too intensely, her fingertips troubling the flame like a fan. Sometimes, on the final scoop, there was a stretching wisp of white and the smell of candle smoke. We watched as she put out the flame with her devotion, we watched her fallen face as she sniffed at the air. It was unbearable: the smoothness of her eyelids, as tears seeped under the fringe of her lashes. The dimpling of her chin as though God would not visit the table that night because Franny, in her fervor, had extinguished his invitation. When this happened, we had to shut our eyes tight to keep from feeling her shame on our faces. And we resented her for making us—Franny who had never learned the art of a straight face and never would.

She said the words of the blessing like we said the words of the murder notes. *Baruch atah, Adonai*, she prayed. Our lips only formed the shapes of the prayer words, while in our heads we said, *Mam that negro hire down here did this*.

We had seen Franny copying the Hebrew alphabet, with its blocky letters—a backward language for forgotten people. Her pencil dragged from right to left, the fat edge of her hand smearing graphite over every labored letter. A smudge of it stained the crook of her curled pinky, even after soap and water.

One of us tore a strip from Ana's sketchpad for Franny to write the shem upon. How could we deny her? She engaged the task as she did everything: seriously and with flared nostrils. In spite of her practice and earnest effort, she was naturally ungraceful and unlucky, and the letters she conjured were thick and ugly. Her nerves made her grip the pencil in a fist and she carved into the paper with such force she snapped off the point and had to finish with a blunt tip. The bare want on her face embarrassed us, so we looked at her hands instead. The slightest among us, it seemed an unfair miracle her hands could be so heavy, and we wondered if she might float away if they were chopped from her wrists.

It's wrong, she said, fat tears falling to the page, which she swept roughly, streaking it. She rubbed her eyes with her palms, smeared her right eye with graphite sheen, and we said *shhh, it's all right*, and took her hands in ours to feel the weight of them, to feel our hands light.

We erased the letters. *See? Gone*, we said to her hands, but they weren't. They were engraved on the page, letters legible by touch, on top of which we wrote his name: *Leo Frank* on the bed of ugly, ghost-marked Hebrew. It was the only thing we could think to do, the thing we most wanted. Then we waited for midnight. The animating hour was not made clear from what we knew of the stories, but we all agreed that midnight was the most powerful time. When each of the clock hands pointed due north, we folded up the strip of paper, tucked it into the golem's mouth hole, and braced ourselves, holding hands.

First, there was a time when nothing at all happened. The nervous sweat on our joined hands turned sticky and then dried. You could feel it in a person's palm when she sighed, just like you could feel a pulse. We unlaced our fingers. It was an eternity of time, hours maybe, that we sat in our circle, staring at the thing, the night suspended in full black.

Some of us recited prayers we half-knew, patching over phrases we'd forgotten with Leo and Frank. Some of us developed headaches from such great concentration, and we had to remind one another to unknit our brows so we wouldn't develop wrinkles. Our legs, folded under us, pricked pins and needles and we unfolded ourselves, pointing and flexing our feet. One of us had good ballerina's arches, one of us had soles flat as matzo. We kept our yawns inside our mouths so that our jaws strained behind closed lips. Some of us had begun to let our shoulders slump soft and round. Our eyes gave in to slow blinking, like the light of a dying firefly, with more and more darkness in between until someone gave a haphazard flick to the corner of the slip, which had been poking out from the hole of the golem's mouth like a tiny white tongue. A last, disappointed gesture before sleep.

Most of us had closed our eyes already, breathing quite slowly, and all together. A nursery quiet, eased by the gentle sound of snoring, like rice being poured in the next room. The lamp's twin wicks were burning low and the attic was pale with predawn.

And then the golem's mud-colored voice stirred us awake. That voice—so quietly choked, as if by a boot sole over a mouth or a noose around the neck—hardly a voice at all. At first we thought we had gone to sleep and dreamed it up all together. The words he spoke weren't Hebrew or Yiddish or any of the old bubbe languages. In fact, he didn't speak any language at all, only the shem we'd fed him. *LeofrankLeofrank*, he said, with no space between the two names.

Leof rankle ofr ankl eofr an k k k, he sputtered, coughing dirt, clearing space for sound.

Le o frank o frank. His body yet unmoving.

His terrible voice sounded without pause for breath from the hole that was his mouth, and we wished we had not dug so widely the hole whose earth became his body.

Shhh, we said, holding up one finger in a weak warning, but he would not be quieted, did not understand our pleas for silence. His eyes, blue hydrangea blossoms, blinked petals in response, *kleofran n n*. A gray centipede emerged from his left leg, crawled across his body and retreated into his right shoulder.

A monster, said one of us, and suddenly we were all shy without our nightgowns. Some of us tucked our knees into our chests, some of us draped blankets over our shoulders, and sweat collected in the creases of our stomachs.

Spider's Nest Reprise

A reward of $1000 is offered by detective William J. Burns for satisfactory information in connection with reports that Leo Frank is a pervert or is immoral. Burns . . . made public his wish to receive any information that Frank is sexually abnormal.

—ATLANTA CONSTITUTION

By our third night of slumber parties, the golem had grown so much that we had to turn him sideways to fit him into the closet when it was time to go to sleep. We could have let him stay with us, sleep among us. We had no proof he was anything other than docile, but some of us weren't sure. How could we know what inclinations might stir in him as we dreamed? We even jammed the closet door up with the high back of the desk chair, though we all knew that if he got it in his mind to leave, an old wooden chair wouldn't prevent him any more effectively than blinds prevent the sun from roasting the sitting room on a summer day.

O! O! he said ceaselessly in the closet dark. We tried to teach him into our Leo. Who better than us to make him into the man we loved? We played "Vissi d'arte" for him (Leo was a patron of the opera), we set a chessboard before him to tempt him into play (Leo was a chess enthusiast), we pitched tennis balls softly in his direction (Leo had played at university), but they only bounced dully off his body. We fashioned a wreath of pencils for his head, but he would not become our man. He gave us only monotone *O*'s.

Remember Alice and her magic cake? said one of us, her voice barely floating above the dense silence of our pretend rest. We had all read the book together for English class in grade five. We memorized her recitations and performed them for our mothers as they made the coffee. We stood on our chairs and cleared our throats: *How doth the little crocodile improve his shining tail?* we asked, snapping our teeth, and our mothers asked us for quiet. But we were not yet finished. We clasped our hands behind our backs and continued: *And pour the waters of the Nile on every golden scale!* Our mothers did not care for Alice or her adventures. We were scolded for our poor table manners.

Remember how it made her shoot up so tall that she couldn't reach her shoelaces to tie them?

Just think, said someone else, *how scary it would be.*

And we did. We thought about the walls squeezing in, the ceiling lowering itself over our heads, crushing the curls flat out of our hair.

Remember how she grew so terribly big that her head struck the roof?

One of us, lying on her stomach, lifted her neck to pantomime striking her forehead against the floor. For extra measure she slapped the wood at the same time with an open palm so that her head seemed to make a displaced splat. Another, fooled, let out a sympathetic yelp and from the golem a great big *O! O!* Then footsteps on the stairs, the heavy scrape of adult feet, and a stern rapping on the attic door.

Girls, said Mr. Wulff.

No one answered. Two of us scrambled to the door to brace the knob with our hands.

Girls, he said again in a familiar way, a way we knew was meant to sound like, *What are you doing in there? What is all that noise? Why can't you keep quiet?* But all he really did was call us what we were, a simple matter of identification. We looked around to see who would reply, and Ana nodded.

Father, she said, in her best, deep father voice. *Father*.

After a too-long silence he said, *All right then*, which meant he didn't want to bother, and we heard him recede down the stairs to the place where he belonged, which was anywhere far enough away from the attic door that he could return to forgetting we were there. We were certain that when our fathers pictured us, we were always sweetly sleeping.

But we weren't sweet, we were spiders. Or at least we tried to be. We hadn't quite figured out what to do with the golem. He didn't disobey us, but neither did he obey, exactly. He wouldn't sing or dance or tell jokes, not that Leo would have, either. He was too respectable for all that. The golem could go in and out of the closet perfectly well, and one of us discovered the air around him was slightly cooler than the rest of the attic, like the shade under a tree, so we sat around him, and stared, and felt the pleasant cool his mud skin gave off—not exactly what we'd imagined when we brought him to life.

We decided to play spider's nest plus golem, which was similar to regular spider's nest, only the says had to be about Leo, and since we couldn't decide who should get to be next to him, and also because he wasn't really flexible enough to twine with all of us, we laid down in a circle with our mudman in the middle, using each other's feet for pillows, all of us with a hand on the golem's blockish feet.

The says:

They say Mary Phagan died defending her honor.

Against Leo.

No, it was her virtue.

But that isn't true!

Well, it's what they say!

It was her honor, *which she got by* virtue *of being a girl.*

That's funny, one of us said, *because Esther would die to be rid of hers.*

No names! We laughed anyway.

What makes you think I haven't already, said the one of us we weren't supposed to know was Esther.

Everything, said someone else.

You're just jealous no one wants yours.

So, it's just a thing you're born with? one of us asked. *Shouldn't honor have to be earned?*

I've never felt my honor. How do I know if I've got any?

Just reach up your nightgown and—

Don't be disgusting, Rose.

No names!

Let her finish. I want to know.

We all reached under our nightgowns. The thin current of air our hands admitted was welcome in the stuffy attic, and if it was our honor we were feeling, it was very hot.

Not everybody's born with honor. Only girls. Men aren't born with any honor at all. That's why they work so fiercely to defend ours.

That's how they get theirs, by keeping ours safe.

What happens if a man can't find any honor to defend?

We didn't know.

He probably has to make some.

You can't just make honor.

Sure you can, we made an honor.

Through our slitted eyes, we saw a foot poke up from our spider circle to trace the golem's belly at the beltline and watched the toes descend. Some of us kept our hands under our nightgowns, making ourselves hot-cold with our fingers.

A fat muddy honor.

O! said the golem.

Don't be cruel. Another foot kicked the first away.

He likes it.

I don't want it to happen to me. What happens if I need it back?

What do you think it's like—getting dishonored? Does everyone know when it happens? Does it hurt? Did it hurt Mary Phagan?

We didn't know.

The feet beneath our heads had begun to sweat and dampen our cheeks, and toenails dug into our eyelids.

It's like this, one of us said, breaking the spider apart and leaping to her feet to give the golem a raspberry, which, to our delight, sounded perfect and wet.

Pinky Swear

"It's fight and never tire,

The devil is to blame,

But fight him with the fire,

And he'll beat you at the game."

**—FOLK RHYME REPUBLISHED IN THE "JUST FOR GEORGIANS"
SECTION OF THE *ATLANTA CONSTITUTION***

The night we made him, we promised to have slumber parties as often as our mothers would allow it, and not because slumber parties were such a great deal of fun, either. Sure, the first night was: away from our beds, the creaking attic our very own den, and us, lying all together like that. Spiders in nightgowns. But the more we had them, the less fun they became.

For one, the attic floor was cramped for space, which wasn't a problem for holding meetings, but it was torture if you wanted to sleep. Several of us had grown quite a lot in the last year and had to sleep with our legs tucked up. We tossed and turned all night, unsticking our skin from each other, pinning ourselves to the floor. We weren't growing a foot a day like the golem, but we felt we had some understanding of his plight.

One morning, we woke quietly, looking around to see who would let the golem out of the closet, but no one got up.

He likes being in the dark, one of us said. *He's a night creature.*

But it wasn't that. He had indicated no preference for time of day. He was no more lively at dawn than dusk. The true reason we hadn't let him out was that he was a so-far failure. We suspected he was capable of much more, if put to the test, if forced into action. But none of us wanted to seem cruel, or underdevoted, so we pretended his limited performance was satisfactory.

My mother doesn't like me away every night, Franny told us. *She says I have too many slumber parties.*

We all murmured our agreement. Now we could confess it too: we weren't allowed to be gone so often. We all had to go home to our separate houses, separate families, and do whatever it was we did on our own, but we couldn't be without him, either.

It's Rule #1, Esther reminded us.

Sarah suggested he move between houses: first hers, then another's, then another's, kept each night under a different roof, but we had no way of sneaking him about.

It's the only fair way, she whined. *Otherwise, he's always at the Wulff house and Ana has him all the time.*

We can't move him, you simp, said Rose. *It's impossible, use your brain.*

If he had stayed small, we might have been able to stuff him in a book-bag, carry him down the stairs with some effort, but now he was far too large for smuggling.

Slumber party slumber party slumberparty, Esther laughed. *Try it.*

We were all exhausted and flitted with ease between vexation and glee.

Slumberparty sluhmbrpardy slmbrprdy. It seemed funny now that we were cheery again because it didn't feel like a party, and we hardly slumbered at all. The pursed-lip consonants made it sound as though the room was filled with the stuttering engines of tired motor cars.

We settled on a pact: *No one acts alone. We bring him out of the closet together or not at all.* And we swore to it, solemnly, like this: we stood in a ring and looped pinkies with one another. Rings were good for swearing, they kept promises from getting away.

> *Pinky pinky*
> *kiss kiss—*
> *If you aren't true,*
> *then little Mary Phagan will send*
> *the Night Witch after you!*

I bet Ana breaks the pact on purpose. She fancies the Night Witch. Don't you? said Rose, who had no respect for the solemnity of swears, even though she had made ours up. She was good at that sort of thing.

She definitely *fancies the golem*, Sarah taunted, touching Ana on the tip of the nose. *I'll bet she has chills just thinking about the both of them.*

I don't! Ana protested.

I saw her shiver just now, said Sarah. *Do you need a shawl, Ana?*

Cut it out, said Franny.

Ask me nicely, Franny, said Sarah.

I'll bet you lie awake at night waiting for your Black witch to come and take your honor, said Rose. *You probably pray for it.*

Shut up, Rose, Esther commanded. *You're ruining the swear ring. Ana, do you know where the Night Witch takes the dishonored souls she claims?*

Ana was quiet, blank.

It's miles below the basement of the pencil factory, Esther continued. *Miles and miles below, where no light ever enters.*

My father says there's no such thing as—Sarah started.

What does he know about anything? said Rose.

Ignore her, said Esther. *Listen to me. Are you listening, Ana?*

She had to be. We all were. Esther was normally quiet about subjects not pertaining to feminine expertise.

It's so far down there are no sounds, said Esther. *No one talks or sings. Even your tears are silent. You can't feel or see anything, not even the ground. You can't hear your own footsteps. It's impossible to tell if you're running away or running toward it.*

Toward what? asked Franny.

Once she has your honor, Esther continued, *she devours it in front of you and when it's gone you can't ever come back.*

Why? asked Sarah.

Now Ana doesn't really want to break the swear, said Esther, *do you Ana?*

No.

Good then. Let's seal it.

None of us wanted to be touching fingers anymore. Everyone wanted to be done with it, wanted the sun to rise and never sink again. We all kissed the pinkies we were looped with. First the left, then the right. Everyone had both pinkies kissed by different lips. *Mwah, mwah.* Done, double-sworn. We could finally let go. We wiped our palms on our own thighs to get the others off them.

> I have so many questions! And with every question answered,
> a dozen spring up in its place! Why would God fill people
> with such terrible curiosity?
> **—DIARY OF ANA WULFF**

Esther had done all right with her story. It was chilling, in a way. But she had it all wrong. Ana had considered cutting in and setting the record straight, how the Night Witch was really a friend and escort to the dying, but she bit her tongue. She'd spent years retraining herself to think of the older girls' stories as purely entertainment, taking nothing to heart. Ana, like Franny, was sticky with the need for belief. The difference was that Franny was flypaper; she couldn't help what stuck to her, and everything did. She was covered over by belief, whereas Ana had brought her stickiness inside. She could choose when to close herself to a belief as easily as holding her breath in a graveyard.

The others hadn't seen how she'd crossed her fingers, middle over index, on both hands for good measure. It wasn't that she was afraid of the curse. In fact, she would welcome a second chance to explain herself to the Night Witch. She only crossed her fingers because she didn't want to break a swear to her friends. All the same, she needed time alone with the golem to test the limits of his capability, to figure out his role in the story, and it was common knowledge that crossing your fingers negated a swear, just the same as putting an X over a wrong answer. Whatever you swore with crossed fingers, you couldn't be held accountable for. And besides, if it had been any of their attics instead of hers, they'd have done the same thing, probably worse.

If no one had ever done any kind of prodding into the nature of fire, people might still have thought it was some kind of magic light, when it was really the natural result of something flammable, say a sheet of paper, being exposed to a source of heat, say a lit match, with a temperature high enough to produce the chemical reaction, combustion, and a flame.

If people had seen fire turn water into steam and simply stood in awe with no concern for why and how, they'd never have invented the steam engine. There'd be no Union Station at which to board a train, and it would take eight awful hours on a good day to travel from Athens to Atlanta by carriage.

She and the others couldn't make magic, yet the mudman *was* magic, in a way. Like fire and steam, they were impossible things, or they had been, before they were studied. And that was what Ana intended to do; to bring possibility to impossible things. For Leo she would study the golem with any means at her disposal.

Film Star

I had a dream once that we were all in a gag picture together,
like five Charlie Chaplins. Decking policemen, zipping along
clotheslines, falling out windows. We couldn't be hurt, it was
great fun.

—DIARY OF ANA WULFF

Since Leo's lynching, Mr. Wulff had been uncharacteristically
somber. But today (*Happy birthday, dearest one!*), standing alongside his wife, he was giddy as he presented Ana with a card featuring a rouged field mouse in a hoop skirt. Inside was an advertisement,
clipped from the paper, which Mr. Wulff recited over Ana's shoulder.
CHILDHOOD FOREVER, it read in bold letters. *Preserve the living
actions of your children in Motion Picture, which you can project yourself.
Don't let the little smiles and joyous antics of your children become mere
memories.*

I don't understand, said Ana.

You will in a moment, he beamed conspiratorially at his wife. *You can
come in now*, he shouted toward the front door.

On cue, something large clattered against the door, followed by grunting.

Mrs. Wulff winced and Mr. Wulff's grin fell a bit. *Wait here*, he said,
and he hurried for the door, opening it (*sorry about that*), exchanging greet-
ings with an unfamiliar voice, and then additional clatter.

Ana, darling—Mr. Wulff's smile had returned—*this is Mr. Fairfax.*

Having shrugged off her father's instructions to wait alongside her mother
—a small, expected disobedience—she was now staring into the face of
the very same overstuffed man from Greenburg and Bond, with the same
huge mustache. The same stupid man and the same camera—a dull black
box—that had filmed and winked and guffawed over Leo's body.

He's the photographer for The Constitution. *All those pictures on the front
page of the paper? Those are thanks to Mr. Fairfax here.*

Pleased to meet you. Fairfax extended a hand, which Ana shook only
after her father laid his own on her shoulder.

*But Mr. Fairfax is also a skilled documentarian with his very own film
camera.*

You mean I'm the subject?

*Yes. Well, no, not entirely. It's quite expensive to produce a film, as I under-
stand it.*

Yes indeed, said Mr. Fairfax. *But I think you'll find it's worth the price tag.*

What I mean, said Ana's father, *is that Mr. Edelstein and Mr. Cohen and
some of the other members of the temple, we're splitting the cost of a film, a
documentary shot by Mr. Fairfax here, about—well, about Atlanta, I suppose.
Our lives and our community.*

What have I got to do with all that? said Ana.

You're part of that community, sweetheart.

This was the same camera that had made Leo dead forever, dead on
film. And now here it was, this killing thing, in the foyer of her home.
Here for her.

Ana looked up at her father's pleading face.

And you're my daughter, he said. How could she deny him?

What your father means, Fairfax took over, *is that no matter who you were
yesterday, today you're a leading lady. You're Lillian Gish.*

Ana prefers Mabel Normand. Don't you, sweetheart?

Ana nodded.

Talkative, said Fairfax.

I saw one of Mr. Fairfax's pictures last spring. Capital City Club commissioned it, and there was a public showing.

Yes, sir, that was a pleasure to shoot. The cameraman's eyes glistened. *Keys to the city, as they say.*

It was sensational, Mr. Wulff continued, speaking to a place between Ana and her mother, *to see these familiar locations and these people, real people, living their real lives on screen. I had the profound sense that I was seeing the crossroads of history and future. And I thought we ought to have one too.*

Well said, Mr. Wulff. Fairfax clapped him on the back.

A film for Jewish Atlanta, said Mr. Wulff with the smile of someone who feels they have done a very good thing, the kind of smile that intends to be reflected by others. He raised his eyebrows to cue his daughter that now would be an appropriate time, but Ana couldn't bring herself to do it, and Mr. Wulff's tenuous smile flattened.

Let's get you set up, shall we? Her father invited the man farther into their home. *What's the best spot for this picture, do you think?*

Out the front door, thought Ana, two streets over, out of town.

The parlor is always a good choice, said Fairfax, already in motion. Mr. Wulff followed close at his heels and Ana dragged behind, still holding the field mouse birthday card. *I see your wife has beat us there*, he said to Mrs. Wulff, who hadn't in fact moved at all.

Sofia, this is Mr. Fairfax. The photographer for The Constitution, *and today a film documentarian!*

Pleased to meet you, Mrs. Wulff.

Likewise, she answered. *Coffee?*

No, ma'am, said the cameraman. *Fairfax.*

Mr. Wulff laughed alone.

A moving picture in our very own parlor, he murmured to his wife. Then he turned to Ana and got down on a knee: *Nothing to worry about in the city or the country or the world. The day belongs to you, so how about a smile, Ana, darling?*

But she couldn't smile. She couldn't give her father the one little thing he asked for. She closed her eyes so as not to see his eager face, and saw instead the wormy scar on Leo's neck, as if the backs of her eyelids were a projector screen.

She couldn't smile because she was a selfish, selfish girl. What would a smile cost her? What had her father paid for this gift? He looked so tired.

For whom would childhood be forever? Not for her. She would grow old and all the while there would exist another version of her on film. One that would be always just-fourteen and maybe very pretty soon, everyone said so. A version of her that would always be the age little Mary Phagan nearly reached.

No, she couldn't smile for him—what was there to smile about?—but it didn't matter. They would find a way to make her smile and curtsy for the camera. Or maybe the film girl ought to envy *her*—trapped like that, in apparent good behavior and silence. Even if the girl were to scream the rudest words Ana knew, at the top of her lungs—words she'd never said before an adult—they wouldn't be heard in the film. They would be like water on oilcloth and anyone might make up a script for her, might say, *I am sure she recited a lovely little verse. Why, just look at her. Precious thing, of course it was poetry.* And in other people's minds the forever-child version of her would be always reciting some horrid Wordsworth about a field of buttercups.

Film is nothing more than a mirror with a memory, Ana said, and set the card down on the walnut coffee table where they usually received guests.

I, for one, am quite glad mirrors can't remember a thing. She thought it sounded very smart leaving her mouth.

Mr. Wulff laughed and stood up. *It's a good deal more complex than that,* he said, picking a stray piece of lint from Ana's shoulder. *You'll see. You'll be thrilled when it's all up and working. It's a modern miracle.*

The photographer unpacked himself noisily, grunting and huffing, as some men are inclined to do, so that everyone knows what difficult work they're taking on. He lugged his tripod into the center of the parlor, pushing back the settee on the far side to make room. The heavy three-sided stand scrunched up the rug, tugging at its tassels. Mrs. Wulff's mouth twitched. The cameraman hoisted his camera to chest height and mounted the unimpressive box atop the stand, whose legs could be widened or narrowed by spinning the metal barrel that connected them. He fussed with a sliding piece beneath the lens, sort of jiggling it, then fogged the lens with a big puff of breath and wiped it clean with a handkerchief.

Any creature with six legs and compound eyes was classified as an insect. Though Fairfax and his camera had only five, Ana liked insects, and she preferred to think of the camera and its man as a rare sort of memory bug. A new, five-legged specimen, with a mustache.

Ana sat on the couch opposite him and watched his preparations. On the right side of the box was a handle with a silver knob at the end like the crank of a meat grinder.

In I go whole, thought Ana, out I come in strips.

He glanced up at her and wiped at the thick veil of perspiration that had begun to find passage to his eyes.

This is just plain backward, said the cameraman. *It's me that's meant to watch you, isn't it? To film you being your precious self. Now,* he said, *stand up straight and let me see who I'm dealing with.*

He didn't remember her. Good.

How does it work? Ana asked.

Magic, said the photographer, with a wave of his stubby fingers.

It isn't, said Ana. *You can't really expect me to believe that.*

How can you be so sure?

I'm not a child. I'm fourteen this year and quite clever. You and your film camera are my birthday gift, which means you must answer any question I ask.

All right then, he said. *If you're as clever as you say, why don't you tell me?*

You have two reels. Ana knew this much from a feature in *Collier's.* *One is full of film and the other is empty. When you turn the crank, the empty reel fills with the film from the full reel until the one becomes the other. That much is clear.*

Well done, and what about the picture?

The picture is made by the eye that's watching behind the glass, she reasoned. *The camera sees and remembers exactly what the eye sees and fills its empty reel with the eye's view.*

How amusing to hear science imagined by a young girl's mind. Such a delight! The cameraman laughed. *Film lesson number one,* he said: *What looks to be a moving picture is actually many still pictures taken close together and then projected so quickly that they have the appearance of movement. It's all an illusion, so it is, as I said, magic!* (Again, his ridiculous finger wave.) *As a matter of fact, the very flash paper so popular with magicians—the source of their combustible tricks—is cousin to the nitrate filmstrips that capture the film pictures. Their high nitrogen content makes them susceptible to flame. A boon to magicians but a nuisance for those of us in the film business. Good thing you've got a professional here,* he said, and winked.

Ana looked at the camera with new interest. *Is it dangerous?*

It is in the big studios, but not to worry. This camera, the Pathescope, it's called, is made especially for home use. It's shot on nitrate, but once it gets developed, the company sends back diacetate film stock for projection—safety film, it's called.

It was incredible how he made such a fascinating subject a bore.

Let's practice, shall we? I'm going to stand right here, in back of the camera, because I've got to keep the crank going at a steady pace. While I'm filming, you'll need to stay between the arm of that rocking chair and the back of that armchair, and in terms of depth, you shouldn't come any closer than five feet, which is right about—

Ana stared straight-faced at the cameraman and scrunched up her right eye. She made a circle with her hands, thumb on thumb, and framed her other eye, peering out at him.

Action! she shouted.

The cameraman scowled. *It seems we've got an amateur on our hands.*

Could you stand a little farther back and suck in your belly?

Ana! said Mr. Wulff, wrestling down the corners of his mouth.

And which side is your good side, would you say?

Miss Ana, said Fairfax. *A film is a record of your behavior, a permanent record that can't be changed once it's captured. Think carefully: Is this conduct the way you want to be permanently recorded?*

Definitely not your left side, said Ana.

That's enough, Ana, Mr. Wulff warned gently. *Be good now.*

I'm a perfect expert on my own behavior, thank you very much, she told Fairfax, and turned her back to his camera.

Ana, darling, said Mr. Wulff, *Mr. Fairfax has been paid already.*

Has he? said Mrs. Wulff, frowning.

Please, Ana, said Mr. Wulff. *Don't you think you'd like to look back on this one day? To see yourself preserved as you are now? Don't you think it would be a treat for your own children to watch?*

Do I need a map for the back of my own hand? said Ana.

Mr. Wulff opened his mouth but said nothing. A fish on ice.

Such a sharp tongue, said Mrs. Wulff. *If you aren't careful, you're liable to cut your own cheek.*

And besides, said Ana. *I'm not having any children.* It wasn't something she had spent much time thinking of before: the having or not having of them. It was the natural way of things, so why had she never considered it? Then again, breathing was natural, and she didn't spend time thinking about that either. The difference was that when she thought of having children—natural—and tried to breathe—natural—she found she couldn't, or not easily. Unnatural. And there was more to it than that. More than the ridiculous bulging belly, like a heaping scoop of ice cream. There would have to be someone else. She had seen insects mount, houseflies in the kitchen. The bottom one pressed against the morning paper, its legs bowing under the weight of the one on top. And her father would grab the swatter and end the dishonor. She felt her face growing hot, the color in her cheeks rising like mercury in a thermometer.

Ana was suddenly ashamed of how curt she'd been. Then, as though she could change the record of it, she smiled into the camera, her most charming smile. She was grateful, now, for the film. Without words, it could all be taken back, rewritten better. The title cards, white slanted letters with curlicued ends on a black screen, could read like this—

Her father would say: *Ana, darling, how radiant you are today!*

Her mother would say: *Yes, our perfect girl. Without you, our lives would be sunless.*

Her father would say: *Forever our princess.*

She would say: *Mother, Father, you are both so kind it brings tears to my eyes!*

The cameraman would say nothing.

She would say: *Mother, Father, I have not always been honest with you. I have not honored you and sometimes I am so angry it frightens me.*

She would tell them something that was true, they would forgive her, and their forgiveness would be recorded on film. The truth can rewrite wrong things. Already, this was how she had chosen to remember it.

She's really a good girl, Mr. Wulff promised the cameraman. *And deathly clever.* He grinned at Ana, who grinned back. This was the face her father wanted.

Yes, she told me so.

Did she? His smile fell.

It's just that I'm nervous, said Ana, who hated to disappoint her father. There were rules to follow, rules of adult custom, outside of logic: if someone pays you a compliment, you are never to refuse it, but neither are you allowed to assert it on your own behalf. You must always behave as though their saying it is the first time it has ever entered your head.

All this talk of permanent records, she said, gazing at her toes. She thrust her hands into her pockets. *I feel as if I've been punished in advance for a crime that I now must carry out.* This was another rule: contrition must be visible.

You see, that must be it, Mr. Wulff laughed. *No one is punishing you, sweetheart.*

Why don't you and your missus give us a minute? said the cameraman. *If it's nerves, then she'll be better off without an audience.*

You're the expert, said Mr. Wulff. Happy, Ana imagined, to escape the room before she had another chance to disappoint him.

Her father's parting wisdom as he made his way to the back door: *We all know you're clever, darling, but you needn't be clever all the time.*

Could one choose?

Mr. Fairfax is only here to film you, let down your guard a bit.

Before she shut the door to join her husband in the back garden, Mrs. Wulff issued her own wisdom:

But never too much, hmm?

The cameraman let out an audible puff of air from his inflated cheeks. He righted himself and smoothed invisible wrinkles from his trousers. Clownish gestures.

Film lesson number two: each reel is three hundred feet, which works out to about ten minutes of film. And believe me, that ten minutes goes fast. Your father paid me a pretty penny to record you today. Let's shoot ten good minutes for him. What do you say?

Ana nodded.

Terrific, he said. *Now let me have a good look at you.*

I'd prefer you didn't, said Ana, twisting herself around to watch her parents through the bay windows. The parlor had a clear view of the garden.

Don't be shy, said the cameraman. *It isn't as though this is a real motion picture at the theater. Only your friends will see it. And trust me, you'll be glad you've got it once we're through.*

I'm not shy.

You know, you look awfully familiar. The cameraman squinted as though he had spent so much time looking through the glass box of his viewfinder that he was unable to see clearly without replicating the conditions of filming.

And you look awfully strange, countered Ana.

But I can't place you—not yet, anyhow. He stooped once again to the level of the camera. *You begin to feel that way as a cameraman, as though you've seen everyone in the world already.*

Ana frowned. Another effect of spending one's life behind a camera must be that the glass deflects insult.

No pouting, Fairfax said. *Not on film. Now, the picture won't record your voice, but I always tell folks to go ahead and talk as they normally would.*

I find it helps them feel comfortable in front of the camera. Go ahead, he urged. *Pretend it's only me you're talking to.*

I'm not supposed to talk to strange-looking men.

Then why don't you introduce yourself, he said, and began to turn the crank in steady circles, *so I won't be a stranger anymore.*

Through the bay window, Ana watched her parents in silhouette. The window had three panels, and through this tryptic, their sun-washed faces looked remarkably unburdened, as though they might be figures in the background of a watercolor, happy daubs of paint. Her father picked idly at the orange petals of an azalea bush, presenting them to his wife for study, and she accepted.

But we've already met, said Ana, tired of the man and his idle conversation. Why did her parents never behave so freely with her? Perhaps they didn't like her. Surely, they loved her, as all parents must love their children, but was it her cleverness they didn't like? Out the window, Mrs. Wulff crushed the petals between her fingers and held the orange-stained tips before her husband's face. He smiled and kissed her palms, as figures in a watercolor might.

It was only the other day, at Greenburg and Bond. You said it yourself, we're familiar.

Frank's viewing. Of course! I remember you now. What on earth were you doing there without your parents?

Ana curtsied, a deep bow, the toe of her trailing foot pointed just so. She smiled at the camera. She could do it, be the sweet girl her father wanted, so long as it was her way.

That's my business, isn't it? she said, making her face bright and simple, like her mother's in the garden. *I don't nose about into yours.* She imagined pressing her face into a life-sized portrait of her parents as they now appeared. Their heads still wet with paint, she would roll her face over her mother's. Slow and even, left to right, to keep from smearing the pink, brown, and beige that would cover her own face so completely she would smell nothing but the raw turnip smell of acrylic for days. When she peeled her face away: a perfect transfer, like a mask. She accepted an invisible flower between her forefinger and thumb, mouthing the words *for me?*

I'll gladly tell you mine, he said, his hand turning the crank with practiced speed and steadiness.

You shouldn't have. She tucked the invisible flower behind her ear.

I was working. Doing what I'm doing now, making history. I've been following the whole thing. What I wouldn't give to have filmed the lynching. Not that I agree with the way it was handled, mind you, but boy, when Georgia puts her mind to a thing, he said. *Someday soon we'll have feature-length moving pictures that are strictly news. They'll run the papers right out of town.*

Who decides what's history? said Ana. *Is it you? I've got complaints.*

Did you know Frank, is that it? They say he was something of a well-known man in Jewish circles.

Oh yes, said Ana, gathering the corners of her skirt, *I know him very well.* She pulled herself into a wobbling pirouette, like a music box ballerina.

That's great, said the cameraman. *How about doing one the other way?*

Even better than your camera. Dizzy from her spin, which caught one foot under the ankle of the other, and sensing the impending fall, she leapt instead, surprising herself with her own nimble grace. *Which only knows him dead.*

Shame you had to see him like that, said the cameraman, laughing. He was so impressed by her trick that he applauded with his free hand against his thigh. *But you really shouldn't have been unaccompanied. Why anyone might have—what's that you're doing?*

Ana had begun to grow a shadow puppet, her forearm climbing the wall.

A giraffe? Ever seen one of them in person? Incredible necks.

The figure craned and bent, and her fingers spidered out into branches.

A tree?

An oak. In Frey's Gin, said Ana. *Might have what?*

Say, you're awful good at that. How about another animal. You like ele-phants? How about doing an elephant like that old circus elephant they've got at the zoo?

The tree branches curled back into the trunk, which began to fold over on itself, like an aging cut rose whose stem can no longer bear the weight of its bloom.

Between you and me, I think they got the wrong man. I'd put a week's paycheck on Conley. And he's still out there, free as a rabid dog, if you need a reason to be careful.

It wasn't him either, said Ana. *Shame on you, gambling on someone's life.* She made a sharp bend in her wrist and the trunk became a writhing snake, flicking its finger-tongue in search of unseen prey.

You can't mean you think it was Frank. Sure, he was a brute, and I don't mind saying I'm glad those New York Jews couldn't save him in the end—no offense—but he wasn't a killer. You only need one look at him to know he didn't have the brass for it.

No, said Ana, releasing both of her hands. The oak, Frey's Gin, the snake, all razed flat in an instant. *It wasn't Leo.*

Come on now, it had to be one of them. I saw Phagan's wounds. Photographed the body myself.

I don't know, said Ana. *Maybe it was you.*

Now why would you say a thing like that? The cameraman sounded hurt, but what did she care?

Why shouldn't it be you? Did you think she was pretty?

Now wait just a minute. You can't go around saying things like that.

It sure made a great story, didn't it? I'll bet you got a lot of good film from that camera of yours. How much does a photo of a dead girl go for?

Where do you get off talking like that? said the cameraman, his lip curling with outrage as easily as a script falls open to a well-rehearsed scene. *This is the problem with the world today. We don't keep our girls away from nasty things.*

Like the films you make?

And they end up with such nasty ideas in their heads, said the cameraman, his fists tightening into hot, red balls.

Girls like you, he said, *you're not proper. Something ought to be done about it.*

Maybe it was the Night Witch, said Ana, drawing her arm across her face like a villain's cloak with only her eyes uncovered.

All right, kid, said the cameraman. *Why don't you go back to your ballet? Haven't you got any dolls, anything else your father bought for your birthday? That's the kind of thing he'll want to see in the film.*

With the crook of her arm still shielding her face, Ana slinked toward the lens until she was close enough that she could have touched the camera with her fingertips.

You don't believe in the Night Witch? I've seen her in person.

I believe in a paycheck. Say, maybe you've got a career in the pictures after all. Quite the show, he said, pawing for his pocket watch. *Anyway, you're too close. You'll be a blur in this film if you don't step back.*

Disbelief doesn't make it go away. If it did, I'd choose not to believe in sweeping the floor, said Ana. *Or you.*

I think you're letting your imagination run a little too wild. I'll bet your parents call that being clever.

You'd do better to believe in everything, said Ana, lowering her elbow just enough to uncover her mouth, *so you're never surprised by anything.*

Run and get your father, why don't you? I'd like a word with him.

For example, said Ana, so close to the lens now that her eyelashes batted the glass, *you ought to believe that I have my very own Leo Frank in the attic just up these stairs, and that I made him out of mud and powerful ancient golem magic. Jewish magic.*

Would you stop? said the cameraman. *Look, you're getting the lens all dirty.*

And what's more, she continued, *you ought to believe he's deeply loyal to me, as his maker. He protects me, that's his job. And if I told him there was a man here who stood by and filmed his dead body and filmed all the horrible people who came to take pleasure in it, and filmed while those same vile people leered at me and threatened my safety, just what do you think he would do?*

The cameraman stopped turning the crank and Ana imagined she saw through the lens to his eye, fishbowled by the glass, and hazy. A dusty pewter iris and into the blunt cogs of his mind, how they labored to turn, to work out what would come next.

Won't you have a guess?

The cameraman huffed an unanswer through his nostrils.

They say the golem is stronger than ten ordinary men.

If you were my daughter, said the cameraman, *I'd—*

You'd need a wife, said Ana.

That's not the—

Point, no. You're supposed to be guessing what he'd do for me.

I'm not interested in—

To you.

The cameraman stood and squinted down at Ana, his small eyes like the lumpy bullets of an old musket.

You're just a spoiled little Jew who thinks she's a cut above everyone because her father pays for whatever she wants, he said. *Maybe protection isn't what you need.*

That's what I've been saying!

Maybe you ought to have a taste of the real world. Maybe what you need is a hard lesson and someone to give it to you.

Is that so? said Ana, smearing her nose against the camera lens. *Would that someone be you?*

I think I'd better tell your father about your wandering alone, said the cameraman, heading for the front door. *It's not safe.*

While you're at it, Ana stopped him, *accusing him of being unable to keep me safe, would you mind mentioning how you've threatened me?*

The cameraman turned on his heel, the vein in his red forehead bulging.

Go on, say it just the way you did a second ago, said Ana, opening the back door for him. *Say, I told her she could use a hard lesson. Say "I'd like to give it to her."*

The cameraman dabbed at his hairline with his handkerchief and called out the door to Ana's father.

I beg your pardon, Mr. Wulff, he said, casting about for his hat, *but I don't think I'll be able to finish the filming today.*

What was that? Mr. Wulff called back. *What's the matter?* He hurried back to the house, no longer a watercolor. It was only the distance that had made him seem so.

Your daughter has made her displeasure known.

What's the meaning of this, Ana? said Mr. Wulff.

She made her displeasure known, said Mrs. Wulff. *He just said so.*

He deserved it, and she deserved a little fun. But all she ever did was make people cross. All she ever did was make her father worry. The lines between his eyebrows grew deeper every day. Not a painting at all.

I'll refund your money, Fairfax said, *but I won't be terrorized by an unruly child. I'm a professional.*

I'm terribly sorry, said a reddening Mr. Wulff. *You say she terrorized you?* He stared down at Ana with his eyebrows drawn tightly together, and she thought for a moment that he might cry. *She's isn't normally like this. She's just been a little—I don't know—upset.*

Disturbed, said Fairfax. *That's what I would call it.*

It's good, said Mrs. Wulff, *to be disturbed now and again.*

I'll send a boy over for my equipment tomorrow, said Fairfax. In six heavy-footed strides he was out the front door. Good riddance. Bad riddance. No difference.

Shadow Puppets

I used to dream of being a shadow puppeteer and traveling the country. They would bill me as "Ana Fantastic, the Greatest Talent to Come from Atlanta." How silly to think of it now.

—DIARY OF ANA WULFF

M r. Wulff went to bed that night without supper. *Upset stomach*, he said. It was the third time in a fortnight. Though this time his mood was clearly linked to Ana's misbehavior. She too was sent to bed without supper.

Disrespectful behavior must be starved, said her mother, *so that it does not grow*, and retired shortly after. Ana heard her parents' bedroom door shut. Too tired, she guessed, to bother fixing anything to eat. They had all gone to bed hungry.

Her bad behavior had led to a good outcome. With her parents gone to bed early, she would finally be left alone with the golem! And though it was undeniably good fortune, it troubled her. Goodness ought to be the rewarded quality, and yet here she was. Increasingly, she found this equation to be true. Or if not true, then common, at least. Either there had been a change to the world that had shifted the natural balance of goodness and wickedness, or—and this was difficult to imagine—there had never been a balance. There was really no incentive or reward to preserve goodness.

She maintained, however, there was *some* justice to it. The cameraman, bossy and smug, deserved her abuse. But her father had not deserved the shame he suffered apologizing for her bad behavior. It was difficult to adequately punish oneself, but perhaps the golem could be instructed to punish her in strokes equal to the grief she had caused. This would be the best outcome: to get her way and to be punished for the means of achieving it. Balance.

The beds in the Wulff house were creaky, awful Victorian things. The others agreed. Ana had made each of them lie down, in turn, to sample her torture. *This is what it's like to be me.* Mrs. Wulff wouldn't allow their hard-earned money to be spent on modern spring coils when the beds they had worked just fine. *Once you're asleep, what does it matter if it's a stone slab or a sultan's mattress?* But when her parents tossed in the night, Ana could hear their bed groaning as if it were saying *paaaatience, paaaatience, paaaatience.*

Tonight, however, she didn't have to be patient. She wouldn't so much as lay a finger on her bed. Never again! Tonight, she had the golem all to herself. She didn't have to share, and soon she would know everything there was to know about him (Rule #8). Though her resources were admittedly few, solitude—time alone with a subject, as every great scientist knew—was not a resource to be discounted. What was one voided swear in service of such a task? She made a mental note to give her feet extra prickings.

The quietest way to climb was barefoot, on your toes, never letting your heels touch; that was how cat burglars did it. The third to the last step had a creak, but it was simple enough to skip over as long as you kept count.

Ana opened the attic door, just a crack. The golem was awake. She could hear the dull plodding of his feet from inside the closet. They hadn't thought to articulate his toes from his heels, so his feet were soft blocks that went *pom pom pom / pom pom pom.* Pacing the length of the closet. Was he anxious? Who wouldn't be, trapped alone in the dark like that? Though perhaps he never slept. Perhaps he would remain awake until he worked himself down like a candle and went out in a plume of smoke. Wasn't that the way magic worked—*poof!* this and *poof!* that?

For my first trick, thought Ana, and plucked a matchstick from the tuck of her braid. One's hair is the safest hiding place. All the more reason not to let Isaac brush it out, for if it were smooth and unknotted, everything would fall out. She went to the desk at the back of the room to light the lamp. The moonlight spilled from the window behind it, but Ana wanted more. She removed the glass chimneys and lit the wicks of the lamp. A cold glow issued from her hands (*I am a little blue sun*), and she carried the lamp over to the closet, setting it down beside the door.

She had expected to be more afraid. When the others were with her, she could feel it: that shallow dread just beneath her skin. No telling what Leo might do. There was a human anatomy figure in their science classroom, a bust that has been made to look like a human body with all of the skin removed. On the bottom, it was just a pole, but from the waist up, a raw red tapestry of woven bands and muscle. When the others were around, all of their anatomies were on the surface, just like that, snapping and tensing. If one of them flinched or gasped or sneezed, then all of their red underskins tightened. But now, alone, that snapping red feeling wasn't with her. Instead, there was something softer, sparks of woolen static or cottony summer thunder. Curiosity apart from fear.

In homeroom, Miss Albright sometimes picked on her. Before the entire room, the teacher would say, *Miss Wulff, tell the class how the cat died.* It was something she did, Ana had observed, whenever she asked a question Miss Albright didn't feel like answering.

I'm sure I don't know, Ana always replied, but everyone laughed anyhow. Even the others laughed. Everyone liked to watch someone else being made to feel ashamed. Ana laughed too because she wasn't, and she meant to show them: *See? I am not. I am laughing.*

It was a silly adage, anyhow, because she was a good deal cleverer than a cat. Besides, curiosity was a quality possessed in large store by very admirable people like explorers and scientists, people about whom schoolbooks were written. What Miss Albright really meant was nosiness, which was something Ana had been told many ladies were afflicted with. As far as she could tell, though, the greatest difference was that the value of one thing was to know it privately, and the value of the other was to know it as loudly as possible and make sure everyone else knows you know it as well. And if that was true, Ana would rather be nosy, which, as far as she knew, never killed any cats, *so there.*

Here kitty, kitty, she smiled at the thought of her mud Leo lapping cream from a saucer and rubbing against her leg. The key plate of the closet door, behind which Leo paced, had a keyhole shaped like a chess pawn. If Ana crouched, she could peek inside and see pawn-shaped blackness. With her eye to the hole, she put a hand on the cut-glass knob and began, as quietly as possible, to turn it. The very slightest rotation of her wrist like the second hand on a half-speed clock. Suddenly, a shock of blue in the black and she lost her balance and tipped over, grasping for the knob to steady her. But her sweat-slicked palm slid over the glass instead and turned the knob, *click,* just a slim shadow ajar with Ana on the floor, arms curled about her head, ready for the Leo inside to charge like a starved, crated beast.

But he didn't. In fact, he didn't move at all, as though escape had never occurred to him. She lowered her arms slowly. Sudden movement could startle a creature into violence. He was bent over from the middle, head level with the keyhole. His eyes, those flowers, had been the blue of her surprise. Spying! Just as she had been. She laughed, and the golem startled and scrambled out of view.

It's all right, it's all right, she whispered into the slip of black the cracked door yielded. The closet was lined on either side by wooden racks on which hung parallel forests of musty clothing, a small alley of space between them. They were the Wulffs' out-of-season things: the heavy winter wools, topcoats, her mother's fox stole, and, farther back, the clothing cut in styles that had become old-fashioned looking. They were the drab pieces with dripping trains, the silhouettes so pinched at the waist they looked as though you might have to give up breathing to fit into them. No one wore those fashions anymore, but her father was proud of their dramatic tailoring. *The best darn garments in Georgia.* On the lining of each piece, a white patch was stitched into the center back, just below the neck. And each patch was embroidered with gold thread curling into the letters of his shop's label.

The golem had retreated to the back of the closet. He stood a foot from the back wall, poorly concealed under the skirt of a moth-holed dress. Poor mudman. How could she coax him away from the safety of hiding? How was she to tell a creature with knowledge only of the dark that light could be a kind thing, a guide? And was such an invitation wise? Being the first of his kind, or at least the first golem Ana had met, she had no way to anticipate his behavior. He was an unknown variable.

Would he, like any animal, need to be fed and, consequently, to relieve himself? His chest, barely visible in the light of the lamp, betrayed no rise and fall. No respiration and so, perhaps food was similarly absent from his list of needs, even the first item of which she had yet to establish. Well, except safety, she thought as she watched him. Funny how in the golem story, he was the one providing the safety, the one doing the protecting, the brave man.

She picked up the lamp and held it as far in front of her as she could make the light reach without setting foot inside the closet. When it was angled just so, the light caught the golem, twisted up in lace, and splashed his shadow against the closet's back wall. Upon seeing his own flat black shadow towering before him, the golem began cautiously to back away from it, but with every step of retreat from his own projection, he came one nearer to the light of the lamp at the closet door, and his shadow against the wall grew and loomed larger. The shadow, now wider than the back wall, curled freely up the sides of the closet. Its outline was periodically hidden and revealed and hidden again in the racks of clothing.

When the golem was no more than four feet from her lantern, he backed into a stack of hatboxes, which toppled, spilling plumed hats and crinoline veils, and set the hangers to rattling. He clapped his hands together in front of his face, a sticky-sounding thud, and tried to turn his back to the shadow and clatter, but they were everywhere.

To his feet, he murmured *O O O*, soothing himself, a primitive lullaby as he rocked himself with difficulty. His blockish feet prevented the movement granted naturally by the flexibility of an arch. Having no true heel on which to catch himself, he rocked too far back and tripped on a fallen hat form. In the shock of unbalance, his petals flared open and he saw Ana and the flame of her lamp. Trapped between two nightmares, he sank to the closet floor, then shut his petal eyes tight, hiding like a child in his own blindness.

He must have supposed the shadow was a living thing. And since a shadow was a kind of darkness, why he might understand the whole of darkness—the entire night—to be one great, living shadow. How could he not be petrified? The only relief for it would be closing his eyes. There was something traitorous about blindness. People closed their eyes to shut out what frightened them, and what did they encounter there but more darkness?

When she looked back at him, though yet unmoving, he appeared relaxed, even docile. She had estimated it would take at least a quarter hour for the golem to resolve his fear through a series of testing—opening his eyes just for a flash at first, then for a couple of seconds, and eventually for longer periods until he could be assured that nothing in the closet would cause him harm. All creatures learn and adapt by experimentation. And yet here he was, only a minute after his tumble and already unafraid. Remarkable. Indeed, he appeared to be so absorbed in the peace of his thoughts—what could they be?—that Ana couldn't bring herself to break him from his spell.

On top of the rosewood desk lay the discarded rope they'd hustled from the vendor outside of Greenburg and Bond. They'd forgotten it, she realized, as soon as they put it down. It had felt so good to get what they wanted, to listen to the rope slap the road, to jump and turn and call together, like a strong machine. She drew the curtain open to let the moonlight in and found that here on the desk it was transformed into a common object. It might as well have been a hand mirror or a hairbrush. When she picked it up, though, she felt a hint of another sort of meaning, the meaning that had made it a souvenir in the first place. Ana took up the rope with her free hand, drawing one end of it over the other side and then under the point where the two sides crossed. This much was familiar. Like tying a shoe. How many inches around was a human head—she moved the elbow of the rope up and down—and how did the knot slide shut? She lowered it over her own head, and tightened it to fit her neck, leaving it to drape like a rough scarf.

In another corner of the attic was a small heap of ancient playthings: faded rattles, a rag doll in a red floral bonnet, a miniature dust-covered wire pram. Without the others there to distract her, the attic yielded up delights. She glanced back to the golem, meditatively calm, and went to inspect the objects. Had these forgotten things once been hers—toys she had played with and cared for? She felt a twinge of guilt for not remembering. She dislodged a wooden alphabet block from under the split head of a doll, whose batting she thumbed back in place as a small means of apology.

She set the lamp down behind herself to cast the best shadow on the wall, and tossed the block above her head, the big blue *B* tumbling over itself and changing to a butterfly, a bear, and back again. Up it went, the spinning edges blurring soft against the attic wall. Its dark reflection traveled the length of the ceiling and dropped over the doorframe of the closet along the opposite wall where the golem now held his hands cupped above his head, as though to catch it.

You're awake, Ana marveled. She tossed the block again and the golem, like a rooting infant, tracked its climb with his whole head moving to trace the rise and fall of the block. Mouth, face, hands reaching as he stepped, trancelike, out of the closet and into the attic. Something about the alphabet block enticed him. He was an infant by all measures apart from appearance; perhaps he had an infant's instinct for toys.

There it goes! she sing-sang. But this seemed to be something more than mere curiosity. His movement seemed compulsory, as if he were magnetized.

She would need to test the limitations of the golem's behavior. Defining specific limitations could make the unknowable knowable. For instance: snakes must shed their skin in order to grow and fish must breathe through the gill slits in their necks, and humans stopped breathing if their neck was squeezed shut by a rope.

In her left hand, she took up the lamp once more, and with her right, she tossed the alphabet block, this time with her back to the golem. She tossed the block a little ahead of herself and took two quick steps to catch up with it. She tossed again, another moving toss, and again, letting each toss lead her closer to the attic door. If she was very light with her steps, she could hear a faint plodding trailing her.

She opened the attic door and began her way down the stairs. In one hand she held a lamp and in the other the wooden block, which she held above her head—one torch for herself and one for the golem. Halfway down, she heard a groan—the golem had found the noisy step. She held her breath, but no parent noises followed, no one had woken, no creak of *paaaatience* from under the door of their room, so she continued down to the parlor, moving slowly, lighting the way for the both of them.

It was silly to be menaced by a shadow, all those villainous men in nickelodeon pictures stalking around in the dark. Nothing to a shadow but equal parts black and air. At the landing, she pocketed the block and hooked her thumbs together, palms in. Her fingers shadowed along the wall of the parlor: a bird's reaching wings. She turned her wrists this way and that, piloting its shadow flight, and the golem watched her.

The flying bird was the simplest of all shadow puppets. Anybody with two hands could give a feathered bird flight. It was the very first shadow puppet Ana had taught the others. *Here, like this*, she had told them, *now soar!* They became a room full of birds, gliding with the grace of a shadow flock. Never a collision, they passed through one another. Sometimes, their shadows overlapped, and they dissolved into one bird for a moment until a slight change of direction peeled their shadow bodies apart. They didn't think of speaking. There was no reason for it.

She could have done the fancy stuff. A crow perched on a wire or a thirsty goat or a circus elephant. They had taken her months of practice to perfect, but everything was a cinch once she learned the tricks: how the curve of a flexed thumb looked just like a panting tongue, how to move the index and middle fingers, the ears of the beast, perked and twitching to indicate alertness or lying flat with fear or vexation. And so, the golem's first puppet would soar. Her open-winged bird, a falcon, climbed the wall, periodically catching a draft, so that her silhouette, cutting sideways through imaginary wind, dissolved into a black line.

How strange, thought Ana, that of all the things expression permitted, imitation was thought to be the most impressive. The closer a copy came to matching its original, the more praise it received. Portrait artists, for example, were judged on their skill at rendering a good likeness. It would be unthinkable to sit for hours for a portrait only to discover the artist had painted the sitter as a milk bottle with sympathetic eyes or a bicycle with fingers for spokes. But really, why should it be? Why bother with replication, which, at best, was mild failure, when you could have absolute fantasy, which needn't compete at all? The golem had never seen a real bird, so for him, her shadow falcon was the original, and its feathered counter-part—should he ever see one—would be the copy. Every new thing she showed him would be the original form, the true form. She cast a furtive look over her shoulder. A small movement, so as not to frighten the golem, a replicate creature himself. The truth was that the soaring bird, which looked less like a real bird than it did the way a heart might look if it were light enough to fly, was the single most beautiful thing a person could do with her two hands in the dark. And she was happy to show him.

A sharp updraft and her falcon appeared again, wings spread wider, driving up, up to the moon, that pallid splash of light. The wall's moon was where the bird had laid her nest of moon chicks. A homecoming with her beak full of glowworms.

On her way to the moon, her shadow flight was eclipsed by the hunch of a mountain. If she were a day bird, a real bird, then even in the absence of her shadow, she would be a thing to herself and the shadow of another thing would be no impediment, but since she was a moon bird, a shadow falcon only, she was no bird at all when her shadow couldn't be seen. And with no shadow falcon, who would feed the moon chicks? Ana climbed her bird, wrists at full tilt, to crest the mountain top, which seemed to grow as she climbed, like a monstrous loaf of rising bread.

Logically, she knew it was all a matter of perspective. Her shadow falcon was not actually being swallowed up by a growing mountain of shadow. That was impossible. In reality, the shadow bird was merely approaching a place on the wall where some shape was already casting its own shadow between her bird and the moon nest, and the decreased distance between the bird and the shadow created the illusion of growth.

To prove it to herself, she suspended her falcon mid-flight, hovered her just below the lip of the mountain's cliff, as though she were flying into a strong headwind. And naturally, the mountain, in respect to the constant position of the falcon, did not grow but was itself constant.

Reassured, she soared the falcon over the lip to crest the mountain at last. Only a small stretch of wall separated her from the moon, and she drove her bird with straight arms right up as if to shoot clear through the night and come out on the morning side.

There! She'd done it! Her passing shadow draped the moon chicks in their mother's dark, and she imagined tipping the glowworms from her beak like tiny falling stars raining over her chicks for them to catch in their own mouths.

In and out of the moon she passed, circling her chicks in figure eights, but their happy chirps below were cut short by eclipse. The mountain's shadow was climbing again! Growing! Thrusting itself over their reunion like a curtain over a play. Not only did its appearance ruin her finale, it was completely incomprehensible because once an object is under you, it ought to remain under you.

From the mountain, two fingerless hands emerged, which reached toward her falcon's wing.

It's you, Ana whispered, still facing the wall. She didn't want to startle him. *Of course it's you.*

She let her falcon reach back, the pinky of her wing pulling away from the rest of her finger feathers until the slice of wall it revealed was closed by the shadow of the golem's thumb, which melted into the falcon's wingtip.

O, O, said the golem in response. As if he'd been caught doing something wrong, he peeled his shadow from the wing of the falcon and began to recede, his shoulders hunched.

Don't go, said Ana, but what good were words to a golem who had none? She would have to speak another way. She raised her left shoulder and bent her ribs to the right, angling her shadow falcon so that if it were a compass, it would have pointed northeast.

Then she set the bird to flight, following the line of its lower wing down and across the wall in the direction of the golem's shrinking shadow. Not too swiftly, a gentle rock in the shoulders, the shadow falcon balancing on a tame night breeze. When she was six inches from his shadow, she hovered the bird before him.

For you, Ana whispered. The golem's shadow ceased its shrinking, and he reached out one cupped hand to the bird, like the lobe of a question mark. Ana guided her falcon toward it, then over it, hovering directly above until she saw a little lift in the golem's hands, his reach her cue to climb up, up as far as her arms could stretch. She balanced on tiptoes, like a ballerina. She spread her wings as wide as her fingers would reach, then flipped her wrists. Wingtips arrowed down—*come catch me*—she sent her falcon in a deadweight nosedive for the floor. Down, down she plummeted.

O! said the golem, struggling to fold his bulk like a slow and bumbling avalanche. Both his hands now wobbled around, trying to guess the course of the falcon's fall to make a nest. She timed the falcon's descent to match him, slowing the plunge to an earthbound drift. At the very last moment, before the shadow of the falcon's nearest wing feather kissed the floor, there were the golem's hands—just in time for rescue.

Well done, Leo, she whispered. *My creature, my good boy.*

The golem had lowered himself into a catcher's squat and his hands gave cradle to her falcon, which rested just long enough to rustle its finger feathers as though settling down to roost before transforming into a pair of walking legs, which moved, at first, with tentative steps, over the shadow nest of his hands, as though sneaking over a creaky floor. First the index finger, then the middle, then the index again, which she pulled back gingerly—testing an especially noisy floorboard.

Creeeeeak, said Ana.

O O, said the golem.

She ran the shadow legs all the way up his arm and up to the top of his head. He raised a hand to grab them and Ana leapt them to the other side of his body. He reached out again, the mitt of his hand opening and closing, blinking against the wall. Ana perched behind him, nesting her hand into the shadow of his until they were one shadow.

O, he said, hunching lower and ducking away to reveal the rope she had forgotten she was wearing, which must have grazed his head.

O, Ana imitated, moving her fingers to the rope. She raised the trailing end and traced the letters L-E-O, watching the shadow name scrawl itself against the wall.

Leo o o, said the golem.

The knot, she now saw, wasn't right at all. It was loose and poked out at the ends, unlike the sleekness of the real thing with its many loops, and she set about fixing it and tucking in the stray ends. Yes, that looked better. A convincing replica, at least in shadow. She raised the trailing end high above her head, tightening the slack.

Le-O, Le-O, the golem rose from his squat with surprising speed and grasped at Ana's shadow: *FankaFrank-O!* He dragged his mitts against the wall as though trying to scrape the shadow of the rope clean from the wall.

Shhh, said Ana, amazed at the speed of his apparent understanding, and let the length of rope drop as she backed away, her shadow growing longer and blurred. *See?*

The golem, too, took a step back from the wall, and his shadow came into focus before his eyes.

Le-O, he said, mesmerized by his own shadow for the first time. He raised himself up to his full height and cocked his head, first to the left, then the right. Up and down. He watched his own body blacken the wall.

Ana retreated silently to the camera Fairfax had left behind, still perfectly posed in its insect stance. She turned on the standing lamp next to the sofa and stood on her toes, but the tripod was positioned for a taller operator. She carried an ottoman over to the camera and stepped up so that she was able to look down at the box and line the viewfinder up with the golem.

There you are, she whispered, and began to turn the crank. The camera watched him watch his own shadow. He was a blur against the night-washed wall. She had to squint to make him out, to watch him move every way his thick body would allow, lifting his legs and arms in isolation, bending each joint. What it must be like to discover such ability, a whole body he alone could move.

The golem began to revolve, his blue eyes fixed on his shadow for as long as he could before turning over his shoulder and facing the mechanical gaze of the camera. A booming *O* as he brought his arms before his face to shield himself.

His *O O O O*'s growing louder, closer together, until it was one sustained *O*, filling up the room.

Ana hopped down from the ottoman and rushed over to the golem, her hands springing up to his mouth to stop the sound from coming, but it did no good. His sound came from everywhere.

Shhh, she said. *Shhh, you must be quiet.*

And then there were stirring noises above. The *paaaatience* moan of the bed under the shifting weight of a mother rising. She couldn't take him back to the attic, there wasn't time. Ana grabbed the golem by his thick wrist and pulled. Her hand could only wrap halfway around. Why had she made him so bulky, so slow? She couldn't make him move any faster than she could have leash-walked a boulder, and his *O* kept coming.

Please, she whispered and brought her hand before the golem's face. It was wide enough to cover both of his eyes like a blindfold. *Calm down*. For a moment, his petals fluttered in panic, she could feel them beating against her palm, and she worried they would bruise. But he quickly settled into the peace of blindness, and his voice subsided.

She pulled at his wrist again, gently this time, and found he was no more difficult to move than a shadow. Up they sped, she and the blind golem, floating up the staircase in silence, as if they had no feet at all. She closed the door to her room with both of them safely inside just as her parents' door creaked open from the other end of the hall. Her mother would be groggy, slow-moving, but still, she had to be quick. She led the golem to her wardrobe and guided him inside, then shut the door. She turned down the twin wicks of the lamp and set it by her open window, smoke wandering into the sweating night, then took herself to bed.

She yanked at the rope around her neck, but the loop was too tight to slip over her head and the rough fibers of hemp scraped at her jaw. She could hear her mother's small feet drawing near as she tried frantically to loosen the knot, which wouldn't give but tore a broken nail from her finger. She drew a sharp breath and pulled the sheet clear up to her chin as her mother turned the handle—*Hold*, she told herself, *hold still, hold breath, hold perfect* and when the door creaked open, how serene a picture Mrs. Wulff was invited to witness.

She could feel her mother's eyes appraising the scene she presented. The squint of her mother's scrutiny like a too-tight hug. Mrs. Wulff stepped lightly inside and drew a deep breath through her nose. Like a hound sniffing out danger, but Ana was sleeping, see? Dreaming. See, Mother? So deep asleep I am dreaming of dreaming. Only this, only bed, only night, only safe, only the penny-carrot moon in the sky, see, Mother?

Mrs. Wulff poured a deep sigh of blessing over Ana's pillow and pulled her curtains shut over the night. Then she closed the door and was gone.

Silence, creature, Ana said with her mind. *Silence is safe. Stay hidden, creature. Hidden is safe.* She imagined her orders seeping through the painted cedar doors of her wardrobe, into the golem's mud heart. *I am your maker, I command you.*

And then she felt foolish for thinking it.

Once she could no longer hear the small sound of her mother's feet traveling the hallway, once the bedroom door at the end of the hall was closed, and the bed gave its moan, she counted to one hundred the very slowest she could make her mind count and still remember the number that came before. So slowly it almost hurt, like new teeth growing through gums.

Then back to him. There was still so much time before sunrise.

Shadow Puppets: Part II

(LATER, THE SAME NIGHT)

The muffled rustling in her wardrobe sharpened when Ana pressed her ear to the crack between the double doors. She heard a familiar note, the bright *plih! plih! plih!* of splitting thread.

Before her father's shop moved downtown, he had only a small place, half a room that he shared with a secondhand jeweler, so he'd done his sewing at home. Ana had been a fussy baby: scrawny, yellow, and colicky, according to Isaac, and when she cried and wouldn't be put to bed, he would carry her into her father's workroom where the hum of the sewing machine and pluck of ripping seams put her to sleep like nothing else could.

Too eager to be cautious any longer, Ana flung open the doors of the wardrobe.

Wolves! the golem blurted at her, and groped around with mud mitten hands for the hem of the nearest dress to cover his mouth and face.

Wolves wolves wolves. The word came again, a low mutter, and since his voice didn't issue from his mouth exclusively, it hardly mattered that he had covered it.

Ana stifled an excited laugh. A new word! But where on earth had he gotten that word? There weren't any wolves in Atlanta, and certainly not in her wardrobe. How strange that of all the available creatures, the golem should conjure imaginary wolves to hide from. Wolves were giant

189

dogs with razor teeth that lived on the crests of snowcapped mountains. They roamed the desolate landscapes of the Old Country looking for carrion. Ana had only ever seen illustrations of them in fairy-tale books. It even seemed possible wolves had been invented just for scaring children into behaving. That's what the Old Country was: a warning, the threat of danger, something with teeth.

How had he learned the word in the first place? It wasn't as though they had set about teaching him to recite cautionary stories. The attic was not a schoolroom. There were far more important things to learn. For example, almost anything. And besides, thought Ana, he probably already knew loads of things, if she could only figure out how to prove it. "Wolves" might easily have been a random combination of sounds that only resembled the English word. Perhaps he was actually saying *vulfs* or *oolvz*.

Wolves, he said. *Leo o o wolves.*

It certainly sounded like *wolves*, but even if it was a nonsense homonym, where had he gotten the individual letters? He had thus far only spoken his own name and combinations of sound derived from it.

After a few minutes passed, his apprehension seemed to wane in a way that suggested less that he had overcome it than that he had forgotten it, and he babbled to himself:

O frala frank made. At la lanta wolves in. Made Le O Frank. O lan made fra.

So many new sounds! The shape of his head beneath the hem of the dress turned slowly, as though he were scanning the underskirt, and he pawed the objects around him in search of something unknown to Ana. He snatched a felt porkpie hat and drew it under the hem of the dress so that all she could see was the unwilling ripple of heavy wool. The accompanying sounds: a small tear and then the ripping of thread, the soft kissing sound of clay against clay. He had neither tongue nor teeth, and she had not previously seen evidence of a working jaw, but there was the sound.

Then the plop of the crumpled hat on the floor, the label torn clean, and the booming growl of his stomach that echoed as though he were hollow, like thunder in a canyon.

Pflthhh! He spat the label, which landed a foot or so in front of him, face up:

WULFF'S *Made in Atlanta*

Not wolves. *Wulff's!* said Ana. *Of course.*

Wulff's, the golem agreed.

But if he could translate the letters on the label to spoken words, then he must be able to read, which should have taken years of practice. Many grown men couldn't even read their own names on a postcard. And here he was, six days old and reading three-syllable words, but did he understand the words he spoke?

I am Wulff, said Ana. *And my father is, and my mother. Do you understand?*

Glumly, he gummed with his empty mouth and sighed *O.*

Then it dawned on her that the golem might have been starving. He'd had nothing to eat since his birth. And the week before that, when he'd still been in the ground, Atlanta had been in a drought, so quite likely, he'd been born parched and starving. Poor thing, so hungry he'd resorted to cotton moths and clothing labels. Her own stomach rumbled in sympathy, and she checked her pockets for something to eat.

She sometimes squirreled food away before bed when no one was looking in case she should become hungry at night, which she often did. Something about the utter darkness made her stomach ache. It was terrible how ravenous the hours after midnight could be.

The others never mentioned hunger in their version of the golem story. Once awakened, their golem seemed to subsist on Old World rations—davening and despair, that sort of thing—so perhaps Leo was the golem of her mother's telling, after all. Perhaps her mother had been telling the truth. A boy born with a stomach for a heart. Though looking at the golem now, this would-be Leo, squat and timid, she couldn't believe he belonged to that story either. He was a new kind of golem, Ana decided.

In spite of the havoc the clayboy's hunger wreaked, there was something pitiable in it. It wasn't his fault. The old couple erred in their construction. Their fingers too stiff, their spirits too heavy to perform the finer work of creation. How unceasingly the hunger must have gnawed at him as he emptied a whole barn into his mouth. It was the only way he could think to stop the aching. Her golem slunk, dejected, onto the floor of the wardrobe, his face still covered by a long wool frock.

Me too, said Ana.

But was his story really so monstrous? In homeroom, the pendant below the sun-stain on the wall where the Jesus had been read, *Receive Christ into Your Heart and Be Saved*. To get him there inside you, to keep him there in the walls of yourself. That was the aim, that was how you kept yourself from the ache.

In the left pocket of her nightgown, Ana found a cluster of table grapes, days old and puckered where they were fixed to the vine.

Are you hungry? she asked, plucking one for herself and rolling a second along the wardrobe floor so that it caromed feebly off the golem's block foot. He snatched it with his right hand, and with his left, he lifted his veil of wool just enough to reveal the place in his flower eye where the blue began to fade into the creamy yellow of its center.

Like this, she said and popped a grape into her mouth, bared her teeth, and bit down. The golem, likewise, brought the pinched grape to the hole of his mud mouth. She hadn't dug a well for his throat, and she wondered if the grape would just sit there in the nook of his mouth until it rotted. But she didn't wonder long because the golem spat the grape out almost instantly and moaned in toneless displeasure.

Had the grape gone sour from too much time in her pocket? Perhaps grapes weren't to a mudman's taste. Though, surely, he was young enough that his tastes were still malleable. Then again, lion cubs were born hungry for fresh meat and mother's milk. A shiver seized her as she imagined what he might eat instead, but she shook herself from its grip. *I dug him,* she reminded herself, *I shaped him, I made him alive.*

What do you want? she asked him, but he didn't even *O* in response.

On her dresser, there was a music box with a dancing girl on top. A French ballerina, her father had told her, made of bisque porcelain so that she looked more lifelike. When the crank was wound and the song possessed her, the ballerina's thin legs wobbled in their red slippers like insect legs capped with matchstick heads, and she spun convulsively to flourishes in the tinkling music.

Ana didn't have much use for the box; she didn't care for jewelry, she didn't press flowers. For a brief time, she collected the bodies of the lightning bugs whose glow she and the others had taken, but Isaac had gotten rid of them, mistaking the shrine for neglectful housekeeping. Now, though, the box held the small ten-cent Nabisco tin the Night Witch had given her, all of the wafers minus the one she used—for real or for show, she was still unsure—to bring the golem to life.

She opened the lid and peeled back the paper with great care, selecting a wafer from the middle where there was less chance of breaking it. She was hesitant to give one away. Suppose he spat it out as he had the grape. Then she would have wasted the Night Witch's gift, surely an egregious mistake. Still, hunger was a terrible thing, so she pried the halves of the wafer apart—if it was a mistake, at least she'd only be wasting half—and offered the half without the crème, NABISCO-side up, in the flat of her palm to the golem.

This is special, she told him, *magic food. Magic like you.*

With his face still half-covered by the woolen veil, he reached his arm out in front of him, but he wasn't near enough to grab it. Slowly, his whole face slid out from beneath the veil as he leaned toward the offering. Magnetized in the same way he had been by the alphabet block.

He blinked rapidly as the hem grazed his top petal lashes. His stomach growled again and he rocked himself from out of the wardrobe, pouncing at the wafer in her palm, which he pinned between his mitts with Ana's own hand caught between them.

O, he said, *O Wulff's.*

Before she could think to pull away, he had drawn the wafer to his mouth and her fingers with it. She flinched as her fingers passed into the hole, waiting for the pain of a bite, but there wasn't one. Only a pleasant pressure, like having your hand squeezed for luck.

She could have snatched her fingers away; there was time. His eyes were closed, and the hole of his mouth open with toothless chewing. But she kept two fingers there like a pacifier, middle and pointer, and wiggled them down beneath the wafer softening in the damp of his mouth, down below the loose dirt to the flat, filled-in part at the bottom of his mouth hole that would have been the wormy space beneath his tongue, if he'd had a tongue. She dug there with both fingers, scooping out a small pit of dirt, to make a hollow. She flicked his mouth dirt into her palm, withdrew her hand, and closed her fist tight around the small plunder. A soil sample! She hoped it hadn't hurt him, but her curiosity had won out against her concern for his comfort.

N A B I S C O! wailed the golem, this new word still melting in his mouth.

Incredible, said Ana, as crumbs of wafer fell from his open mouth.

Nabisco! Nabisco! he chimed.

It was funny to hear the mudman speak the wafer's name—so very ordinary. But then why shouldn't he be allowed to say ordinary things? He needn't recite incantations or utter prophecies exclusively. He should be free to rattle off the entire contents of the pantry if he liked.

Marmalade, said Ana. *Lemon creams, Maxwell House, Block's Saltines.* Should she write them down?

Nabisco, said the golem.

She emptied his mouth dirt into her pocket and ate her own half of the wafer. The one who got the cream got a wish—or maybe that was a chicken bone. Wishes were like stars, anyhow; you could only look at them and think about how far away they were. Better to have a chicken bone, and still better to have the cream side of the wafer, which she scraped off with her two front teeth. Then she licked the word side, left to right, dissolving each sugar-printed letter, her tongue tip a pencil-top eraser, until they were all gone. The letters slipping about and winding through her stomach and the golem's mouth, both flooded with Nabiscos.

Na-bis-co Na-bis-co, he said and teetered like a happy metronome.

Na-bis-co Na-bis-co, she cooed, as mothers did with their babbling babies. She had seen them at it, strolling their prams along sidewalks, utterly absorbed in their nonsense. They had always seemed foolish to her, but now, the echo came thoughtlessly from her throat, as though someone had reached into her and gently lifted it from some dormant place inside. That shared sound, a warm place for them to rest.

Best of all, for an instant, they were no longer ravenous. A moment of pleasant suspension where she could not foresee, nor did she want to foresee, anything beyond the just then. Satisfied in mind and stomach by the Night Witch's Nabisco. *Thank you thank you thank you!*

But it wasn't just the wafer, she thought. Not just the sweetness, not for him. Why hadn't she realized it before? Hadn't he been captivated by the alphabet block, the clothing label, and the wafer? All of them words, and he wasn't reading them, he wanted to devour them! He wanted new language. But was it *only* that? Only sustenance?

Or do you understand?

Leo Frank, he answered.

And suddenly she was ashamed for her cooing. Her echo was for the pleasure of the shared sound, whereas the golem's was for want of other choices. He was confined to the few words he'd been fed, as he was to the closet where they kept him. He would be trapped, forever, if they chose, to say only "Leo Frank" and "Wulff's Made in Atlanta" and "Nabisco" over and over again, trying, by means of repetition and recombination, to say so many other things they would never understand. One "Leo" could mean "I am unhappy" or "I wish to say more, to explain how I feel" or "I wish to be set free to become whatever it is I am capable of becoming," which is the natural aim of any living creature. A caterpillar wants to become a swallow-tail, a tadpole wishes to be a bullfrog, a hatchling a wood thrush. Only how could she know the metamorphic stages of this mudman—which words would sustain him? Which would grow him into his potential?

You're a Mudderfly, she said, giddy with her own cleverness. *What do you think?*

Leo Frank, he answered.

Perhaps the simplest way would be to let him have absolute freedom over which words to eat. The caterpillar knows instinctively to eat from the leaves of the lilac and willow. Yet mothers wouldn't dare let their infants choose for themselves. They'd gorge themselves all day on cakes and jellies, or worse. A good number of things that would be dangerous to swallow present themselves very prettily. Shimmering pieces of broken glass, for example, resemble the jagged crystals of rock candy. To let him loose on the entire expanse of the English language—to say nothing of all the other languages in the world, of which she was only faintly aware—was such a thing conscionable? To give him "cruelty" and "libel" and "violence" and "tragedy"? All the awful things expressed by language—and yet, could language really be the culprit?

What kind of havoc would you wreak if I let you loose on a dictionary? she asked the golem. *I'd let you if you'd promise to be good and civil.*

Nabisco? he asked, and it sounded like *more?*

I'm sorry, she told him. *I'm responsible for your safety, and mine, for that matter. I'll need some time to think it over. If only you could promise to stay good.*

She watched him closely for hints of recognition. If you wanted to know how a person truly felt about a thing, the answer could be found in their eyes, which were the single most expressive part of the face. That was how you could tell a liar from an honest man—he wouldn't look you in the eye; it was a fact she had read on a tip sheet inside a pack of playing cards. But the golem's eyes, the petals of his flowers, were unreadable, or perhaps it was just that she had no practice at interpreting the expression of flower petals. She fluttered his petals with the length of her index finger and made a mental note to study in the garden later, diagram the expressions of the hydrangeas and zinnias and other late-summer bloomers.

For now, she would begin to exercise her other deductive skills. She observed, for example, that he had stopped tottering and come to a rest, that he waited to speak until she had given a question, and that he faced in her direction when he answered. The last point of evidence was, admittedly, the most contestable because it was difficult to determine exactly in which direction a flower was looking. In any event, she interpreted these observations as signs of comprehension. Better to give him the benefit of any possible doubt than to write him off.

She sighed and he began again to totter, an agitated movement that made him look like a windup toy keyed to its tightest point. So much for her observations.

Wulff Wulff Wulff, he said, like a child imitating a dog's bark.

I'm sorry, I don't understand, said Ana, *but I'm trying to.*

Wulff madly o, he said, which wasn't possible because no one had yet fed him "madly." It simply wasn't a word he had in his internal possession. She instructed him to repeat himself, but he wasn't bound by her command and seemed content with the communication he'd made.

Wulff madly o, Ana repeated. *Wulff mad lyo. Wulff mad leo. Wulff made Leo. Wulff made Leo!*

But even as she said it, she couldn't be sure it wasn't just a random combination of the words in his stomach. Certainly, it was what she hoped for—that he should know. The possibility of his intelligence prickled at her as though a draft had cut through the still heat. They *had* made the golem and she, Ana Wulff, had made him most of all. And he was—at least they had meant to call him—Leo, though once awake, that name had mostly fallen away.

Wulff made Leo, her good boy.

Now be honest, she said, holding open the petals of his eyes between her thumb and forefinger, *Do you know what honesty—*

Frank, he interrupted.

What? said Ana and then felt supremely dumb because, *Jiminy cricket, a joke. You made a joke! And you've only got seven words.* Most people had thousands of words and couldn't manage to make anyone laugh.

You're brilliant, she said and kissed his forehead. *Tell me another!*

Frank, he repeated.

On deaf ears, she sighed, but quickly corrected herself. *I didn't mean—*

She had never sculpted him any ears. Their small folds and ditches were too complicated for dirt to hold. The effect was that his head looked slightly wormish.

I only meant that you seemed not to have heard what I said.

In this dim light, he appeared unfeatured and slick. And suddenly she was no longer interested in jokes. She wiped the dirt from her lips.

The golem said nothing.

OK for now, she said and patted his damp head. *Nabisco.*

Snoops

One day, I'll take Leo to the picture show. I should love to watch his face.

—DIARY OF ANA WULFF

Ana awoke the next morning to a thick and salty smoke creeping through the floorboards of her bedroom. Her mother had a habit of distraction where cooking was concerned—*you try waiting all day for a pot to boil. See if your mind doesn't wander.* Her youth, spent as her father's butcher shop apprentice, had given her a taste for decisiveness in all things, but especially the kitchen: the plucking of feathers, the cleaving of joints, the swift open-and-shutting of the cash register. These tasks, free from waiting, were the sort to which Mrs. Wulff and her temperament were suited. Isaac had learned early in his housekeeping tenure of this particularity and he made certain the Wulffs' supper was never ruined because of it.

Isaac! Ana called from her bed. There was no response, and she hadn't expected one. When she was a young child, Isaac had come to wake her up most mornings and braid her hair while she was still too sleepy to fuss, but that was many years ago. It wouldn't be appropriate for him to visit her bedroom now, but she still called to him sometimes, just to remind herself he was there. Her room was stifling, the August heat doubled by grease smoke. Thick bands of undaunted sunlight pressed orange patterns on her closed eyelids. Still she clung to her bedsheets, pulling them up over her head, drawing in a hot breath.

Flecks of dirt fell into her open mouth and she moved her tongue around her gums, collecting the taste of earth. She spat, frantic. Small granules of sand scratched at the backs of her bare legs. Why was there so much of it? How had it gotten there? She tried to breathe slowly as she peeled back the light cotton summer quilt. Her sheets were streaked with brown and black. A pill bug huddled beneath her pillow. A single blue hydrangea petal stuck to the skin over her ribs and she suppressed a shudder as she pulled it free and balled it up between her fingers. An eye, she thought, a night watchman, a sleep spy, but it couldn't be. She threw open her wardrobe, but the golem was gone. She was struck with fresh panic. Where was he? What was he doing and who had seen him do it? A part of him was with her, stuck to her, in the cracks of her molars, the crunch of sand when she ground her teeth. But where was the rest of him?

The hand mirror on her dresser reflected the blackened corners of her eyes and mouth. Specks of dirt flecked her face like freckles and settled into the fine rings of her neck, which, she now saw, was otherwise bare. Her breath slowed down, and she chided herself for her hasty fear. The lynch rope was gone with the golem. He was only doing his job, protecting her. She popped her thumb into her mouth and used it to wipe the black rings from her neck as she imagined him pulling down her covers and sitting at the edge of her bed, working the knot free in silence so complete he might have been the dark itself. How he must have worried it—even with his crude hands—with such gentle manipulations that he never once woke her.

Bless you, she thought. Bless us all for making you.

But there was still the matter of her soiled sheets, which she shook out of her bedroom window, beating them free of his left-behinds. She washed her face clean. How would she explain the mess to Isaac? She brushed the soot from her hair too, but the wet, rooty scent of the mudman remained.

Her mother still needed tending to. And she was tired. And his dirt was under her fingernails. And the smell of smoke was strong. And where was the golem? And where was Isaac?

Still in her nightgown, she took a big breath and walked the hallway to the stairs. Just halfway down.

Thoughtless klutz, her mother mumbled from the kitchen.

Who? said Ana. *Who are you talking about?*

Mrs. Wulff acknowledged her daughter's voice with a frown of concentration.

A man with a butcher's knife, a battle-ax, she said. *What's the difference?*

What was the point of such questions? Why not just say it straight?

He cut the entrails in with the fat, said her mother, as if this accounted for the gurgle and hiss of boiling chicken fat slopping over the rim of the pot. *Ruined the render.*

Perhaps you should open the window? said Ana from her cautious perch on the first landing, as though her mother, like the pot, might boil over and scald.

Where is Isaac?

Always asking for Isaac. I'm told other children ask for their mothers.

Well? Ana persisted.

I fired him. I gave him the afternoon off. I sent him on an errand.

Was she meant to choose between the three? And what if she got it wrong? Ana liked the orderliness of consequence. And while she professed to esteem logic beyond all other virtues, she was a deeply superstitious girl. For, what other tenant could so easily assign culpability? It was a great relief to her to know the exact origin of a seemingly random mishap. In fact, it had been Ana who invented the Smutch one day after she skinned her elbow falling from a bicycle when she was eleven, though she had tried very hard to forget she was its creator, preferring to believe the Smutch to be a natural and inevitable fact.

The outcome of this particular riddle, she felt certain, would not determine her own fortune, but Isaac's. She was responsible for the future of Isaac's employment, or worse. And though he sometimes irritated her, forcing her to do chores she despised and say polite things, Isaac had been with her family since before she was born. When Ana came down with scarlet fever as a toddler, it was Isaac for whom she had cried out, with her swollen throat, in the throes of those fevered dreams.

I fired him. I gave him the afternoon off. I sent him on an errand. Three possible answers. One to three odds, thirty-three and one-third percent. The first option had three words, one syllable per word, and so perhaps that was the correct answer. Her fingers tapped her knees as she counted. Each of the others, six words, still divisible by three. The second, eight syllables, and the third, seven. She was not strong with fractions. Or else it wasn't numeric at all, but alphabetical. In the first two answers, the verbs began with *f* and *g* respectively; a sequence which the third did not follow, and yet the third seemed the most likely of the answers. But did the three answers correspond to the reality of Isaac's absence or were they code for something else? She peered over the balustrade, hoping for a clue.

Won't you just tell me? said Ana.

Her mother was inhabiting one of her strange moods. Sometimes riddles must be cracked not with cunning but by force. Furthermore, Ana got the impression that her mother didn't know her own riddle's answer, which meant that even if she got it right, offered the true answer, her mother might cast it aside, preferring the puzzle. And Isaac's fate might be suspended until her mother came to her senses.

Tell you what? her mother said, glancing up at Ana. *Oh, that. He's fetching something from the store. It's only us here, your little friends will be here soon, though.*

But I'm not even dressed, said Ana, descending the bottom flight.

Your father relented, not me. Mrs. Wulff sat at the kitchen table, ignoring her smoking pot. Her gaze was anchored past Ana, fixed in the parlor. *He can forgive you for both of us.*

The render needs stirring. It's burning, that's all, said Ana. *It's not ruined.*

A boy came by this morning, said Mrs. Wulff, ignoring her daughter's advice. *To take the camera back. He had dirty shoes.*

It's gone?

Fortunately.

And he took the film?

I'm told your father will have his motion picture before the month is out.

Ana scrambled over to the place in the parlor where the camera had been, searching the room for what wasn't there. All she found were three equally spaced dents in the carpet. If the film was developed there would be evidence: of lying to her parents, of breaking her swear to the others. But also of the golem, of his realness and his body and his goodness. Which were only hers now, and how could she give him away? She had to stop the cameraman from sending off the film. She traced a triangle with her toe, connected the dents in the carpet just as four fists beat at the front door. Answer the door, stop the cameraman, stir the pot. Or was it stop the door, stir the cameraman, answer the pot? Three immediate charges.

Ana! called the others.

Ana! called her mother.

Get the door, said her mother.

But the pot must be stopped.

So must the banging, said Mrs. Wulff. *Get the door.*

The others poured in.

It stinks in here, said Rose, making a screwed-up face. *Doesn't your mother—*

Don't, said Ana.

Doesn't her mother what? Mrs. Wulff called from the kitchen.

Look lovely today, Rose called back. *Can't say the same for you, though.* She looked Ana up and down.

You're a mess, Sarah giggled.

I woke up late, Ana mumbled over her shoulder as she moved into the kitchen. She stirred the render and took the pot off the flame.

The rest of them followed, stopping only to bow their heads in an embarrassed chorus of apologetic greeting to Mrs. Wulff, who ignored them entirely. Then resumed their path through the house, which by now was automatic: past the parlor, past kitchen, past the powder room to the landing. They were all here to see Leo, after all. Rule #1. And what if he wasn't there? What could she possibly tell them? *Don't worry, he was in my bed last night, he can't have gone far.* The truth would only make things worse.

Ana rushed to the landing and spread her arms across the width of the stairs.

What are you doing? said Esther.

We should go outside, Ana blurted. *We should have a picnic.*

But Ana, you aren't even dressed, Franny said with a little laugh.

It would only take me a moment, Ana countered. *And then we could—*

We didn't come here for a picnic, Rose bossed. *We're going to the clubhouse.*

She pushed past Ana and climbed, with Sarah in tow. Esther lagged two steps behind.

Franny took Ana's reluctant hand and tried to lead her gently up the stairs: *Come on. You and I can have our own picnic later when it cools down.* Ana pulled away and raced up the two flights to the attic door, but Rose was already through and Ana said *wait!* but no one did. They were all inside now, and in six more strides, someone had a hand on the cut-glass doorknob of the closet. Everyone's eyes were trained on the promise growing in the widening angle of darkness.

And there he was.

He had returned himself to the closet and stood dormant in the shadow. Nothing out of the ordinary, almost less exciting than before! And there too, on the desk, the rope he'd loosened from her neck. A film of grateful tears warped her vision.

Thank you thank you thank you, Ana thought to her golem.

You spied for the Day, you lied for the Day,

And woke the Day's red spleen.

—FROM "THE DAY," BY HENRY CHAPPELL, REPRINTED IN THE *ATLANTA CONSTITUTION*

Who'd have thought this—said Esther, fake-yawning at the open door where the golem stood unmoving—*would be it.*

What are you looking at, pinhead? said Sarah.

Who knows what he's looking at? said Rose, *thanks to Ana's brilliant sculpting job.*

I like his eyes, said Franny. *I think they're pretty.*

Ugh, Sarah complained. *He's the worst Leo Frank.*

Maybe he needs upkeep, Ana suggested. *Plants need watering, don't they? And bread must be kept warm so it can rise. Maybe waking him up wasn't enough.*

One of us suggested a blessing. We knew blessings for lighting candles and blessings for the morning and blessings for eating all manner of food, but no one knew the blessing for an occasion precisely like this one. And furthermore, there was the problem of address. We weren't sure if we ought to pray in the normal way, *Barukh atah Adonai,* and so forth, or if we ought to pray to the golem himself. Or perhaps we ought to pray to Leo Frank, from whose name and likeness, roughly, the golem borrowed. One of us thought we ought to pray to the Night Witch because Ana had actually seen her, and so she would probably answer quicker, wasn't that right?

Sure, if you believe Ana about it, said someone else.

But we didn't want to upset any powers by saying the wrong blessing, giving credit where it wasn't due, so we made a list instead. We thought of all the things we could do with the golem, because what was the use in having him around if he was just going to be a lame lump of dirt? It wasn't worthwhile magic unless he could at least do a trick or two. Even dogs could be trained to shake and roll over. Chickens could run around with their heads lopped off. And if that wasn't some kind of magic, well.

The golem looked even worse in the daylight, his incongruity and lumpiness on full display. Except for a low gurgle and the occasional flutter of his eye petals, he might have been a very ugly statue. We didn't know exactly what we'd expected him to do, the precise way we'd wanted him to act in the world, how he should regard us, but we knew we wanted something more than this imbecile staring. We thought he would need us more.

Ana, however, watched him with a degree of interest we had never earned from her. What did she know that we didn't? And what did we see that she couldn't? Our two disappointments: one squat and earthy, the other very much like us, familiar, but changing, we could see now, into someone different.

Do something! we said. He made no sign of understanding our command.

We stuck out our tongues and wiggled them around. Two of us could fold our tongues into clovers. They were extra lucky and would have many suitors.

We pulled the corners of our mouths open with our index fingers like hooks and stretched our lips tight, the surprise of dry skin splitting, the warm pain, the salty taste of blood we lapped from our lips before it trickled down our chins. One of us, growing bold with idleness, prodded the golem with her toe and then recoiled, anticipating retaliation that never came.

Don't, said Ana.

But why not? We wondered what it would take; how far we would have to go, if Ana would let us.

We could teach him to recite poems, one of us suggested.

You must be joking, said someone else. *That's worse than nothing at all.*

We could teach him to dance, one of us said.

I know the Grizzly Bear, someone offered, but we didn't have any music.

We could dress him up in all the old clothes in the closet.

We could even dress him up like a lady. Teach him manners.

We could take him apart and make him better this time.

We could marry him and make him do our chores.

Of all the possibilities, this one was the most appealing because we didn't like making our beds and sweeping the floors and canning peaches for the winter and blah blah blah. And besides, our families all had maids whom they paid to do the same dull work they insisted we do for free.

But if you marry someone, the person you marry has to do what they're told, including your chores. Our fathers told us about how, when they were our age, they had many chores—chores that lasted from sunup to sundown. But then they married our mothers and now our fathers never have to do any chores at all. This was how it would be with the golem, though he could only be married to one of us at a time. Otherwise, we'd be heathens.

Rose thought it ought to go in order of birthdays, which, of course, would make her the first bride. No one else liked her idea.

We should let him choose, Ana offered, laughing. But we could tell she meant it.

I bet you think he'd choose you, said Rose.

I don't—Ana stammered, *I just*—

Who'd want to be a monster's bride anyhow? said Rose.

Don't call him that, Franny said quietly. *What if he understands you?*

I hope he does, Rose shot back, and wrapped on the golem's soft head with her knuckles. *You hear me in there?*

But what if he believes it?

We prayed he would. That he'd believe it and turn into a monster, that he'd monster Ana; she'd deserve it for thinking she was better than us. And if it looked like a romp, we'd hope he'd monster us too.

Na—said the golem, as if to weigh in on the matter. Na, I am a monster. Na, I am not.

Na— Na—babbling like a toothless baby.

Franny? said Franny. *Are you trying to say Franny?*

No one was ever trying to say Franny. Even her own mother forgot her name sometimes, called her by her sister's name, Emma. A better name by all accounts.

Ana, said Rose. *It's Ana, our dear little Muscovite princess.*

Na— said the golem, which Rose took as agreement and she flicked her palm open in Ana's direction as though tossing a fistful of flour at her.

Oh, get on with it! Rose screamed, as if the golem's delay were causing her genuine anguish. *An-YA*, she spat out the second syllable. *It's her, isn't it? You want to marry her!*

The golem blinked his petal eyes twice and then, with a measure of calm, said *Nabisco*.

Ana absolutely lost her head giggling. Like a madwoman, or a volcano erupting with laughter.

There you have it, she blurted, barely able to squeeze the words out from between her bursts of laughter: *A cookie!*

As though it were the funniest joke in the whole wide blue world since the beginning of time. But it wasn't funny. It was a terrible betrayal. No one could have taught him that word but her, and she'd sworn an oath. We wondered what else they had done together, without us.

He wants to marry a cookie! What a riot! She slapped her knee. *Standing at the chuppah as he's circled by a tin of tea biscuits!*

The rest of us didn't laugh. We didn't even smile. We only watched her and the golem, who muttered *Nabisconanabiscona* under her laughter, their lunatic sounds making an ugly braid. After a few moments, Ana managed to mostly hush herself up.

Be careful, Ana, we said with our silence. We made the rules too. Now we get to make the punishments.

She pursed her lips shut so no more sound could get through them, but her shoulders shook and her eyes watered and the shaking made her nesting tears run down her cheeks. She had plump cheeks, piggy pink cheeks that our parents made much of. Like a modern-day cherub. That's what they said. A precious little lady who would one day make a very beautiful young woman. Then she turned her back to the rest of us, hiding her lying face from our scrutiny.

What else, she said. *What else might we do? I'll record what we've got so far.*

She wandered over to the rosewood desk, fussing with her back to us over thises and thats that no one cared about. She struck a match and lit the twin wicks of the marriage lamp that sat on the desk, adjusting their heights when there was already too much sun.

This isn't a slumber party, said Esther. *What do you need the lamp for?*

You're right, she giggled. *Just a habit.*

She went around the desk and made a show of the top left drawer being stuck, even though it had never been stuck before, before fishing out a pad and a pencil. Any excuse to prolong avoiding our eyes, avoid revealing herself as traitor and liar.

Plans for the golem, she said, scribbling with great intensity. *Friday, August 27th, 1915.* As though it were some kind of formal document instead of what it was: chicken scratch on some scrap paper and a ploy to distract us from what we already knew. Ana was breaking our rules. Even very clever girls don't always get their way.

We could let him loose on Mrs. Dillard next door, she rambled.

Sarah fake-yawned.

We could do it when she's just gotten up from her afternoon nap. Imagine what a fright he'd give her! Stop her old heart cold.

She chanced a look up to us. We made our faces hard and she quickly returned her eyes to the pad, writing now with frantic strokes. *Clitch* went the tip of pencil, which was common enough, but Ana, flustered by her own lies, said *Hell!* and slapped the desk with her palm, which sent the pencil rolling off the desk onto the floor.

Why, Ana, said one of us. *Not a very nice word.* It was a mock-scolding because what did we care about "hell" or "piss" or "damn" or any other swear word? But it was a real scolding, too, because completely beside the fact that Mrs. Dillard was a perfectly decent neighbor and made excellent gingerbread soldiers, we all knew that showing the golem to anyone else was strictly out of the question.

Besides, said one of us, *that would be violation of Rule #9.*

We wagged our fingers at Ana, willing them full of lead bullets. If we wagged them hard enough, we could hit Ana square between her clear blue eyes. And the blue would drain out and stain her pig cheeks blue, too. She deserved it for being a rotten cheat. For cheating the Felicitous Five. And really, didn't the Felicitous *Four* sound just as good?

It was just a suggestion, mumbled Ana, now on hands and knees before the desk, searching for her dropped pencil.

We weren't naive. Ana might have been twice as smart as us, but she was only half as smart as she thought she was. Our suspicions were confirmed and now we had proof—Nabisco! such a dumb mistake for a clever girl—proof she'd been coming alone to visit the golem and breaking the vow she had made with us, just like we knew she would, because Ana thought there was something special in store for her. Everyone told her so. Something apart from us, some future we couldn't join. And fine, if she thought she had to break her oath to be special, there were other ways to keep her bound to us. Rule #4, withholding is a serious offense.

The pencil had rolled to Sarah's feet. She kicked it away and it hit a steamer trunk with a loud crack.

Ana coughed nervously.

Rose draped the back of her hand over her forehead and gave a pitiful moan.

I'm coming down with something ghastly, she said. *Ana, why do you never cover your mouth when you cough? It's repulsive. Moreover, it's infectious.*

It just from dust, she tried to say, *I'm not—*

But we wouldn't let her speak. Her rotten, lying tongue would stay in her rotten, lying mouth this time.

You know, Rose, said Sarah, *I'm feeling a touch of a sore throat, too. It must be her terrible hygiene. Ana, you have to change your rags when you bleed, you're liable to make us all ill.*

Why would you say that? said Franny.

Oh! Sarah, said Esther, ignoring Franny, *that must be the source of that dreadful smell.*

It's the smoke from the kitchen. How could you think it was me? Ana said, horrified. *I . . . I haven't even begun to . . .* she couldn't finish the sentence. *I would have told you,* she finished weakly.

We took up places in a semicircle around her, pinning Ana between us and the desk.

I don't believe you would have, said Esther. *Doesn't seem in keeping with your character.*

That horrid smell, said Sarah. *It turns my stomach. Didn't your mother teach you how to clean yourself?*

If it isn't the smoke, said Ana, *then it's the mildew from my father's clothing and it can't be helped. You know how damp it gets up here.*

No, said Rose, stepping closer to her and inhaling deeply, *it isn't that. It smells distinctly of filth.*

It's the golem, then, said Ana. *Clearly, it's the golem. What do you expect when we keep a mudman shut up in a hot closet?*

We all began to sniff around. Short, audible huffs. We sniffed the dust in the air. We sniffed the moth-holed lace curtains, *Not it.* The insides of hatboxes, *Not it.* The gilded frames of old pictures, *Not it.* The wooden legs of the desk, in front of which Ana knelt, *Getting closer.* The pad of paper in her hands, *Closer.*

Then we sniffed her: the linen of her dress against our faces, her heaps of hair. Two of us flanked her and pressed our hands into her palms, threading our fingers through hers, her fingers clasped in our fists. We hoisted her to standing and lifted her arms to shoulder height while the other two sniffed down her sides from her armpits, over her ribs, down her waist, and lower. She didn't resist. She made no response at all.

It was only a game to start. Ana was the Smutch, the one to blame. We were only going to pretend disgust, pretend to sniff her out like something rotten. To set things right with her before they went too wrong. Disloyalty mustn't be allowed to go unpunished. But the invention of every new game creates a new way to lose.

What else did you teach him? one of us said. *Did you teach him to say "Ana is a wicked liar"?*

Or "Ana is the real Smutch"?

I suppose you taught him to love you better than the rest of us. How did you do that?

It wasn't like that, she said quietly. *I was going to tell you tonight.*

The dust and the mildew and the candle wax and the dirt and her buttermilky skin smell and the rose petals in her pockets—all of the things we had loved so completely, so stupidly—and the mad tears tearing down our throats. All of it turned to filth, turned to sweet, nasty, rotten, the chicken coop, the barnyard.

A pigsty! one of us gagged and staggered back. And then we all smelled it, her filthy piggy stench. We felt sick and not pretend sick anymore. Real, salty pain burning in our guts. Waves of nausea clenched at our stomachs as we doubled over in woozy squats. We crowded around the open attic window, we covered our noses and mouths with the crooks of our arms. We tried to breathe in only ourselves. We smelled of nothing at all.

Just like a piggy rooting through its own filth.

And eating it!

You're being disgusting, said Ana, her arms crossed tight against her, fingers gripping her own shoulders as though she were afraid we might steal her beating heart from her chest. Her eyes were glazed with tears, drowning jelly eyes, like a dime-store doll.

Shut up, pigshit! one of us shrieked, delighted by the word.

Ana tried not to cry. Blinking and biting her lip and digging her fingers deeper into her shoulders. But we would make sure because that's what you get.

Such obscenity, Sarah, Rose fake-chided.

Sarah gasped and clapped a hand to her mouth.

There, there, Rose said, rubbing her back. *It's all Ana's influence, you mustn't blame yourself. That's what happens when you breathe in the same air as a filthy, unclean piggy.*

Sarah got down on all fours and began to gag.

Are you really going to be sick? said Esther, and Sarah shot her a look.

That's why we keep kosher in my household, said Rose.

Now I am besmirched! Sarah croaked from the floor, the back of her hand pressed theatrically to her forehead. *Ruined by the evil nature of a trusted friend!*

That's enough, Rose commanded, tugging her up from her knees.

Franny, said Esther, *do you think Ana keeps kosher?*

I suppose so, said Franny, who never picked fights or scabs or anything. *Of course I—*

Liar! shot Rose. *How can a piggy keep kosher? Let's see your hooves, Ana. That's why the golem's an ugly oaf. Her dumb pig hands made him this way.*

He isn't, Ana whimpered. *He's good.*

If Leo weren't dead already, Sarah chimed in, *this hideous thing would send him to his grave.*

How can you say that?

Why can't you ever shut up? said Rose. *Never a moment of peace in this pigsty attic. All I hear is squealing.*

Soo-ey! Sarah did a pig call, her voice low-highed like a seesaw, which made Esther laugh, which made Rose angry. Franny covered her ears.

You used dirty magic on him, said Rose.

No, I never—

You did! Sarah agreed. *With that voodoo-hoodoo abracadabra you did.*

No, it wasn't—

It was *real,* said Esther. *You said so.*

Or do you admit you're a wicked liar? said Sarah.

I wish you hadn't done that, said Franny.

You probably made a deal with the Night Witch, Rose pressed. *What did you promise her?*

Ana wiped her eyes, drew a long breath, and seemed to grow taller with it, as tall as Rose, even, which was impossible because Ana was supposed to be the baby.

None of your business, she said, the frightened whine wrung from her voice.

It should be, said Esther. *We were supposed to do everything together.*

Anyway, it's our business now, isn't it? said Rose. *All of us. You were double-sworn and you double-crossed, which means you've double-cursed us.*

I didn't promise her anything, said Ana. *I just did what you asked. I did a dare. I did what I could for Leo, and for us. Which wasn't enough.*

You're just saying that to make us feel bad, one of us said. And we did, but we couldn't stop.

I bet you promised her our hearts on a platter! said Sarah.

Stop being so dramatic, Esther sighed, tired.

You made Leo into a mutt full of dirty magic, said Rose.

Without asking us, said Franny. *Why didn't you ask us?*

He's just like any living thing of bastard parentage—man or animal, said Rose. *Unpredictable.*

Isn't that the thrill of it? said Ana. *Isn't that what we wanted?*

You left us out, said one of us. It wasn't an answer.

Not like this, said someone else. We had wanted a thrill we all made together. We had wanted a Leo to share. And now what could we do?

We didn't say: you hurt us.

All right, fine, said Ana, throwing up her hands as if in surrender. *It's my fault. I get it. All of it's my fault; I know how to play.*

It doesn't matter anymore, one of us said. *The game is over. You're perfectly hygienical.*

It's my fault rain's wet. My fault the summer's hot. School is dull, wool is itchy.

Let's get back to the golem, one of us said. Being angry was exhausting. *Forget the whole pig game, we're through with it.*

But Ana wasn't.

It's my fault Rose's father got laid off and now he gets handouts from the JEA.

Take that back!

I know how this goes. It's my fault Sarah thinks being bossed around is the same as being loved. It's my fault Esther's mother drank so much gin she ironed a hole in Esther's party dress.

Stop it, Ana!

She gave Esther a pitiful smile. *You probably wish you'd been wearing it when it happened.*

We hugged each other's waists.

It's my fault Franny was a spinster by her tenth birthday, but at least she's kind. It's my fault I'm not. And you know what else? said Ana, and she lit up as though she were about to reveal the answer to a riddle that had been stumping everyone.

Go ahead, guess, she said. As though anyone would want to.

It's my fault they lynched Leo Frank, too. It's all my fault. I'm the best Smutch we ever had.

All our bad things were coming for us.

I want to go home, said Franny, who was the second-most baby after Ana, who was acting now, not like a baby at all, but like the monster we partly wished the golem had been. This was supposed to be his role, not Ana's. Ana's role was supposed to be our friend.

Esther sat down on the floor.

It's your fault they killed Leo Frank, said Rose, her voice caught halfway between disdain and dread.

What are you—a parrot? said Ana, which might have been funny if only it absolutely wasn't. The parrot line was Rose's. She got it from some kind of vaudeville act and said it whenever she was feeling sour and though it was none-too-nice, we were used to her shtick. When Ana said it, with a nasty little wink, it felt like the meanest thing we'd ever heard.

That's what I said. It's my fault they killed Leo Frank.

And how exactly do you figure that? said Rose, who never ever backed down. Not even when it seemed like she really wanted to.

Why, Rose, Ana beamed. *You know as well as anyone how it all ended. Have you forgotten so quickly? I put a noose around his neck.*

Why would you say that? Franny pleaded.

Blaming the Smutch was how we were supposed to get rid of all our awful things: by pinning them to the Smutch, where they would hang forever and be no longer ours to carry. But the Smutch was supposed to be far away, forgettable to us. If the Smutch could play along, if the Smutch could make us wish we'd held on to our awful things, the little handfuls of darkness we had earned, then everyone lost. You can only push pins into a Smutch that doesn't know they're being stuck. Otherwise, they might find the pins and take them out and stick you with them.

I'll show you the rope I used to do it.

We said we're not playing anymore, Esther whispered. *The game's over.*

Who's playing? Ana said. *I brought it home for the museum. Souvenir of the century! Those postcard photographs are a dime a dozen, but I've got the genuine article.*

From a pocket in her nightgown—why had she kept it?—she withdrew the rope we'd hustled off the vendor outside Greenburg and Bond. Once the golem came to life, we had stopped thinking about the museum, our artifacts, our real Leo, whose life had ended with a rope just like that.

And she'd tied it, too. The coils of manila rope like fingers in a fist, choking up the hangman's knot. She gathered it to her like something loved, scooping the frayed end in her palm, and twisting the thing into a loose bundle in her arms.

And if we weren't done playing, said Rose, *you'd be losing, anyhow. Obviously, that's the rope we all skipped the other day.*

We wanted her to be right.

You tied that knot yourself. Did you really think we would scare that easily? Sarah, Rose commanded, *go check the knot.*

Sarah's father had been an inspector at the docks in Brunswick before her family moved to Atlanta, and he'd taught all his children how to tie knots and scale fish and do all sorts of things we'd teased her for.

I don't know, said Sarah without moving closer to inspect, *I was young when I learned. I can't remember how many loops are in that knot.*

Come take a closer look, said Ana, taking hold of the knot and rolling it between her palms.

Who cares how many it's got, said Esther, *do you think it would hold?*

It looks pretty sturdy, said Sarah, who hadn't moved so much as an inch.

Don't just stand there, said Rose, pushing her forward. *Pull on it or something.*

Go ahead, Ana encouraged. *Give it a try.*

I don't want *to pull on it, Rose. How about* you *pull it. You've got hands, haven't you?*

Just look at it, Rose protested. *The knot's all lumpy, and the rope's too long at the end, and it's fraying.*

What do you think? said Ana. She shifted the rope bundle to one arm and took up the lamp in the other hand, daring each of us in turn to examine the rope under blue illumination: *Would you like to give it a try? Go ahead, Rose. Come on Sarah, what do you think? How about you, Esther?* None of us responded, none of us looked at her. We crossed our arms over our chests: No, no, no. She turned toward the golem and hummed a few notes of a Russian lullaby her mother sometimes sang. They floated away like the last snowy feathers of a dandelion.

It was more than Hebrew scribbles that woke you up from under the garden, wasn't it? she cooed to him.

The golem gave no reply, but his petal eyes made small adjustments, slight rotations and contractions.

To us she said, *Did you really think I was so naive I believed Night Witch magic was as simple as chanting over a cookie?*

We had, and we had wanted to believe it ourselves.

Wulff's made Leo Frank, said the golem.

That's right, she said, her hands on the slumps of his shoulders. She used a different voice for him, a secret coaxing voice, as though there was something else hiding in her words, something only he could hear.

You all fed him a paper scrap, rubbish, she laughed, *and you thought it was you. You thought you woke him up just like that.*

And one of us said: *We all did it.*

And were all supposed to share him after, another agreed.

No, said Ana. *I used real Night Witch magic. Blood magic.*

What do you mean? Whose blood?

A life for a life, that's how it works. So I made him, he's mine.

O O, said the golem, rocking himself as though in pain.

We all knew he was going to die, so I made his death useful. That Leo's life for this one—for my Leo's.

O, said the golem. *O O.* He had begun to build momentum as though preparing himself to tip.

No, don't be upset, said Ana, turning to the golem. A breathiness edging into her voice, as though to a tearful child on the verge of tantrum. *Shhh, quiet now, Leo. You know the truth.*

The golem's eyes stirred, focused tightly, the petals drawing toward the center, an unblooming.

Franny, who had crept forward while Ana was turned around, reached for the rope, though timidly, as though reaching to pet a dog with bared teeth, but Ana whipped around and slapped her hand away.

Not you! she shrieked, snatching the rope bundle away. *Don't you dare touch it.* She turned her back to Franny, shielding the rope from her.

Why not me? said Franny. *You've tried to force it on everyone else.*

I know, said Ana, *but I shouldn't have.*

Isn't that what you wanted? Franny pushed back. *For all of us to be afraid? To know how awful you can be?*

Not you. She retreated a couple of steps, and held the lamp out in front of her, waving it like a torch. *I don't want you to. Please don't.*

Well, too bad, said Franny. *It's what I want. Give it here.* She was shaky on her thin legs and grabbed wildly for the rope. *I want to hold your stupid noose. I want . . . I want to be angry. I want to be awful. I'll see if it . . . if it really works. Give it here!*

She stammered, but we didn't interrupt. Sometimes we forgot Franny had a voice.

You think you can scare everybody into believing you're not scared. She stood before Ana, breathing audibly through her nose like a small, agitated horse. *You all do,* she said, turning to us, and we believed, for the first time, that Ana could hurt us, if she had to, if she wanted to. Franny batted at the bundle of rope, knocking it from Ana's arms. Franny could, too.

There, she said, stomping on it. *Am I awful? Am I scaring you?*

Yes, said Ana, scrambling to the floor to push it behind her. *Yes.*

Good. I'm sick to death of all of you, Franny spat.

You were right, the rope's a fake, said Ana, now on her knees. *And there is no Night Witch magic. I just wanted to scare you. I wanted you to leave us alone.*

Which is exactly why we never will, said Rose, grabbing the rope from behind Ana's back. *Help me tie her up,* she said, lunging for Ana's arm, but Ana was too quick.

We watched the pink blur of her whip free. We watched the blue blur of the lamp streak from her hand into disappearance at the back of the closet. And then the colors changed to orange.

Fire time displaced clock time and set flame to the darkness. We saw what there was to see: the graveyard of dead clothing brought back to life in heat and blaze. The hems caught first, where the kerosene had pooled. Cottons and linens took up fire, the orange spilling up their skirts in reverse stain. The wools and furs invited a slower, darker burn. We grew hot and immovable.

Only Ana was in motion: her arms, her fingers, her face reaching for us like a scream we could not hear and could not answer. Fire time held us watching as she went in, stomping at small things ablaze on the ground. She ripped an overcoat off its hanger and flung it over a flaming dress. A smoking hatbox toppled and rolled out of the closet, coming to a stop at our feet. The lid fell open and a flat-topped black felt hat plopped to the floor—brim up, a beetle in October.

Help. Ana coughed. *Help me.*

The golem moved with new speed.

Wulffs, he moaned, his block feet crushing the felt hat as he ambled to the flaming closet, to Ana, who needed him, to Ana who loved him—and whom he loved.

The spell of fire time was broken, and back in clock time we sprang from the attic, ticking down the stairs, calling for Mrs. Wulff, who was already climbing as we descended. She overlapped us in silence, and we ran out the front door, taking one last orange look at the attic window.

Suddenly, it seems, nothing is a game. Perhaps nothing ever was.
—DIARY OF ANA WULFF

Ana came to on the front lawn. Pain flared in her blistered hand. Sweat
burned her sun-stung eyes and the parched crabgrass poked through the
thin linen of her summer dress. How many days since it had last rained?
When was the last time her mother had taken to bed with a migraine? She
sometimes wondered if her mother faked the headaches just to be alone.
But now, Mrs. Wulff lay next to her. Unmoving, except for the light breeze
that stirred the wispy blond hairs around her temples. Ana wanted badly
to touch her mother's face, but she was afraid.

She's not dead, thought Ana, but it was bad even to think the word.
Thinking not dead made dead possible. Her chest stung at the thought.
She slipped her Leo locket—the one they all wore— under the neckline of
her nightgown so that it touched her bare skin. Its scalding heat replaced
the pain of thought until her mind was clear. She's sleeping, Ana corrected
herself.

Awake, Mrs. Wulff had a face that drew, not unpleasantly, toward the
middle. She was a habitual squinter, which gave her a look of shrewd skepticism, and she frequently pursed her lips, which doubled the effect. Until
fairly recently, Ana had been convinced her mother could see inside of her
head—the contents of her thoughts appearing to Mrs. Wulff as legibly as
the items on a grocery list, each one priced to the penny. But asleep, her
features unknit themselves and eased across her wide face as though floating, nothing quite tethered. Everything waiting serenely to be arranged, a
childish quality that made her face look like Ana's own.

My dead face there, thought Ana, but prettier. Dead pretty, enough to land on the front page. But not dead. Don't think dead. Don't think it. Don't think it.

Asleep, she said aloud. The word punched at the hot, still air.

And a man's voice said: *Ma'am?*

Ana hadn't known anyone else was around. But there, along the line of sugar maples that hedged the Wulffs' home from its neighbor's view was Fiddler's slight silhouette, perched on a stump, his stupid fiddle in a pillow slip at the base. He pushed up the slipping cuff of a sweat-yellowed shirt-sleeve and nodded to Ana.

She wake yet?

Always sure to be anywhere you'd want to be alone.

Go away, Fiddler, Ana whispered.

Can't do that. I saw it.

Saw what?

The wail of the fireman's siren and the clang of the bell. They were far off now but getting closer. Such clamor must have made the horses' hearts race like mad, thought Ana.

Mrs. Wulff's eyes stirred beneath soot-creased lids. Ana wanted her mother to wake and she wanted her to stay asleep.

The whole thing. String of little girls running out the door. And the strong feller carried you from inside, one of you in each arm. Brought you right out here and dumped you where you now lie. Hell of a thing to do, with all that smoke pouring out the house. Hell of a thing to see. Then he went back into that deathtrap and poof!

Poof?

Poof. Fire was out. Smoke was out. Magic.

Ana looked back at the house. Apart from the smoke in the air, there was little proof of the fire. A little blackening of the paint around the attic window, and a new crack down its center.

There was no one in the house but us, said Ana, *and the girls from down the street. Mother sent Isaac out on errands and father's at the shop until supper. You don't know what you're talking about.*

Maybe not, never was much good at talking. Know what I saw, though.

An attic fire is what you saw.

That, yes, and the feller.

What fellow?

Funny type. More than that I couldn't say.

What do you mean "funny"?

Fiddler shrugged.

Tell me, Fiddler, Ana pressed.

He pursed his lips and shook his head, wisps of orange hair bobbing emphatically.

Do you want payment, is that it? said Ana. She didn't have any money with her, no rings or jeweled brooches, but she had one thing worth trading. It was against the rules to be without Leo's photograph, but what did the rules mean anymore with everything coming apart? She fished her Leo locket out from under her nightgown, pulling the chain over her head with her blistered hand and winced.

Can't hurt none, said Fiddler, eyeing the locket. He weighed its worth against his eyewitness, then approached, crouched, and held out his hand to receive it.

He lifted you both no problem. Might could have done it one-handed, he said, fiddling with the pendant. It had a tricky clasp she had always found frustrating, but now she was glad the locket wouldn't yield. *Strange feller. Didn't look like any man I ever saw around here before.*

Is that so? Ana sized the man up: a missing button at his chest, slackened purple skin beneath his eyes, barely covering his small, frayed veins.

And what if I said we walked out on our own? she countered. *What if I said you're drunk and out of your head?*

Don't know what. Not a fortune teller. You could give it a try, said Fiddler.

He didn't care. Fiddler's word was good, even when it was rotten. They both knew it. Drunk or mad or healthy, it was all the same. The siren was louder now, it was coming. Noise enough to knock her ears off, to scramble her thoughts. And soon others would come out of their houses to see the spectacle. Ana and her mother sprawled on the lawn, it was just the kind of thing to add interest to their boring day. Fiddler was a siren too, orange and wailing, fiddling and spinning stories to the highest bidder. Too much noise and Ana's ears were ringing. Fiddler had no loyalties. No amount of pleading and tears would sway him. A siren is insensitive to sympathy. But money. Money was a reliable argument. A siren's wail might be bought into silence. Anything might be bought.

Listen, Fiddler, Ana bargained. *I've got a dollar in my pocket and I'll give it to you if you run ahead and flag down the firemen.* She made herself believe that lying didn't count if it was a liar you were lying to. *Tell them to turn their horses around. The fire's out and we're safe. Tell them not to bother coming any farther.*

You haven't got a dollar in there, said Fiddler. *I might look like a fool, but you never seen a smarter Fiddler.*

My mother does. She always keeps money with her. She insists on it.

Does she? said Fiddler. *Smart woman.*

Mrs. Wulff moved her sleeping arm from her side to brush a fire ant from her cheek and Ana dove her quick hand into her mother's unguarded pocket, snatching out four wrinkled dollar notes. Fiddler's lip gave a tentative twitch and the scar that curved from the left corner of his mouth to just under his left nostril deepened as if his mouth were being pulled into half a smile by a black fishhook.

And what's more, said Ana, *I'll give you another on your successful return.* Even a leery dog can be tempted by the smell of food, if you hold it close enough to his muzzle.

She needed the siren gone, she needed Fiddler gone. Everyone, every sound, gone gone gone. Her mother shifted in the dry grass, revealing the prints at the back of her dress, a dark smudge at the back of her thighs. It was a broad mark that widened into the shape of a baseball mitt. Hands were impossible to sculpt. No great wonder all the old Roman sculptures were only busts.

She waved the bills before his face in an effort to distract Fiddler from seeing them. *Go on*, said Ana. *Take it!*

But Fiddler knew one thing for certain: people weren't charitable by nature. If someone gave a stray dog some food, it was only to keep his own food—better food—safe. Only a sucker would mistake fear for charity. He lowered his hand over Mrs. Wulff, his fingers hovering inches above her dress so that his hand's shadow lined up with the mitt-shaped smudges. He followed the line of prints across the backs of her legs— the shadow of his fingers slats across her thighs—then he snatched the notes, all four, and sprang to his feet, but he was stopped in his tracks by another voice.

What are you doing there, Fiddler? a neighbor man called from the side-walk in front of the Wulffs' house. *Mrs. Wulff!* he hollered. *Mrs. Wulff, can you hear me? It's Mr. Fink, Esther's father.*

Stink, thought Ana. Perfect. Esther had probably gone and tattled right away. First Fiddler, now Stink, next the whole neighborhood. Stink with his stupid, nosy starched cuffs and his starched-looking face. All business, all proper, all the time, never any time for his wife and daughter. How good it was that she and her mother were Ana and Mrs. Wulff and not Esther and Mrs. Fink. How much better to be lying, with singed hair and skirt hems, on their yellow front lawn than to have a father like Stink.

Sir, Fiddler nodded. *Looking in on young Miss Wulff and her mother.*

More like stealing from us.

Come now, Ana, said Mr. Fink and gave her a stiff-necked bow of the head. *Don't be unkind. Fiddler is here to help*, he said, *isn't that right? Esther told me there was some kind of fire. But she was too hysterical to give a complete account.*

There was a kitchen fire, said Ana. *But it's out, as you can see. We don't need any help, thank you.*

I'll stay with the Wulffs until the ambulance arrives. You may go, Fiddler.

Fiddler pocketed the crumpled bills. *Thank the good Lord they made it out unscathed by the fire, but I feel obliged to tell you, Mr. Fink*, he said, his face bright—a dog begging on his hind legs, thought Ana—*that is, a concerned citizen like yourself with a wife, and daughter, and so forth ought to know that in the midst of all the pandemonium, I seen something awfully strange. Awfully strange, indeed. Gave me quite the start.*

What is Mrs. Wulff's condition? Fink said, ignoring Fiddler.

She's fine. Just faint is all. Two gentle ladies such as the Wulffs, without the man of the house around to protect them, said Fiddler. *Vulnerable, I'd say, to unsavory circumstances.*

Mr. Fink nodded. *And what exactly did you see, Fiddler? Why don't you step away and give the ladies some room to breathe.*

It was Mr. Fink's belief that unless you were helping a lady directly—guiding her elbow, for example—as she walked over a patch of ice, you shouldn't touch her. Even extended proximity could elicit an undesired response of nerves. Fink preferred to admire his wife and daughter from a distance, which is why Mrs. Fink spent so much of her time replicating the looks she found in her ladies' magazines. In grade four, she had dressed

Esther in nothing but lavender for two whole months after her husband had remarked that some or other dress in a shop window was nice. Now Esther refused to wear purple.

Fiddler did as he was told, scratching a scab on his scalp beneath his feathery hair.

I'm having some trouble remembering, he said, beaming. *What with all the drinking I do, I sometimes lose track*, he told Fink.

Easy enough, said Fink, impatiently and only halfway listening.

Maybe I'm out of my head, Fiddler said and winked at Ana.

Oh, I doubt that, Fiddler. You seem fine to me. A little weary, maybe. Why don't you bring home a nice cut of meat for your family tonight? Go to bed full and early, said Fink, and handed Fiddler a crisp five-dollar note from his wallet.

Much appreciated, said Fiddler, bowing once to the man, and once to Ana, a little too deeply.

Now can you manage to remember?

I can tell you what happened at no lying cheating stealing cost at all, said Ana, her voice rising. *Absolutely nothing.*

That's enough now, Miss Wulff, said Fink, holding up a silencing palm to Ana.

Knowing I'll get a decent night's sleep tonight, I believe I can, sir.

Very good, Fiddler. That's very good.

Why isn't anyone listening to me?

Ana was so angry that she had to bury her face in her mother's shoulder to keep from screaming. Her hair tickled her mother's neck, the final gentle prod to consciousness. Mrs. Wulff's face, instantly alert, pinched together in prompt evaluation: Ana, the lawn, the siren, the fire, Fiddler, Fink. Ana watched her mother's eyes dart around the scene like a threaded needle, animated by some enchantment to string together a room full of mismatched quilt squares.

I was just over there, Fiddler told Fink, pointing to the tree line, *when I started to notice the windows of the downstairs pouring out smoke. I thought I'd better see if anything was wrong.*

Naturally, said Fink.

I was about to go to the door when it swung right open and out came some kind of monster.

No need for embellishment, said Fink. *I'm not in the habit of tipping for that sort of thing.*

Well, that's how he looked in the smoke, Fiddler backtracked. *Wasn't a white man but didn't appear like a Black one, neither. Didn't appear like any man, matter of fact. Kind of gray in color and strong as a monster. Sure, strong as a monster is what I meant. Carried both Wulff women, one in each arm, the young Wulff here like a baby.*

I don't believe I've ever seen a gray-skinned man in Atlanta, said Fink. *It must have been the smoke that made him appear thusly. The Wulffs employ only one hired man—Isaac, a Black man. And I dare say he's too old now to lift them.*

I already told him so, said Ana. *But he's an incorrigible liar.*

The man you saw must have been on loan from a house nearby. Did he wear a serving man's clothes?

Didn't appear to.

A workman's?

Not at all.

A vagrant? What then?

Nothing.

What do you mean nothing? Irritated again. It was easy to rile Mr. Fink, bat him into a fit.

And I don't pay overtime either, said Fink, as though Fiddler cared about his managerial habits.

Appeared to be wearing nothing. Nothing dressing him but his own skin.

You mean to tell me this man was—Fink's lips wormed about, searching for a shape that might protect him from discomfort—*indecent?*

If that's what you call your natural state.

Fink's eyeglasses slipped down the sweating bridge of his nose as Fiddler slid his fiddle from his pillow slip. I'll sing it for you, he said and positioned his fiddle under his chin, dragged his bow across the strings, and crooned:

> *Squat and ugly feller, skin like dry gray dirt*
> *Bent over your poor mama, thinking he might flirt.*

This is hardly the time! said Mr. Fink in an embarrassed whisper.

> *But pretty little woman was sure out like a light*
> *and when he saw ol' Fiddler, he took off quick all right!*

Mr. Fink reached for the neck of the fiddle to strangle the song and his sudden movement sent his eyeglasses cascading from his face. Mrs. Wulff, who had propped herself up to seated, caught them with one hand, while the other rubbed at her temple with two practiced fingers.

Oh, thank goodness, said Fink, reaching for his eyeglasses, which Mrs. Wulff did not offer, *you're awake. Though better perhaps if you had slept through this account, Mrs. Wulff. It's shaping up to be highly upsetting. And utterly unsuitable for young Ana.*

His speech was quick and clipped with nerves—or was it anger?

She'd be better off at a relative's home for a time. Your husband has family in Decatur, isn't that right?

Mrs. Wulff focused her efforts on righting herself and rose to a wide-kneed crouch. How wonderfully unfeminine! Ana crouched beside her. Two wild cats, ready to pounce.

Now Mrs. Wulff, you'd better not do that just yet. You're liable to be unsteady. Let me help you inside. Then Fiddler and I will wait together for your husband's return to discuss the matter further.

Oh no, Fiddler won't, said Fiddler.

She should see a doctor, said Ana to Fink. *Won't you go and call one? Take Fiddler with you.*

I don't need a doctor, said Mrs. Wulff. *And I don't need your help, Mr. Fink. My daughter will help me up, and we will go inside when I am ready.* She nodded to Ana, who sprang up behind her, digging her hands into the moist nook of her mother's underarms for purchase, lifting her, so light, to her feet. Feather mother.

Pardon me, Mrs. Wulff. I feel I really must get to the bottom of this account, and given the troubling nature of the details Mr. Fiddler has disclosed thus far, I must ask that you and your daughter go inside immediately. This is not a conversation for polite company.

You're pardoned, then, said Mrs. Wulff. *You and Fiddler, both. You may leave.*

I'm afraid I don't understand.

Were you in the house when the fire caught, Mr. Fink?

No, of course not, but—

And was Fiddler?

No, ma'am, said Fiddler, *but I saw—*

Well then, said Mrs. Wulff, *if you weren't involved, and you, Mr. Fink, weren't even a witness, the best you two can do is gossip, and I don't abide gossip.*

Now Mrs. Wulff, be reasonable, said Fink. *Fiddler saw a dark, unknown man walk into your home in broad daylight, with—forgive me—his indecency fully exposed, and carry you both out the door. And if he hadn't seen Fiddler and taken off running, well I shudder to imagine.*

Be careful now, warned Mrs. Wulff. *Don't say more than you mean.*

On the contrary, Mrs. Wulff, Fink said. *There is a great deal more to be said.*

No sir, you've got it wrong, said Fiddler. *Nobody walked in.*

What are you saying, Fiddler? You can't mean this deviant was in the house already.

You should call him a hero. said Ana. *We might have died otherwise.*

What is it you want, Mr. Fink? Why are you here? Mrs. Wulff swayed once on her feet. Ana put a hand on her low back to brace her and she could feel her mother's weight relax into her palm. She imagined draping her mother over her shoulder, grasping the backs of her legs, carrying the small woman as the soft weight of her head thumped against her back no harder than a rag doll's might. All of her lifted and Ana beneath.

Naturally, Mrs. Wulff. I'm deeply troubled and should like answers. I should think you would too. Fink was the kind of man who felt so certain his conclusions were logical, he deemed all questioning a waste of time. *And I want your safety ensured, of course. If Isaac—*

It wasn't Isaac! Ana shouted.

—or any other man, for that matter—

It wasn't!

—is wandering into our homes with—I'm sorry, ladies—lecherous intentions, I have an obligation to protect the virtue of my wife and daughter. Now, I think you both ought to be examined by a doctor.

I have told you, Mr. Fink, my daughter has told you, and I am telling you yet again: Isaac was away on errands. There was no one else in our home.

Then I shall wait here for him to return.

Not on my property, you won't. It seems to me, Mr. Fink, you already have your answers. You had them before you ever talked to Fiddler.

I'm afraid you've misunderstood me, Mrs. Wulff.

Then as I misunderstand you, Mr. Fink, Mrs. Wulff said calmly, *you would like to find a man whom you have never seen, and very well may not exist, but whom you somehow imagine yourself capable of identifying. You imagine that if you find this man, you will bring him to justice for accusations of harm you suppose have been committed against my daughter and me, though we have told you plainly they were not.*

You're making me out to be ridiculous, Mrs. Wulff. Fiddler saw the man.

Even though we have told you no such man was in our home and we are unharmed.

Even though he would be a hero if he was! said Ana.

Mrs. Wulff wiped at Fink's lenses with the apron of her dress. The soot clung to the oil in black streaks. *And you would like us to stay out of the way while you investigate an imaginary crime.*

I'm summoning the police, Mrs. Wulff.

I can't stop you from speaking with police. And Fiddler, no doubt, will sell some story or other to the papers, but you will leave me and my family and our employee alone. I have work to do. My clothes and my daughter's clothes need scrubbing before they're ruined. As you can clearly see, our house needs imme-diate attention, dinner must be remade, and the day is getting on. So, I invite you to take your speculation elsewhere.

But Mrs. Wulff, Fink protested, *surely—*

Mr. Fink, I insist on it, she said, handing him back his blackened eye-glasses. *Good afternoon.*

Fiddler, who was not beholden to customs of invitation and dismissal, and less still to answers, was already halfway to the street.

With Fink reluctantly gone, though he promised to *return to see the matter through to his satisfaction,* Mrs. Wulff turned her attention to Ana.

How did we get out of the house?

We walked out. You don't remember?

I know we didn't.

Isaac came back.

You're lying to me, Ana. When did you become a liar?

You wouldn't believe me.

Come, said Mrs. Wulff, pulling Ana by the hand back toward the house. *If Fiddler's story catches on, a lot of people could be in danger. Isaac most of all. Because of us, because of you.*

But I don't want to get anyone in trouble, said Ana. *I didn't mean to.*

It doesn't matter what you meant. It doesn't matter what you want!

Back inside, the air was hazy. Ana's eyes stung, so she closed them shut. Mrs. Wulff guided her blind daughter to the kitchen table and pushed on her shoulders until Ana's knees bent and she sat.

Then tell me what to believe, said Mrs. Wulff.

Ana could feel her mother's gaze bearing down on her. She laid her hands on the table, which was coated in a fine layer of new ash, and took a deep breath, a truth breath, she was ready to tell. But the ash caught in her throat and she coughed until her eyes teared up.

I can't, she said, her eyes streaming. *I want to*. She really did. She wanted to tell her mother the whole truth, to be good, but she was sworn by Rule #9—until death do us part. And if she was good with her mother, that would make her bad to the others and to Leo, and she had already betrayed them once by breaking her oath and twice by giving her locket to Fiddler. And even if this danger her mother warned of was more important than her swear, how could she make the truth sound true?

You must, said Mrs. Wulff, *because if you can't convince me to believe, how will we convince anyone else?*

Truth and belief were not bound to each other as they should have been. There was nothing to ensure that telling a person the truth meant that they would adopt it as their preferred version of the circumstances. Belief was as far from science as the funny papers. It was all so complicated, and was a lie that kept people safe more true than the real truth?

There was another man in the house, said Ana. *Sort of.*

Mrs. Wulff gripped the back of Ana's chair. *Oy, gevalt, tell me who, Ana. What was he doing here?*

I will, but you must promise to believe me.

I won't be held hostage to what you've hidden from me! said Mrs. Wulff. *Please*, she said, softening, *Ana, I am asking you as your mother.* Her hands moved to Ana's shoulders. *As clever as you are, you can't know all the dangers that surround you, and all the ways you can be dangerous. Unfair as it may seem, it's true you can be both at once.*

I don't want to be dangerous, said Ana. *I just want to be good.*

You can be, my Ana. If you tell me the truth before it gets away from you.

She could be good, she would be. She would tell the truth and her mother would believe her. Mrs. Wulff was the most willful person Ana knew. Whatever was wrong, her mother could fix it.

It was the golem, said Ana, turning over her shoulder to look her mother in the eye. *We made one, and he saved us from the fire today. He saved our lives.*

Mrs. Wulff took her hands from her daughter's shoulders in silence.

Don't you believe me? said Ana. *You have to.*

Mrs. Wulff sat down next to Ana, kicking up a cloud of ash. She put her head in her hands and bent over, obscuring her face from view until Ana couldn't stand it.

You have to, Ana said again, shaking her mother's shoulder.

When Mrs. Wulff removed her hands, her ash-covered face was streaked with clean, wet skin.

Go away, said Mrs. Wulff. *Go to your room. Go now.*

Alphabet Soup

I'm ashamed to say I can't remember what was so remarkable about Leo Frank in the first place. I have tried these last few days, to search our collection for some brave words, a testimony or letter, any scrap that might make me feel as though this whole thing was worth it, and though he is noble in some aspects, he's cowardly in others, like any man. I can't remember him at the temple. I can't remember him in any park or on any streetcar. I can't remember him the way I used to.

—DIARY OF ANA WULFF

To Ana's great relief, the others weren't allowed to come over, not after the fire. *Not tonight, not a hundred nights from now.* No one was allowed into the Wulffs' home. All the blinds were drawn across the windows. Mr. Wulff had to chase off three different neighborhood boys who were trying to catch a glimpse of whatever rumor was most depraved. One—an older boy, almost a man—had pounded away on the door. He had pounded so hard Ana thought he might knock it down. *You can't hide him forever*, he crooned into the mail slot, *you Black-loving Jews*. His voice had poured in through the front door of the house, which had become very quiet, as if all sounds had been coated in ash. Mr. Wulff spent the evening nursing a snifter of bourbon that never emptied. Mrs. Wulff holed up in her bedroom.

Time for bed, Mr. Wulff said to Ana, though it was only half-past eight.

But what if Isaac comes back and no one answers the door? Ana had asked, knowing somehow he wouldn't.

I don't know. Her father took a sip.

Where could he be? He hasn't got any family, has he?

I don't know.

Is it my fault he's gone?

No more questions, Ana. I'm tired.

Her fire, her fault, she had guessed the riddle wrong.

A policeman came to the door at nine and asked to come inside. Mr. Wulff declined, politely. Now was not a convenient time for his family. It was simply too late, and what was this about, may he ask? There had been reports, said the policeman, of a disturbing nature. People were getting stirred up. Mr. Wulff stepped outside and shut the door. Ana, who had been spying flat on her belly, like a worm in the upstairs hallway, hurried to her room and opened the window, leaning her head out so that the men's conversation and the smell of night-bloomers from the garden below mixed with the smell of burnt wool.

You don't mean to tell me, her father was saying, *that you're taking that drunk's word over my wife's.*

It's my duty to respond to any report made in good faith, said the policeman.

Exactly how would you define good faith? said Mr. Wulff. *A Peeping Tom who can be bought with pocket change? Is that good faith?*

Now Mr. Wulff—

I tell you no one else was here. Only my wife and daughter and my daughter's friends.

Not according to a Mr. Fink, father of one of the girls, and a friend of yours, I believe.

What's he got to do with any of this?

Mr. Fink made his report as a concerned father, which I'm sure you can understand.

If he's such a concerned father, said Mr. Wulff, *perhaps he ought to spend his time tending to his daughter and his own damned business instead of gossiping with a fiddling linthead.*

My job, Mr. Wulff, is to protect this community, to protect your family, your safety. Your wife, your daughter, the other girls. All virtuous women.

Don't tell me about the character of my own family.

And if they're in danger in any way—physical harm or reputation—well I'd hate to see something like that happen to a good family like yours.

So would I, said Mr. Wulff, *which is why I am trying to tell you we're perfectly safe. All of us.*

I understand you're upset, Mr. Wulff, but your refusal to cooperate isn't helping the rumors. Now, have you had any recent correspondence with your employee, Isaac Young?

No, said Mr. Wulff. *Now if you'll excuse me.*

Does your wife often host Black men while you're away at work?

The front door opened, slammed, locked.

The policeman lingered at the doorway, surveying the house. Ana should have moved out of view, she should have hidden, but she was tired of hiding, tired of secrets, and she stared at him instead, willing him to see her, which he didn't—*some policeman*—but Fiddler did. He was staring up at her from his post along the sugar maples. He dragged his bow through a cake of wax and raised it to her in salute. He was back, which meant the trouble wasn't over. But whatever it was that was out there, she wouldn't let it come inside. She shut the window and drew her curtains. What she wanted was here in the house, here in the attic.

Leo was past-tense now in the papers, which meant soon he would disappear entirely. For all she knew, theirs was the only remaining account of his life—all those chapters of his story the paper had reported stuffed into the drawers of the rosewood desk in the attic. How fast had the fire moved? How quickly could it eat through wood? She'd been too afraid during the day to venture up to the attic. But it couldn't be over, because it just couldn't. She wouldn't let it. There was so much left to resolve. Ana and the others had charged themselves to carry it on, and to fix it, but instead, they had made it even worse. *She* had made it worse. It was her story now, and she had brought her parents in, and Isaac, too. And where was he? They were never supposed to be part of it, but it had gotten too big, and she couldn't control it anymore, couldn't stay far enough ahead of it to make for it the ending it deserved.

Every day now, the front page of *The Constitution* was filled with stories of the European war: German takeovers and Polish refugees. Ana knew her father preferred this far-off war—*such a shame*—to the headlines about Leo, because a shame that didn't threaten his home was a better shame than one that did. He would sit at the table, paging through the headlines, and say, *Wouldn't I like to be a fly on the wall*, which, as near as Ana understood it, was what you said when you wanted to know something but didn't want to be responsible for knowing what to do about it. But Ana didn't see the sense in that. If you were a fly on the wall, you could be a perfect impartial judge. The True Judge, as Franny would say. The fly on the wall, she thought, should have the *most* responsibility.

A one-hundred-eyed witness. One bead-black eye watching over every dispute. Think: if there could be one honorable person, one invisible arbiter appointed to be the world's fly-on-the-wall, there would be no more conflict. No trickery, no treason, no miscarriage of justice, and eventually, no wrongdoing at all.

The problem was that everyone liked to think, against evidence to the contrary, that he was free from fault, that any harm he wrought could be justified. Furthermore, the fly himself would have to be utterly impartial and utterly good, and who could be both of those things?

The first difficulty was that everyone was absolutely partial. People naturally favor the company and circumstances that reward them. Such impartiality could only truly be achieved through absolute isolation. Only the friendless, loveless person could serve. And such lovelessness would surely make goodness a challenge.

The golem, however—her Leo could be the fly, and why not? He was without parentage, save for the Five, and they weren't real parents. He was without friendships. He had no relations at all, excluding the ghostly legacy of his name. And his character, though it was not yet fully defined, could be made perfectly good. Indeed, he seemed to be much more than halfway there, a hero already! Furthermore, his natural goodness could be encouraged. He could be fed a strictly moral diet. The speed of his learning was incredible. Only a week old and he already knew so much. At this rate, it wouldn't be long until he had sufficient knowledge to begin feeding himself. Given enough time, she thought, he might fix everything. The True Judge, he could write the ending she couldn't.

The night had risen, her parents were silent in bed, the time had come.

She crept to the attic, blackened by dark and doubled by scorching. The door to the closet had burned from its hinges, and still there he was, waiting among the heaps of ash.

You are good, aren't you? Ana said, taking him by his mitt-hands. Small rivulets of soot crumbled away in her grasp. *It's in your nature*, she told him, loosening her grip, and drew him out of the closet.

The answer was obvious. He had saved them all from the fire. Protected them, like the golem from the Prague story. Such goodness merited freedom, and furthermore, his freedom was necessary for her ends, which required some experimentation.

I am—

Of course you are. You're incredible!

—Leo Frank.

So you are, Ana laughed. *And you are more.*

I am Wulff's, he said.

Not just mine, she said, fighting her delight at his exclusion of the others.

I am Wulff's, he insisted. A narrow wind forced its way through the attic window, which had cracked in the fire. The fresh black breeze cut a welcome slash through the choking smell of smoke.

Certainly, she had made him—they all had—but did they own him? A cobbler made shoes, but once sold, they belonged to the man whose feet they covered. A baker made loaves of bread, but once eaten, they were disappeared and had no owner. A policeman made justice, which may have belonged to him, but not only to him; it had to be shared equally among everyone under the law. Creation, it seemed, was no promise of ownership, but perhaps a promise of responsibility.

Ana lit the emergency lantern. The desk had burned in the back left corner, which was nearest the closet. The papers in that drawer would be damaged, but she couldn't slow down to inspect the ruin now.

Instead, she pulled open the bottom right drawer and withdrew one of the early papers from their collection. Nothing from the first week—those were too important—something filed far enough back that it wouldn't be missed. She tore a blank corner from the top page and sifted through the pencils that sat in a tin on the desktop until she found one that was uncharred and whole. The golem's moral diet would start at once! She made a couple of pencil-tip figure eights in the air above the paper as she thought it through. She wanted so badly to initiate the process that would fix the story, correct the wrongs she'd made, but nothing was ever as simple as it should have been. Every corrective effort she undertook carried with it unforeseen trouble.

Wulffs, he said. *Wulffs Wulffs Wulffs.*

I'm thinking, she told him. *I need to be smart about it.*

The setup was important. The choices she made now would determine the whole course of her experiment, but how could she possibly know which words were the most morally nutritious?

The usual way prescribes the teaching of family words first: mommy, daddy, the maker names. One repeats these sounds again and again until the infant's mind is full of them.

The golem shuffled over to a singed portrait of Ana's great-aunt someone or other, which hung on the wall nearest the attic door. The fire had eaten holes in her brow, and the right side of her face was cracked and disfigured. He pawed at the plaque below her face, which identified her as Johanna Noemi Wulff. Three meaningless words, only two of them new, yet he appeared greatly tormented by their withholding. He must have been ravenous, but he would have to wait.

I'm sorry, she told him. *I'm responsible for you, and if you're to be the True Judge, I have to be selective with your diet, feed you the very best words for your development.*

Excessive words would only confuse, and the last thing she wanted to make was more confusion. Then it came to her: the three words it seemed most important for him to eat and to know, if he was to be made wholly good. But was knowing the same as believing? Ana knew her multiplication tables, but did she believe in them? Would she make a sacred oath on seven times nine is sixty-three?

She wrote them down on the torn corner of the paper, taking care to shape each letter with perfect legibility, and the golem craned his thick neck at the sound of pencil scraping paper.

With seven words to his world, what did the golem believe? *You believe in your stomach, don't you?* she said and walked the scrap of paper with its three perfect words across the room, laying it on the sill of the window, well out of reach of his stumpy arms.

This will be your reward, she told him, *once we've finished your lessons for the evening.* It was stuffy, and the reek of smoke was making her light-headed, so she turned her back on the golem to work on opening the window. The pane was sticky and she had to be gentle so the glass wouldn't shatter. She had barely managed to crack it when she heard the scrape of the golem's block feet shuffling across the attic floor and glanced over her shoulder to see him moving with surprising speed toward the rosewood desk, on top of which she had left the rest of the newspaper splayed care-lessly. She scrambled over to it and swept the papers into her arms just as the golem's mitt hand swiped at the desktop. It must have seemed to him like a disappearing feast.

No you don't, she scolded happily. *Too clever. That's what they tell me, too.*

She restored the paper to its proper drawer and the golem's back rounded in apparent woe, though it was hard to interpret his mood with certainty because his face remained fixed in its original formation, only dried, ashen. In the light of the lantern, his face, his whole body, looked gray, just as Fiddler had said. A rill of loose dirt cascaded down his back, leaving a thin ditch where his spine would have been. The fire had wrung the moisture from his dirt, and she wasn't sure how to restore him, but one problem at a time.

Soon, she promised, and returned to her lesson. *Once you have the family words—*

Wulff's Wulff's, said the golem.

—I suppose it's on to the barnyard animals. Chickens and pigs and horses. But what value could they possibly add to the shaping of your infant character?

And what about the unlearned noises? There were many noises that children discovered on their own, simply by blowing bubbles through their lips.

What happens to those unwords? The ones with no duplicate in a dictionary or in adult language? Those our parents deny us? We are forced to spit them out.

Le-O Lalala, said the golem.

Yes, exactly.

She had always assumed she was free to say anything she liked. She had some sense, of course. There were things she couldn't say in front of her parents because she'd be punished for them, but she'd never before considered the idea that there were things she couldn't say because she didn't have the means. Whole ideas, even, she might never learn without the words to hold them. Ana lay down on her cot with her fingers woven in a sling for her neck. *And if we are made by adults, to spit them out again and again, well then, our mouths must stop making them altogether.*

Fra na lala made made made.

Until finally we make only words for which there is a known match, words that are publicly understood, so that there is eventually nothing we can say that wasn't first fed to us, so to speak.

Bisc-at lantana o le le sco, the golem babbled sympathetically.

If that's true, she mused, *how can we ever know anything for ourselves? Perhaps I could—*

She let her tongue go slack and stretched her jaw like a snake's, then snapped it closed and made her throat vibrate to allow sound through. It bubbled up under her tongue and melted into her teeth: *thhhlllllth*. It tickled.

She opened her mouth back up and it went *thlaaaaaaaa*. She touched untouched touched untouched her lips and tongue: *mnaaaaaa mnaaaaaa mnaaaaaaa.*

She sent the sound all the way to the back of her throat as if trying to push it back down to where it had come from. She made every mouth shape she could think to make: pursed and wide and curled and puckered and tucked, scooched to one side, and then the other. But even in the privacy of the attic, with only the golem to see her, she felt foolish. Her days of experimentation with word-making had long since passed, they'd been traded in for an expansive adult vocabulary.

What do you have, she asked the golem, *that I've lost?*

Leo Frank.

Yes, it started there, didn't it? With those two words. Maybe they ought to have left him to feed himself from the start. But how could they have known the feeding of those two words, his very birth, would begin the inevitable shaping of his future? And each word she fed him now would bend him still closer to her way of thinking, which was perhaps—distressingly—no longer very different from her parents' way of thinking and their parents'. And there were no answers in her own head; she had looked exhaustively.

There was nothing Ana knew anymore without its public word naming it. What could a tulip be, or a hair ribbon, or sadness—what could any of them be now without their adult word to call them by? She closed her eyes and tried to draw a picture in her head, divorced of words, but it was impossible. An object had to first be named before it was drawn. Even when she suppressed the name of the thing, she found she named all of its component parts—strip a tree from its name and still she thought *branches, leaves, bark.* Once a thing was learned, it couldn't ever be unlearned. It could only be further defined until it was fixed forever.

If she thought of the words *parasol, parade, pencil, crocus sack, cellar, cinder,* each word should have had meaning independent of the rest, though all together, they meant something entirely different. But now she knew them so well together that even apart they meant the same thing. They were infected by their collaborative meaning,

A parasol was a dead girl. A pencil was a dead girl. A crocus sack was a dead girl.

When she opened her eyes, the golem was standing over her, his face a foot above hers. He blinked three times and she imagined all the flowers on the hydrangea bush in the garden fluttering their petals in unison, saying *yes yes yes*.

We'll do an experiment, she told him.

Yes yes yes.

She opened a middle drawer from the unburned side of the desk. With her eyes closed, she plucked a middle page from a stack of papers and tore it into strips on the desk. Then she stacked the strips with squinted eyes so that she couldn't make out any of the words and shredded them again, the other way. She tore in every direction so that no words would remain intact, no syllables. Each word was to be ripped free of meaning, unmade, which was difficult work. For instance, *O*'s split in half would resemble *C*'s and would have to be quartered, at which point they might appear to be apostrophes, and though an apostrophe had no inherent meaning, it indicated possession, ownership, fault. She shredded the paper until the pieces were so small they were impossible to tear further. Two huge handfuls, the shreds spilling from the cracks between her fingers.

O, the golem moaned with unmistakable longing.

Then she stuffed them in her mouth.

Instantly, her tongue flooded with wetness, the level of water rising to the jagged peaks of her molars. *Saliva*, she thought, pinpointing the word, still perfectly joined to its meaning as it wrote itself in her head like chalk on a tablet. She spoke it aloud: *sa-li-va*, except that with her mouth stuffed, the word she produced was *hu-rlah-rluh*. The soaked shreds floated on her tongue as she considered this accidental corruption. Hurlahrluh, an un-word, was objectively better than saliva, though both were bound to the same meaning.

She tried again, this time to rearrange the word and thus dissolve the bond of the word to its meaning. The letters scrawled in her head, shuddered and shook loose of their line, they floated freely on her mind tablet, each according to its own will. The *A*, as the first alphabetical letter, was inclined to take up the first position in the new arrangement and was then followed by the *V*, for no reason that she could comprehend according to its character, and so forth until a new ordering of letters finally settled into an original word: *avilas*, if you were to read it, though she wasn't certain reading was the correct method for interpretation. A thrill of heat rose in her cheeks as she considered the arrangement. *Avilas!* she thought. Meaningless until she chose to assign it. *AVILAS!* She pictured a cloudless blue sky strung through by daytime stars made of tear-sized mirrors. And if she wanted, she could drain it of that image and start again.

She chewed ravenously, the talc taste of paper steeping her tongue. She mashed the word apart with the full force of her jaw until it was nothing but a chewy wad of word marrow. *AVILAS! AVILAS!* If she could not unlearn, she could at least dissolve it all in her mouth, dissolve the smallest specks of language into a sloosh of sound to be swished through her cheeks, puffed full of pulp ready to be spat into new ways of saying—

O! said the golem and she opened her eyes with a start as he toppled from an overturned milk crate he must have climbed atop—careless Ana!—to reach the windowsill. It was a vexed *O*, not a full stop but an O like an open hole from which more would emerge.

She ceased chewing. The slip of paper, her message, was gone. It didn't matter that she'd changed her mind, decided to give him the freedom to choose. He had fed. *She* had fed him, forced him into a foregone way of understanding, and—was it her imagination?—his face revealed a trace of pleasure; a lipless smile contorted the hole that was his mouth. She'd been so absorbed by her own experiment—selfish Ana!—that she'd lost sight of his.

You can still be the True Judge, she apologized. *After this, no more teaching, no more meddling. You can eat whichever words you like.*

I am— he said, his petals pointed to the floor.

Yes! said Ana. *Let's hear it!* Even if a moral diet was not the solution, a part of her was eager to hear him speak the words she'd chosen, the best ones she could think of.

I am, he said, teetering as he digested the new words.

She tried her best to appear encouraging during his slow rumination.

You are, she said, or intended to say, with her cheeks full of pulp. A simple affirmation. Nothing to hurry or perplex him. Since he only knew seven words, each new introduction must have been a substantial development, altering his understanding of all the words that came before it, and the whole world. How terrifying and exciting to be upended by every entry in the dictionary.

I am. Flirt girl I chum innocent.

What?

I flirt. Innocent girl tries with.

No! That wasn't her message. Or rather, it was more than her message, which also made it less. *That's wrong,* she said. *Say it right.*

Boy made, boy tried in Atlanta.

No! How did you get those words? Had he found them? Had he written them himself?

I am murdered girl.

Stop it, she cried. It was so far from the words she had intended for him to say, to know.

Those words, so flatly uttered, like a false pledge. She couldn't hear them spoken like that, not from him.

Please stop, she begged. *Spit them out.*

O, he said.

She knew he couldn't. They were in him already, becoming part of his knowing.

O, he tried. A stuttering resistance of *O O O*.

Open your mouth, she said. An instruction he could not disobey, his mouth being a hole that could not be closed. She would extract the words herself.

He had grown so tall she could see right down the dark of his gullet without stooping. He was then perhaps half a head shorter than she, and the ditch of his mouth she had dug so shallowly appeared somehow to have no bottom. She considered dropping a lit match down his throat but the possibility that he should be sensitive to pain prevented her. She put one hand on his forehead, gently tipping his head back, and brought her eye to the well of his mouth to examine its depth. A cool moisture rose from his mud face. Her nose rested in the nook below his chin. There was nothing to see.

As a child, she had once drunk poison. The glow of bottled Paris Green had a strange beckoning effect. Fortunately, Isaac had caught her in the act and made her chase it with syrup of ipecac to expel the poison before it could take hold. Surely she could do the same for Leo.

She reached her forefinger into the narrow hole of his mouth, just to the first knuckle, intending to root through the loose insides of him for the tip of the paper. But she felt nothing, as though he had been built entirely hollow. She admitted a second finger, the middle, to help the first seek out his substance, and then a third. Her whole hand all the way to the wrist and still nothing. By the second knuckle, the hollow of his mouth ought to have filled with the mud of his general composition and this is where she supposed the paper, with its new bad words, to be lodged. She had imagined it would be simple to pluck the offending words clean from his body and vocabulary. But it wasn't so. Once her fingers entered his mouth, the urgency of her task drained away as easily as water seeps from a leaking bucket. Strange how easily he yielded to the introduction of her hand. No pushing, no force. The hole of his mouth had expanded naturally to accommodate her growing trespass, which provoked no signs of distress. On the contrary, he seemed almost sedate, like a baby after nursing.

Her own internal state, she noticed, reflected his ease. The excited edge of her curiosity had softened to gentle observation, and she shared in his peace. The skin of her hand, once it was fully submerged within the hole of his mouth, touched no surface, lacked contact entirely. Most things people referred to as holes were not truly holes. They had bases, points where they ceased to sink and where their walls began the climb to their openings. But true holes, like eternity, or God, were nearly impossible for people to comprehend.

The deeper she reached, the more she encountered the nothing of the hole, and the more she began to feel that this was not an average nothing. In fact, it was a something. His hollow wasn't vacant but filled with a something she couldn't remember ever feeling before. She tried: wet, good, dry, edge, whole, all, more. But, for once, she had no formal name by which to understand it. Neither did it have component parts to equal a whole she could name.

Her head was filled with low humming—was it him? It felt so good, a pleasant heaviness that settled into her bones. The golem was patiently silent as she tried to understand this something-in-nothing feeling they now shared.

All this time she had thought she was responsible for his education, but he had known this something his whole life, though his life was then only a week long. He had more than known it; he had been filled with it, composed of it from before birth. His eyes seemed to glow a deeper blue the farther she sank her hand into him. Glowing, she decided, with the pleasure of a shared knowledge.

His knowing traveled as a shock of slowed-down electricity might, from her fingers, which received the thing directly and coursed up her arm, then spread across her chest, down into her legs and up into her head, where it swarmed and tugged at her comprehension. She was so close to understanding his secrets. In an instant, she could have the wisdom of thousands-year-old dirt; whatever the earth knew, she could know too, if only she could make sense of the words buried there, which were surely as numerous as minerals, but how to translate the language?

Just as the golem had no concept of a human word until he ingested it, the language of mud was indiscernible to Ana.

What does it mean? she asked. *I need to understand.*

I am tried truth, said the golem.

I know, said Ana. *Me too.*

Even between humans, a difference in accent could make comprehension impossible. Southerners had enough trouble making out Yankees, never mind, say, an Irishman. And here she was trying to interpret the language of the earth itself!

Make me understand what the truth is, she pleaded.

The truth is, he stuttered. *The truth is made. The truth is.*

Yes!

Wulff's.

My what? Help me.

The deeper she sank herself into him, the nearer she came to comprehension, even glimpsing flickers of it: at the wrist, a tug of intuition;

at the forearm, a blow of perception. Ana felt certain that if she could
only get far enough in, she would reach the threshold of understanding. In
chemistry, there were known temperatures required for a change of state.
Liquid water, for example, wouldn't boil until it reached exactly one hundred degrees Celsius. It would scald at ninety-nine, but without that final
degree, it would never turn from liquid to steam. But what was the boiling
point for the comprehension of pure truth? For that, she now knew, was
the ultimate knowledge, written in the golem's very body.

And then she found it.

Her knuckle grazed something—an actual, nameable something: the
moist corner of paper, on which she had written her message. She pulled it
out as carefully as she could so that it wouldn't tear.

With her other hand, she waved her widespread fingers before his face.

AVILAS! AVILAS! AVILAS! she said, witching him with her new word,
a charm to protect them both.

The golem reacted instantly, folding in spasms, gagging in silence. The
body must be purged of poison.

She brought the scrap over to the newspaper from which she had so
carelessly torn it, smoothing it free of wrinkles, and fitted it as best she
could to its missing page, a headline stacked in three rows above its column:
*FRANK TRIED TO FLIRT WITH MURDERED GIRL SAYS HER BOY
CHUM.* The print on one side soaked into the message she had written on
the other. It was the only thing she had wanted him to know: *The truth is
I am innocent.* The two made one by the transparency of wet paper. The
letters smudged, overlapping, backward.

I am made murdered, said the golem. The wrong words left the hole
of his mouth and his mud shoulders slumped. Words worked faster, it
seemed, than poison.

A v i l a s, she scribbled in the margin of the paper. S a l i v a. Her failed charm merely a reflection. No magic in it. No new words, only pretending. Poison never leaves the body, not all of it, not ever. We keep it with us, shelter it in our blood. And yet, poison is a part of knowing, a part of truth.

I am innocent, she instructed.

I am innocent, the golem reflected.

The Night Witch: A Secret Game

I t wasn't hard to get away. All of us were good, by then, at sneaking. And our parents were good at never finding out. We arranged the planning of it at our usual meeting, which no longer included Ana. It was done before our stomachs had settled the last bubbles of our Coca-Colas, though some of us had made our own plans. We met beneath the oak tree that framed the Wulff house. We kicked off our shoes at 11 P.M. sharp. We came dressed in black, our mourning clothes, so that we would blend into the shadows. Under the tree, before we climbed, we played Not It Knees.

I can't, said the last to take a knee.

You lost, someone answered. *You have to.*

The wood of the trunk curled out over the top of a low hollow. A good enough step to catch a handhold on the first low branches. The shortest went first. We made rungs of our hands for her to step up and swing a leg over the bull's-eye bough. If you made it there, you could climb up easy. The tallest, a natural climber, went last. We handed our fists down for her to grab onto like knots in a rope.

We wove through branches, climbing up the trunk, as ants climbed us down, until we were level with the oval window that looked into Ana's attic. Though we couldn't see in, the black glass had a golden glow to it, and we knew there was a lantern burning inside. *We are coming, we are coming to put your glow out.* One by one, we edged along a branch that overhung the roof until it gave under our weight as we eased ourselves out along its wilt. Just before its snapping place, it delivered us to the roof's eave where our toes could trace the shingles, and we lowered ourselves down in total silence.

We went one by one, one foot and then the other, until only the tallest was left. Her weight was not enough to bow the branch, so we pulled for her, and she slid down, crashing lightly into us. The branch, now free of her weight, whipped back into the air and rained a handful of black leaves over our heads.

We crawled on all fours up the slant of the roof, denting our knees and palms on fallen acorns. One of us tapped the window with her finger. Fewer than a dozen strikes before Ana's face appeared. Naughty girl. We pressed our palms to the cracked glass. No getting around it now. We shoved our hands under the pane; we would force our bodies inside. She had gone and made a mess of it, inviting the whole world in and shoving us out. We pressed harder and she watched, shaking her head. We would break the glass if we had to, we could hear it cracking. We were coming in. The golem belonged to us. The story belonged to us. The magic, the mud, all of it. We would have it. We would take it back. We were coming in.

Open the window. Open the window. Open the window or you'll be sorry.

The smell of smoke poured out and we pushed harder.

Le—she started, but our eight hands pushed with such force that we shattered the window. The glass rained down on her. She fell to the floor and covered her head with her arms as we went in, over her body. We went in and she couldn't stop us.

Now, said Rose, her voice breaking us apart. *That wasn't so hard.*

O, said the golem, his flat panic finishing Ana's cry for help.

Hello to you too, said Esther.

Franny, in her nervous, scuttling way, found a sooty broom and began to sweep the glass.

Cut it out, Rose snapped at her.

Sarah took a thin strip of paper from her pocket and knelt over Ana, pinning her to the floor with a knee on each of Ana's shoulders. When Ana tried to call out, Sarah put her hand over Ana's mouth. The rest of us admired her technique. It kept Ana so motionless and quiet. Sarah rolled the strip of paper into a ball the size of a pea and pried Ana's lips open. Ana tried to turn her head away, but Sarah squeezed her legs in tighter, her shins and knees bracing Ana's head still.

We almost said something, said stop, said harder, said mercy. We hoped it didn't hurt too much.

Na, the golem called. *Na na no. No.*

The evolution of the word made Sarah pause, two fingers exposing the glistening pink of Ana's gums.

No, I can't, she said to the golem. *I won't.*

I don't know why I bother with you, said Rose, plucking the paper ball from Sarah's fingers. *I ought to feed you one of these.*

You wouldn't.

What is it?

This isn't part of the plan, is it? I don't remember this part.

Sure I would. How'd you like to be dead little Mary Phagan?

What is it? I can't see.

I don't believe you. You don't know anything about anything.

Oh yeah, then open up your mouth and let's see what happens. Say "ah" and let's see how much I know about it.

Back and forth, like little starlings squabbling over seed, pecking at each other's eyes until Rose tugged Sarah away, bent over Ana, and wedged the paper ball into the gap of her overbite. Franny yelled for her to *stop it!* and everyone scrambled away as though she were a grenade.

Wulffs, said the golem and lumbered toward us, too large now. Thick as the old oak trunk we'd climbed up and drying out. We saw how parts of him had begun to crumble away, leaving small piles of himself wherever he went, and what must it feel like to be crushed under a falling tree? We scattered, not wanting to find out.

O Wulffs, he said again, and positioned himself in front of her, a wall of protection we could not see through.

What did you do! said Franny, fighting to see around the golem.

Murdered, said the golem. We hadn't known he could say that word and the sound of it, the way it seeped from all parts of him, made us wish we hadn't come.

She's fine, said Rose. *Look at me talking to this ugly lump like he understands.* Then, more quietly: *We didn't even hurt her.*

Are you sure? Franny asked.

We weren't.

From behind the wall of him, Ana's hands shot out, fingers splayed and then they began to quiver and spasm like the legs of a dying crane fly. They tapped at the floor. A code we did not understand, but which we hoped meant safe, meant forgiveness. Then she withdrew her fingers and gasped for air.

What did you put in her mouth? said Franny. *What did you do?*

Never mind, said Rose. *It won't work.*

What won't?

Satisfied our attack was stalled, the golem turned to Ana and held out his crumbling mitt for her to take. Had we ever touched his hand? What did it feel like? We couldn't remember.

She draped her hand over his and rose like smoke from a chimney, a plume of Ana. In the dark of the attic, her nightgown seemed to glow white and turn her body into shadow. She bowed to the golem, eyes cast down, then caught sight of her own feet and sighed, *Tsss.* She examined them, flexing and pointing her toes, as though testing them out for the first time. She looked at her hands, grabbed her own wrists, measuring their thickness, and shook her head.

This little girl again, she said. *I knew she was trouble.*

We braced ourselves for all that we did not know. We shifted weight between our feet and the floorboards creaked.

Franny said *who?* and Sarah elbowed her in the ribs.

I don't believe her, said Rose.

What don't you believe? said Esther.

No, said Rose, *it can't have worked.*

It was a name, wasn't it? said Franny. *You fed her a name. Whose?*

It was just a prank. Sarah was pleading now, on the verge of tears.

Like we did with the golem? said Esther. *But we're already ourselves! We can't be remade. What about what we were before? What will happen to Ana?*

Good riddance, said Ana, who might not have been Ana.

I don't know. I don't know. I didn't think—

You can't be serious.

How do we undo it?

You have to take the name out. That's what the rabbi does in the story.

No, Rose barked, her cheeks red and blotchy. *I'm done falling for her lies. She's faking it, look at her.*

We were. And she looked back at us from under the shadow of her brow. Had her cheeks always been so gaunt or was it the weak light of the lantern?

Girl? said the golem. His voice sounded dusty.

The lantern's flicker licked at her face. Something with terrible depth passed across her sweet features. We could have believed she was anyone but Ana.

Who are you? said Sarah.

You can't actually believe her, said Rose.

Three guesses, said Ana, her voice a low rumble we were too afraid to answer.

What's the matter? said not-Ana. *Newt got your tongues?*

Wulffs, said the golem. *Girl is Wulffs. Wulffs Wulffs Wulffs*, as though trying to convince himself.

The plan was to have a trial, said Rose. *The golem and the Night Witch. So what if she's playing along now? So what, this is even better.*

If you didn't believe it could happen, then why did you do it? said Esther.

This wasn't part of the plan, said Franny. *This is real.*

A real bore you mean, buying into her act. I thought you weren't a baby anymore, said Rose.

Even if it is an act, said Franny. *Even if she's fooling us all, it's still real. What she did, what we did. What did we think we would do to all these real people?*

It's not like that, said Esther. *We didn't do it to hurt anyone. We were trying to help.*

It doesn't matter what we meant, said Franny. *They're searching for Isaac.*

But that's good, said Esther. *Ana really misses him.*

Who's searching? said Sarah.

A mob, said Franny. *I heard my parents talking about it.*

Maybe it's a search party, said Esther.

What will they do to him when they find him? said Sarah.

No, said Rose, pacing. *No, she can't be. The Night Witch is made up.*

Why? said Franny. *Why is the Night Witch made up? Look at what's standing in front of you.*

But that's different. We made the golem by—

Exactly, said Franny. *And who do you think made the Night Witch?*

Wulff's Made in Atlanta, said the golem.

Just because we made it up, that doesn't mean it isn't real.

Ana laughed, a ragged sound like a thorny ball of vines. Whose laugh was that? Esther had begun to whimper, and Franny took her hand.

Who do you think made the Night Witch? she said, in a mocking, fake little-girl voice. *I could fill the seven seas with what you don't know.* Her grin was wide and sharp. *I made myself. I made the Night Witch. All you did was knock at my door,* she said, rapping on the golem's chest. *You don't have a cigarette, do you, baby?*

A run of dirt cascaded down from the spot she had struck, and she opened her palm over it to staunch the wound.

No, of course you don't. I'm so sorry. Then, to us: *I came to take this beautiful creature back with me.* She stroked the side of his face with her other hand and he pressed himself into her palm. *I get lonely.*

He loved her, whatever she was, and it wasn't fair and no one touched us and damn them. Our faces, our throats, so hot they hurt.

Give it up, Rose said through gritted teeth. *Besides,* she said, with more confidence than we felt, *you don't sound anything like a Night Witch.*

Oh no, said Ana, whom we hoped was still Ana, *how does a Night Witch sound?*

Like nothing, she shot back. *We're having our trial,* she said to us. *I'll take the name out when it's over.* She flipped over a milk crate to use as our witness stand.

We had a plan; we would not be obstructed. We would play our game and we would win. That was the plan, but we were no longer sure what winning was.

You are summoned here tonight to . . . to, one of us stammered. The prosecutor's role more difficult than she had imagined.

To answer . . . one of us whispered to prompt her.

To answer for the charges leveled against you, against both of you.

Rule #4: Withholding information is a serious offense. Suspected with-holders will be tried by a jury of her peers, another chimed in.

We needed order. We needed fault, guilt, conviction.

Night Witch, said someone else, assuming her role, *please approach the bench.*

To our surprise, she obeyed, sauntered to the crate, as we had directed her to do, but instead of sitting, she stood atop it so that she towered above us, cast us in her shadow. We faltered, we shrank and forgot.

One of us cleared her throat. *You stand accused,* she said, faking bravado, *of dishonoring our friend—*

Our former *friend,* someone reminded her.

She tried again: *You stand accused of dishonoring our . . . Ana Wulff.*

You too, golem, another chimed in. *You are also accused. And we aim to find out who did it!*

I am innocent, said the golem.

Liar, one of us shouted, forgetting her courtroom demeanor.

Sure you are, baby, the one we hoped was not the Night Witch said, and held out her hand for him to come. *So am I. It's them, they're the wicked ones.*

We're carrying out justice, one of us said.

Oh, is that what you think you're doing? said the one we hoped was still Ana. *Where is this friend of yours? What does Ana say about it?*

Barukh ata Adonai Eloheinu, melekh ha'olam, hamog—Franny stuttered a blessing of protection—*Barukh ata Adonai Eloheinu, melekh ha'olam, halga*—*I can't*—

Well— said Esther. *She*—

None of us knew how to answer.

We hadn't expected her to ask questions. She should have stumbled around with the syllables of her own name, like the golem, dumb and easy to condemn. Though now, he, too, knew things we never taught him. Who was he to say *innocent*? What did he know about it? We were supposed to be the questioners.

You killed her, said Rose. *You and the golem. You probably did it together.*

I thought they dishonored her, said Sarah. *That's what we agreed the charge would be.*

Don't listen to Rose, said Franny.

She'll listen to me if I say so.

You're her, ma'am, said Franny, ignoring Rose. *Sort of.*

What, this rag I'm wearing? said not-Ana, flexing the backs of her hands in front of her face, as though appraising a new dress. *This sad little body nobody ever paid any mind? Believe me, I'm doing her more of an honor than she ever had on her own.*

What right do you have to talk about honor? said Rose. *I should cut out your lying tongue.*

Here it is. The one standing on the crate presented her tongue for the taking. Wet and long and pointed.

—*Barukh ata Adonai Eloheinu, melekh ha'olam, galohem*—No, it's *helgoma*—*melekh ha'olam helgoma*—

Take your time, said the one who towered above us. *Go ahead, baby. Just get it out.*

—*hagomel lahayavim tovot, sheg'molani kol tov.*

Well, that was pretty, wasn't it, she said to the golem, *but we've got our own cauldron to stir, don't we?* She held out her hand and the golem helped her down from the crate.

Sarah put her arms out to block them. *He belongs to us*, she said. *You can't have him.*

She isn't even good at it, said Rose. And then louder: *You aren't even good at it. Do you hear me, Ana Wulff?*

I don't have to be good, said the one we no longer believed was Ana, and stepped toe to toe with Rose. *I just have to be strong. And this little girl can't give me what I need. But you*, she said, running her hands over Rose's shoulders, down her biceps. *Your body is better, taller, older. How much do you weigh? One ten? One twenty?*

Rose batted her hands away and punched not-Ana in the gut so that she fell backward and stumbled over the burnt crate. The golem caught her under the arms.

Oh, that's good, she said with an awful, coughing laugh. *That hurts. There's the strength I need. You'll be perfect.* She got back to her feet. *Just hold still for me now while I come inside. Be brave, little girl. You're the brave one, aren't you?*

We moved in front of Rose, guarding her, and she let us. We could be the blessing Franny's prayer couldn't conjure. We could keep us safe.

She's not any more powerful than Ana is, said one of us.

Less, even.

I'm not brave, said Rose. *Not at all.* The truth of her fear like bare feet on broken glass.

Why don't you take the golem's body, someone suggested.

Yes, look how big and strong he is.

Yes, of course, they belonged to each other, away from us!

I am innocent, said the golem. *Girl says I am innocent.*

You are, said not-Ana. *The only one.* A softness cottoning over her voice, changing it back to something nearly familiar.

Go inside him instead. We'll be better, we insisted, *we'll be so good. Please, just let us go.*

You're right, she said. She had stopped advancing, arrested by his face.

Her earnest consent unnerved us. A warm and unwelcome ease flooded our muscles.

Of course, you're right. I should go inside him.

I no, I no, said the golem.

She reached up for his face, rubbing the withering petals of his eyes gently between her fingers.

Of course you do, she said, examining her fingers, stained blue at the tips. *You know all of it, don't you? Everything. And how to make it right. It's all inside you, I just have to find it.*

I no Wulffs.

Ana laughed a real laugh, her own, like the meat of a walnut, which was somehow more terrible even than the Night Witch's.

Ana, said Franny. *Is it you?*

Of course, of course, she said and scrambled back to the milk crate, stepping up again so that she was level with the golem. With her hands on either side of his head, she brought her mouth close to the hole of his.

Will you help me in? she asked him.

In where? What's happening?

Where's the Night Witch?

See, she faked it!

Talk to us, Ana! What are you doing?

The golem lifted her by the waist without hesitation.

Stop him, cried Franny, but he handled Ana so gently she might have been a swallowtail's wing. We wanted to be so light, so lifted.

Looking over her shoulder at us, she said, *Soon, I'll know the truth and I'll make everything right. With us and with Isaac and maybe even with Leo. He knows the truth of everything in the whole world.* She kissed the golem's forehead. *He's going to show me.*

Show you how? said Sarah. *How do you know?*

I just do, she said, into his mouth. *He's the True Judge.*

Suddenly we wanted to touch her, to spider's nest her, to understand what she knew. We wanted so badly to believe she was right, that we had made a miracle after all, not the ugly, scary failure we had taken him for. We wanted to believe he could help us, that he could do what she believed he could. We reached out for Ana, to hold her hand, but she shook her head.

I know it's my fault, she said.

It's not, said Esther.

Not only yours, said Franny.

But just wait for me to know the truth. It won't take long. I almost found it the other day.

Found what? said Esther.

Be patient and wait for me. We'll all be happy soon.

Where are you going? I don't understand.

You will soon. I'll tell you everything. No secrets. We'll all be perfectly good and perfectly smart. We'll fix everything when I get back.

Back from where, said Rose. *Can we come?* But we all knew the answer.

And we chose to believe her. We believed her as she pushed her fingers, one by one, into the hole of the golem's mouth, as her wrists and elbows disappeared into him—*does it hurt?*—and his eyes flung open in ecstatic bloom. *Ana? Can you hear us?* We believed as he lowered his grip for purchase, clasping below her hips, as she kicked her way in, thrust herself into the expanding hole of him, until her second foot, the callus of her last toe went into him, vanished from us.

And then we waited for our belief to be rewarded. We sat in an arc before the golem and waited for the answers Ana had promised us. We waited to feel good like we used to—better than we used to.

How long do you think it takes? one of us asked, but no one wanted to guess. We watched the golem closely for signs of Ana. The attic window was turning dark blue with early light.

I hope she can breathe in there, said someone else.

I don't think it's like that. She probably doesn't need to.

Every living thing has to breathe.

A sniffle came from somewhere within him, though it sounded very far away. The golem's face was completely blank, and his body motionless.

Was that—one of us started, but a whimper cut her short.

Is she crying? one of us asked.

People cry at weddings, sometimes.

Ana, one of us called to her. *Ana, can you hear us?*

Yes. Ana's voice poured from him, seeping from a thousand tiny holes in his skin. Ana in a thousand pieces. We imagined gathering her from the floor.

Just barely. You sound so far away.

We're here, one of us said. *We're right here.*

What's it like? someone said, trying to sound hopeful. We should have known there were no easy answers.

It's so dark, came her voice. *Will someone shine a light down here?*

One of us scrambled for the lantern and held it to his mouth.

What's in there? said one of us. *How do you feel?*

I feel . . . small. As though I could walk until breakfast and never find the end of this place.

Don't stray! one of us begged.

Can you see the light?

No, came her voice, *but I'm adjusting to the dark.*

What can you see? one of us asked.

Are you almost done? said someone else.

It's not like that. It's not a place for seeing. It's more like . . . well, like Esther's intuitions. And the longer I'm here, the clearer they become.

Come out now. You've been in there long enough.

They're turning into . . . truths. Like an invisible museum of truths stacked to the ceiling. Only there is no ceiling.

Come back to us.

Not yet. I have to find . . .

Find what? said one of us and struck the golem's chest with the flat of her palm. A little trickle of dry gray dirt cascaded down and landed on her foot. *Find what?* Another struck his thick neck. *Find what?* A strike to his back. We're here, we said with our hands. Feel us and come back.

The place with the truths we need, came Ana's voice. *But I'm getting closer. Shine the light down. Can you see me?*

We can't see anything, there's nothing to see.

There's me, came her voice, so small. *I'm here.* Even filtered through the wall of his dirt body she sounded afraid.

We're here too.

What if I don't find . . . and we knew what she didn't want to say. *But I was so sure.*

Come back out, one of us cried, craning over the golem's mouth, though there was nothing to see. *Come out now, we'll figure it out together.*

I just need more light.

One of us, frustrated at her insistence on knowing, and knowing we could not help, said, *Fine,* and shoved the lantern into the hole of the golem's mouth, fed it to him roughly. *There!*

There! Ana echoed. *I can see!*

She took in a deep breath and held it. We pressed our ears to the golem's chest, waiting for her exhale.

Oh, I wish you could be here.

Tell us!

It's so much. There's so much to know.

What is it?

*It's more than I've ever known before. I think it might be everything. Oh, I
can't get it all down, keep it all in my mind. And some of it is so—*

Tell us!

*Huge and difficult and incredible and awful. And every way I think to
describe it is further from the truth of it than the last. It crushes at me to make
it fit into words. It's . . . impossible. But it's here anyhow. Here, as plain as an
exhibition, like books on a shelf, like Leo in his box. All these truths. I'll give
them to you like I said I would. Just let me have a moment to—*

The questions tumbled out faster than she could answer.

Is Leo in heaven? Is Mary?	*There's no such thing.*
Can you talk to him?	*He can talk to me, in a way.*
What's he saying?	*It isn't like that. You have to ask what you'd like to know.*
What cologne did he wear?	*Orange water or nothing.*
Did he kill Mary Phagan?	*Why would you ask that?*
Who did?	
What did Leo see in Lucille?	*She made him laugh.*
Did he ever think about us?	*No.*
Tell the truth.	*He never did.*
Where is Isaac?	*Hiding on a freight car bound for Chattanooga.*
Did Leo tell you that?	*No, the answer is just here in this place.*
Will he be all right?	Ana drew in a sharp breath, the perception of sudden pain.
Do you love us?	*Yes.*
Do you swear?	*I do.*
Will people remember him?	*Yes.* A deep breath, staving off nausea.

Will they remember Mary?

Did we do the right thing?   *No, but we meant to.*

Does that even matter?

Will his name ever be free?   *Mmm*, she moaned. She was

hurting and we knew it, but we

couldn't stop asking. *Almost.*

Did we change anything?   After a long pause,

her answer came: *Yes.*

But not the way we wanted.   *You will.*

Tell us the truth.   *You can. It's still possible.*

How?

The golem shook with her crying, its slumped shoulders shuddered, its face a blank, a mockery of her.

Tell us, please, you have to.   *I want to*, almost a whisper. *But only*

the past is easy here. The future is—

We have to know.   *Tearing me open.* Water poured

from the golem's flower eyes.

Please.   *Please.*

Please, I can't know any more.

We're coming for you, we cried. *We're coming in!*

We were inches from our friend, but she sounded a hundred feet away.

We're here, we're here. But we might as well have been a thousand miles away.

We could hear her ragged crying growing farther from us.

Please get me out, came the whisper of her voice, siphoned through the dirt.

One of us stuck a tentative finger in his mouth, ready to snatch it back, but the golem was inert. *Dig*, she said, and we all scratched at the well of his mouth.

We had to get her out, so we tore in. We went at the golem with all our strength. We struck at him hard enough to bruise ourselves, though we didn't feel anything but our own fury. We struck whatever was in front of us: legs, arms, chest, head, each other. One of us swung hard enough to topple his terrible head, his neck already dried out and weak. A cloud of body dust swelled at our feet and we cheered the toppling and stomped at the dark cloud, as if it might rise and reform. Still his body stood defiant, and we dug into his belly from all sides with all eight of our hands.

We're coming for you, we're coming in! We would rip our Ana out of his crumbling body.

Finally, we met each other's hands in the holes we made in his body and we tore him open. He spilled for us. All of him came undone, mounds of him at our feet. Heaps of his body up to our knees. Nothing inside him but endless dirt. Our heaving breath, our own bodies covered in smears of him, our sweat making him cling to us. One of us fell to her knees, sifting his fallen body for our friend. We didn't stop her. The golem's blue eyes watched her search from the toppled mound of him until one of us crumpled them up and threw them in the closet. The new day cracked the pink yolk of morning over us as we searched.

And then we found it, in the heap of dirt that had been the golem's chest, the only artifact of her pursuit: a letter, still sealed. Some of us cried, or we all did. We hoped it would be from her. Written while she was inside, like the murder notes, but different. An account not of how things came to be as they are, not of how she had become gone, but of how we should proceed—truth notes. They would be instructions on what to do now. How to approach this new day, how to live with it and through it, and what to do with the one after that. Signed Felicitously, signed with all her love.

But it wasn't that. It wasn't from Ana at all. It was a jumble of numbers and dashes. More secrets when we only wanted her voice: bright, clear, wise, stupid.

4-5-1-18 / 13-1-18-25,

9 / 8-15-16-5 / 9 / 8-1-22-5 / 7-15-20-20-5-14 / 20-8-9-19 / 3-15-4-5 / 18-9-7-8-20. / 8-15-23 / 3-12-5-22-5-18 / 25-15-21 / 1-18-5 / 6-15-18 / 20-8-9-14-11-9-14-7 / 9-20 / 21-16! / 9-19 / 1-18-20-8-21-18 / 19-20-9-12-12 / 1-6-20-5-18 / 25-15-21 / 20-15 / 7-15 / 20-15 / 20-8-5 / 16-9-3-20-21-18-5-19? / 20-5-12-12 / 8-9-13 / 25-15-21-22-5 / 3-15-13-5 / 4-15-23-14 / 23-9-20-8 / 20-8-5 / 16-15-24. / 20-5-12-12 / 8-9-13 / 25-15-21-18-5 / 18-21-14-14-9-14-7 / 15-6-6 / 20-15 / 10-15-9-14 / 20-8-5 / 3-9-18-3-21-19. / 20-5-12-12 / 8-9-13 / 25-15-21-22-5 / 1-12-18-5-1-4-25 / 7-15-20 / 20-8-5 / 2-5-19-20 /3-15-13-16-1-14-9-15-14 / 9-14 / 20-8-5 / 23-15-18-12-4: / 13-5! / 20-5-12-12 / 8-9-13 / 23-5-18-5 / 9-14 / 12-15-22-5 / 1-14-4 / 20-8-5-14 / 20-5-12-12 / 13-5 / 1-2-15-21-20 / 20-8-5 / 12-15-15-11 / 15-14 / 8-9-19 / 6-1-3-5!

23-9-20-8 / 12-15-22-5,

6-18-15-13 / 25-15-21-18 / 22-5-18-25 / 4-5-1-18-5-19-20 / 6-18-9-5-14-4

The magic of night was rapidly dissolving into the public of morning, where we would have to account for all we could not. Give words to the unsayable, though our tongues felt shredded in our mouths. We can change things, that's what Ana had said. And it was the truth—it had to be. The dawning light cast urgency on our understanding, and we worked up a conversion table with haste, a translation for every number. It was a simple alphanumeric code. *A cinch*, Ana would have said, a game. We had it cracked within the hour. Not the truth notes we had wanted, but truth notes all the same. Beyond our wishing, our need, our hope, our influence. Written in pen, unerasable.

Dear Mary, it began. And it was signed, *With love, from your very dearest friend*.

Research Note

Research for this novel was conducted in the archives of the Atlanta History Center, the William Breman Jewish Heritage Museum in Atlanta, and the Marietta History Center. Steve Oney's 2003 book *And the Dead Shall Rise: The Murder of Mary Phagan and the Lynching of Leo Frank*, the most comprehensive historical account of the Frank case and its context, served as my research backbone. Jeffrey Melick's *Black-Jewish Relations on Trial: Leo Frank and Jim Conley in the New South* and Nancy MacLean's "The Leo Frank Case Reconsidered: Gender and Sexual Politics in the Making of Reactionary Populism" were instructional as well. Tayari Jones's *Leaving Atlanta* and Philip Roth's *The Plot Against America* were novels also very much on my mind in the composing process. And finally, I am indebted to Paisley Rekdal's *Appropriation: A Provocation* in helping me think through the many, many unresolvable problems inherent in writing a novel that extends so far beyond my own positionality. What I strived for in the writing of this book was a response to Rekdal's provocation for "something messier, something that eludes our understanding of 'right' and 'wrong,' 'accurate' or 'false,' 'self' and 'other,' or even 'good' or 'bad' writing," to make literature that invites the reader to "see more complexity, more nuance, more differentiation in humans, not less." There are surely ways that I have failed in this intention, and the reader will find them. But my hope is that this book, in addition to bringing pleasure where it can, unsettles the reader in a productive way.

Leo Frank's murderers, the self-titled Knights of Mary Phagan, resurrected the KKK in 1915 with Frank's lynching. Earlier in the year, D. W. Griffith's Lost Cause propagandist film *Birth of a Nation*, initially titled *The Clansman*, was screened at the White House for President Woodrow Wilson before its wider release to great commercial success.

I am uninterested in true crime sleuthing, but I do wish to note that the state of Georgia posthumously pardoned Leo Frank in 1986.

Finally, the letter at the end of the novel was inspired by a postcard I found in the archives of the Breman Museum—from Mary Phagan to her cousin. It was a simple, untroubled letter to a friend. The kind of thing that would have been unremarkable if she had gotten to live out her life, if she had never been made a posthumous martyr for the white supremacist cause. Hers might not have been an easy life, it might not have been a wealthy one, but it might at least have been filled with simple exchanges between friends.

Acknowledgments

This book has had a long road to publication, nearly ten years. My biggest supporter along the way, and really in all things, has been my mother, Susan. How does a kid get so lucky? A close second place goes to my partner, Sam, who is always willing to listen. Thanks also to the members of my thesis committee at the University of Alabama—Wendy Rawlings, Joel Brouwer, and Michael Martone—where this novel was first drafted. I am indebted also to the Tent: Creative Writing fellowship and to the St. Albans School Writer-in-Residence program for giving me time and space to work on this project.

To my friends Sarah Edmands Martin, Drew Van Dyke, Ivy Grimes, and Courtney Eason who read my work and helped me along when I got stuck, simply out of the goodness of their hearts: bless you and thank you. Thanks also to Maggie Cooper, Phong Nguyen, Jess Row, Donna Denizé, Joshua Henkin, Jaimy Gordon, and Utz McKnight—writers, thinkers, and lovers of literature who all encountered this story somewhere along its journey and gave me the confidence to keep going.

Endless thanks to my editors, Marisa Siegel and Anne Gendler, and to all of the other folks at Northwestern University Press, without whom there would be no book. My sincere gratitude to Conrad Rosenberg for help with Yiddish and to Dino Everett, who set me right regarding everything I didn't know about early film. And finally, thanks to my dad, Bryan, who wanted a Navy SEAL but got a writer instead: thanks for conceding gracefully.